I0586946

Rabbit in Red

Volume Three

Bury the Rabbit

Joe Chianakas

Four Phoenixes Publishing

United States Canada United Kingdom

Printed in the United States of America

ISBN # 978-0-9976205-8-0

www.joechianakas.com

www.facebook.com/chianakas

This is a work of fiction. Names, characters, places, and incidents either are
the product of the author's imagination or are used fictitiously. Any
resemblance to actual persons, living or dead, events, or locales is entirely
coincidental.

Dedication

For Teresa Anne Chianakas who passed away on 9/3/16.

I remember sitting with my Mom at a cancer center on so many occasions, but in July 2016, there's one session that particularly stands out. I was in talks with Horror Block, and they were considering including *Rabbit in Red*. It was a huge deal, as thousands and thousands of horror fans around the world would be introduced to my book. While this was happening, my Mom and I were awaiting the latest test results. I started bargaining with higher powers.

"Let Horror Block change their mind. I don't even care if the book completely fails. Just let my Mom survive and be healthy."

Horror Block shipped the book to over 10,000 people and the response was "exceptional" enough that we worked on a new deal to even send my second book to thousands around the world. But my Mom got bad news—treatment was no longer working and the cancer had spread.

I finished the first draft of *Bury the Rabbit* later that summer, just a few days before she passed. I hope all of you know how much love and passion went into this series, and I hope you enjoy it as much as my wonderful Mom—my biggest champion—would have. This project is the end of a trilogy that kept me motivated and stimulated during the hardest of times. I say goodbye to it now and give it to all of you. Thank you for being a reader and a friend.

Part One:

Ashes to Ashes

"We make up horrors to help us cope with the real ones."

– Stephen King

"It is the unknown we fear when we look upon death and darkness, nothing more."

– J.K. Rowling

"To die will be an awfully big adventure."

– Peter Pan

Chapter One

During the year that followed the original Rabbit in Red contest, Dexter Lange morphed into something like one of the lesser known characters of *The Walking Dead*. After his adventure at Rabbit in Red, he wasn't invited back. Instead, Dexter went back home to Seattle, Washington.

He had finished high school with passing grades, but he learned a lot more than any high school class ever taught. He learned about coding, he studied psychology, and one more precarious subject.

He learned all about explosives.

Images from the first-year contest consumed his mind and motivated his personal studies. Witches, clowns, and . . . spiders. The spider had dropped on his forehead. Then it had climbed down his nose and almost danced near his eyeball.

How did JB know he was afraid of spiders? He knew JB had accessed their personal information from the first day they agreed to the terms of the Fright Fest 4D app, and so Dexter learned coding.

Today Dexter had received a text that changed everything. He read it and re-read it. Could it be true? Could Rabbit in Red have been destroyed?

On the bed he'd had since he was a child, he sat and stared up at the ceiling. While his old "friends" returned to Rabbit in Red, Dexter spent the year at home. His parents didn't question him. He told them he would take classes online, that he didn't want to deal with people, including them. Dexter only had to open his eyes as wide as possible. His mom would choke, his dad would blink hard, and they'd leave him alone in his bedroom.

He studied ways to make a person's head explode, and he planned revenge.

Sitting on his bed, he stared at the text that just appeared on his phone. *It's gone. RiR. Burned to the ground.* He thought back to that Halloween weekend, the only experience he'd had at Rabbit in Red. He had replayed that weekend in his mind over and over again. Even as he tried to eliminate the old visions, he still pictured himself holding a knife—what had turned out to be a fake knife—and stabbing Daniel's father over and over again.

Of course, the man dressed as Daniel's father had turned out to be JB. It was all a big game, and Dexter had lost. At the end of that first-year contest, JB had gathered them all back in Rabbit in Red's commons to explain. He had a bunch of bullshit to say. Stuff about overcoming fear, becoming a team, helping one another, blah fuckin' blah.

Dexter had stared at JB then and wanted to scream. *You want to overcome fear? Sometimes you have to pick up a knife and plunge it through someone's heart! Especially if that someone was going to hurt you.*

JB had invited those assholes to lead his so-called horror college. Bill, Jaime, Wes, and Rose. Sycophants, that was what they were. Sickos and sycophants. Almost everyone got invited back. JB had even let Daniel return, but he had let his brown-nosers make that decision for him.

And what about Dexter?

"As for you, Dexter, you and I will have a conversation in private." That was what JB had said to him in front of the other first year Rabbit in Red contestants. But Dexter was never invited back.

He started to think of that conversation—more like a lecture—that JB had given him. No, no time to dwell on that conversation again.

He rolled over on his bed and re-read the text message.

"It's gone. RiR. Burned to the ground."

How many times have you replayed that conversation with JB, Dex?

You know how many times. Every damn day.

But did you ever do it?

Get out of my head!

Dexter let go of his phone, threw up both of his hands, covered his ears hard, and squeezed. The voices were getting louder.

JB had known something about everyone. He had known their pasts and their fears. Maybe he knew everything. In their private conversation, he had asked something very special of Dexter. After that conversation, Dexter had thought that this could be a great redemption. Or it could become his ultimate revenge.

As the summer after graduation had approached, he knew the first-year students were working on the new theme. JB had called it "Burn the Rabbit." Dexter laughed out loud in his bedroom, thinking of the text message on the phone. It was as if it were meant to be.

So last summer Bill, Jaime, Rose, and Wes and the rest of the ass-kissers put their teeny tiny brains together and came up with Hellfire.

Dexter had to admit it wasn't half bad.

He had watched every news story he could, and he had followed along with any updates JB had posted on frightfest4d.com. Hellfire took a traditional haunted house and turned it into something that would literally make most people shit their pants. Enhanced by the Rabbit's Eye, an ordinary haunt could turn into anything—it could make the participant feel as if they were falling or even on fire. The Rabbit's Eye was virtual reality on steroids. Yes, that was the real genius of Hellfire—it had tricked their brains into making them think they were feeling pain.

Dexter's jealousy raged. He would have loved to try it.

Dexter watched the stories about the new recruits when they had joined. There was Brandis, who had become the new love interest for Jaime. That made Dexter laugh. He didn't give a shit about love, but anything that would piss off Bill was great. There was Carol, who had a huge girl boner for JB. That part of her made Dexter sick, but Carol was hot. Then there was Diane—Dexter respected her. She got hurt and came back with a vengeance. Dexter had laughed when he heard about Jimmy. Jimmy apparently had an attraction for Daniel, and Dexter laughed at all the ways he could exploit the situation to mess with Danny boy.

There were several others, but Dexter's mind drifted to Ricky next. Couldn't forget Ricky. What a surprise that turned out to be.

Dexter had seen right away that something wasn't right with Ricky. What was that old saying? People can't see what's right in front of their eyes? Ricky reminded Dexter of those *Mission Impossible* movies. Anyone with those resources could change their face.

Ricky, of course, turned out to be none other than Sid Malcolm, Chester's brother. Chester was JB's right-hand man. During the first year, they locked Sid up because he had threatened to call the police and tell them about JB's insane tests.

Moving from his bed to his computer desk, Dexter browsed through photos on frightfest4d.com.

"How did they not see this?" He looked at Ricky's face. "That moustache, c'mon, so fake."

What a year Burn the Rabbit had been. Dexter knew JB had made every effort possible to keep the scarier stories out of the public eye. Dexter knew this because he never saw any news stories about Tara Stein, Jaime's kid sister, who had been kidnapped and nearly got burned alive. He knew that a so-called horror professor had been murdered. He knew that Diane, one of the new recruits, had nearly been killed. And of course there were other deaths—Donnie Chase, the assistant who dressed as Samara, being the one that really caught his attention.

Dexter looked at their pictures online, then turned his attention back to his phone.

He had known all of this because of the texts.

He smiled and thought of JB.

"I learned a trick or two from you, master," Dexter said with a snarl. He loved that he had someone on the inside keeping him updated. Dexter may not have been a big player last year. He had watched from the sidelines and waited patiently for his turn to play.

That time had finally arrived.

Fooling someone online really was too easy.

A fake name, a fake picture, and lots of compliments: he could have gotten anyone to talk.

Dexter understood that the people at Rabbit in Red weren't typically the coolest. They spent their days with noses in books or eyes on movies. Not really with a whole lot of other people.

You deserve better, he commented on someone's Instagram post.

Before long, he had made a friend.

And that friend was inside Rabbit in Red and told Dexter everything he wanted to know.

He knew something was odd about Ricky, but he didn't say that. *That's their mystery to solve.*

Once people started dying, it all got very interesting very fast. Dexter would stare at his phone at night when he couldn't sleep, hoping and waiting for such a text. How great would it be if he received a text that read, *OMG, Bill's head got cut off.* Or, *U won't believe it—Jaime hung herself.*

Dexter snorted. That would have been great.

But today—on this cold winter's day in Seattle—Dexter felt happier than he had in over a year.

He replied to the text. *What happened?*

Then he waited. He hated waiting, but he had gotten so good at it.

We're outside. RiR is on fire. Literally.

Dexter texted back: *Is everyone okay?* He bit his lower lip and hoped for the worst possible answer.

I don't know.

He inhaled deeply through his nose. He needed to know if any of those assholes were suffering. *First, I better play the game,* he thought.

Are you okay?

Not hurt but my brain's a mess. This is crazy.

Good, the bitch was okay. He still needed to know more.

Can I see? Call and put me on FaceTime. He'd love to see what was going on and see Rabbit in Red turn into ashes.

K.

Dexter sighed. He hated the fuckin' *K.* Lazy.

Seconds later the phone rang. He answered, and the camera on the other ended pointed directly at the studios.

"See?"

"Jesus," Dexter replied.

Through the phone, Dexter saw the old Rabbit in Red studios—a place the size of maybe ten city blocks—crumble with flames and smoke. He had to force back a laugh. *That's what JB deserves. Let his dreams burn to the ground. Let all their dreams burn to the ground!*

"Rose! Rose is inside!" That was Wes's voice Dexter heard. It made his smile grow.

There was commotion and panic. His little spy did a good job keeping the camera on all of those fucking rabbiteers.

A few moments later everyone drew their attention to someone walking up to the group. She came from the outside, not the inside. *And where have you been, Jaime?*

Then Dexter heard Bill ask, "Blood? Jaime, what happened?"

"It's not my blood," Jaime said back. This caused more of a commotion, and Dexter tried to focus on what he could see. It looked like Jaime had blood all over her body. But it wasn't hers? *That's too bad,* Dexter thought. Whose was it?

"I did what I had to do," he heard Jaime say. "We're safe now. Finally."

"I have to go," Dexter's friend said.

"Wait. Who else is missing?"

"Looks like Rose and JB got trapped inside. Oh God, you think they're dead?"

Dexter forced back his grin and shrugged. "Text me as soon as you know more." His friend nodded and disconnected.

Leaning back on his computer chair, Dexter laughed out loud. He couldn't stop it. The laughs morphed into a roar. His entire body convulsed.

"We're safe now. Finally," Jaime had said.

This made Dexter laugh even more.

The dumb bitch had no idea what was about to happen. All of the events today . . . fucking icing on the cake. Rabbit in Red burned to the ground. *Looks like one of their good friends and the wizard behind the curtain are dead and out of the picture.* Hell, it looked like Jaime must have gotten rid of Ricky—er, Sid—and in quite an interesting manner. He sure wished he could have seen that fight.

"As for you, Dexter, you and I will have a conversation in private."

11

Dexter thought once again about his final conversation with JB.

Tears were now rolling down Dexter's cheeks, and they sure weren't tears of sorrow. He was laughing so hard he could barely breathe.

Oh, if only Jaime knew what JB had told Dexter back at Rabbit in Red.

"You're not safe," Dexter said out loud. "Not by a long shot."

Dexter stood up and walked to his closet. He bent over, grabbed a duffel bag, and started to pack. Then he looked into the mirror. He had let his hair grow out a bit. It was dark like his eyes. He rubbed his chest. His muscles had grown, bigger than Daniel's ever were, he thought. It made him smile.

It was time to pay a visit to his old friends. Maybe he'd get lucky and catch a funeral or two on the way.

Chapter Two

"Come here, beautiful."

It was Sid Malcolm's voice. The elaborate mask had long been ditched.

"I *said*, come *here*."

He sat in the front of a Chrysler mini-van down the road from Rabbit in Red. He had tossed Jaime into the back seat when they first exited the studios, and then he drove just a bit down the street. He was going to watch it burn.

He turned his head and looked at Jaime and patted the front passenger seat. His eyes repeated the message.

Her body twitched again.

When she didn't move, he thrust both of his arms at her and grabbed her by the shoulders.

"Get up here, you fuckin' bitch." He pulled her in between the seats, but she didn't scream. A moan escaped her lips, but she held back the urge to yell. She banged her elbow on the seat belt and her knee on Sid's seat. He tossed her into the passenger side like she was nothing but a small animal.

"Front row seats while we watch your fantasies burn to the ground." He looked at her, and his brow narrowed. "I should have brought popcorn." He giggled, an awkward sound coming out of an older man.

"Why?" Jaime asked. Her chest moved vigorously as she tried to catch her breath. Goosebumps formed on her arms as he stared at her.

He rolled his eyes. "Fuck you," he answered.

Jaime blinked hard, and in that moment she saw her uncle. Uncle Tim . . . but not the real life Uncle Tim. She saw the way JB had pictured him in her fear simulation during the very first Rabbit in Red challenge. Uncle Tim wrapped the rope around his neck.

Jaime had cried when she saw that, and her words had failed to make any sense of it. So, in that simulation, she had put a rope around her neck, too.

She wished she had a rope now.

"I thought . . ." Jaime swallowed hard. Part of her wanted to run, now. If she opened the door and sprinted away, could he catch her? He was older and heavier, and that would make him slower, right? Another part of her wanted to gouge his eyes out. She looked at her fingernails. Maybe she didn't need a weapon. She'd slice his eyeballs open with her nails. Could she do that? She looked at Rabbit in Red and the first visible flames burst through the ceiling. Yes, maybe she could.

More than just revenge, though, she also desired answers.

"I thought you wanted to shut down Rabbit in Red," she said. He didn't even look at her. She'd have to dig deeper. "I mean, didn't you get locked up? Is all of this because someone locked you in a room for a weekend?" Jaime forced a laugh.

His head snapped her way. "Shut up."

"You're not scary. You're crazy. Revenge for being locked up for a weekend? Didn't I hear that you went back home to live with your mother the rest of that year?" She laughed again, and his eyes grew wide. "That's what I heard. What are you, forty? Fifty? A grown man had to move back home with his *mother*?"

He grabbed her arm and squeezed hard. "You *shut up*."

Jaime winced at the pain, but she knew if she wanted answers, she'd have to keep digging. Her friends were in trouble. Flames flickered sporadically around the studios, and she didn't have much time if she wanted to get back there and help them.

"I can see the news now," Jaime continued. "*Mama's boy throws tantrum and burns down a building for being put in time out.*"

He slapped her. She tasted blood.

14

Then she smiled.

"If that's not the truth, then what is?"

Sid lowered his head. "Chester was always his favorite," he said and nodded at the studio. "JB's."

So, this was all out of jealousy? She didn't say that, not yet.

"Sure, Jay would let me do a stunt or two in some of his movies, but did I get an actual role? Nope." He shook his head. "Years of my life I gave to that man. Behind the scenes was where he kept me. Said he needed my brain, not my body." He inhaled sharply through his nose. "But when he wanted to do this contest, I had all sorts of ideas. If it was really about my brain, you'd think he'd have listened, right?" He shook his head again. "So, I said I disagreed with the contest. Threatened to call the cops and everything. That's why they locked me up, as you know."

He stared intently at Rabbit in Red. From the distance, it looked as if the first group of people had exited the building, but they were too far away to see who they were. Jaime studied his face, and she could tell he wanted to share his story. Didn't all madmen want to tell the world what was really inside their heads?

"They never knew what kind of actor I really was. I didn't disagree, and I never would have called the cops, but they didn't know that. And then after the first contest, JB . . ."

He stopped talking, and several thoughts bounced around Jaime's mind. *JB did what? And wait a minute, I should get the hell out of here!* She eyed her fingernails, and then clenched her fists.

"What about JB?"

He looked at her, and the darkness in his eyes sent a chill through her body. "He did something to me that was unforgivable. Now, shut up and watch your friends burn."

Another group poured out of the Rabbit in Red doors, and Jaime told herself it was time to wise up. She reached for the front door handle and pulled.

Sid laughed.

"Stupid girl. You're not getting out of this vehicle."

Her hands raced over the side of the door looking for the lock, but she couldn't find anything.

"Had them removed." He laughed again. "Just enjoy the show. It's about to get even better."

Jaime sat quietly for a moment, trying to think, but her heart beat about burst through her ears. *If I can't run, I'm going to have to fight. Really fight. That's all there is to it.*

As the flames grew taller around Rabbit in Red, he looked at her again and said, "Get in the back."

"I thought you wanted me to watch."

"There's more to the show."

She looked in the back of the mini-van. Maybe she'd have more room to fight back there. Her eyes scanned every corner looking for any kind of weapon.

When she turned her gaze back at Sid, he hit her in the face. This time it was his fist, and a burst of pain went through her jaw all the way to the back of her skull. Then he grabbed her by the hair and pulled her into the back. He moved quickly, much more quickly than she had expected.

He pinned on her the floor of the van. He got on top, his head facing the front of the van. His upper body strength overpowered her as he pinned her arms on the floor.

"This is the moment I've been waiting for," he whispered in her ear. "JB is dead. Many of your friends will be dead. Your fucking Rabbit in Red is crumbling to the ground while we watch. And now . . . now, I get my reward." He kissed her neck hard, and she groaned in disgust.

"You freak! Get off me!"

"Scream all you want. They won't hear you."

She did. With all of her power, she screamed, but Sid just giggled. Not laugh, but *giggle*. All of his weight crushed her, and it was unbearable. He kissed his way lower from her neck to her chest. He let go of one of her arms long enough to rip off her shirt. With one fierce swoop, he tore her shirt. He grabbed her breasts with his free hand.

But she had a free hand, too.

"Sid!"

He titled his head up, and she plunged her finger as hard as she could into his eye.

She heard a pop.

Sid screamed, and Jaime clawed at his face. She sunk her fingernail into his cheek, hard and deep. She felt bone, slimy and hard. Then she pulled and tore at his face, and the blood shot out like the super soaker squirt guns she and Tara used to play with. It covered her, and she didn't care.

Sid sat up, releasing the great pressure of his weight on top of her. Jaime kneed him in the groin.

He cried out and his head hit the ceiling of the van.

She had nothing but her fingernails, but she dug back into Sid. Now that she had both hands free, she attacked the other side of his face. She clawed and clawed, and blood continued to spray in all directions.

Sid fell back, and Jaime jumped on top of him. She grabbed what her mom always said was the "oh shit" handle near the back window. She held on to it with both hands for leverage, and then she jumped on Sid's neck with her right knee. She pounded him repeatedly. Knee to neck, knee to neck.

When he stopped moving, she put all of her weight and strength into her knee on his neck and just crouched there. She stayed on top of him until she could no longer hear any breathing or movement.

In the distance, she heard sirens. Down the street, she saw her friends.

She grabbed her ripped shirt and put it back on, then crawled to the front of the van and exited on the driver's side. Looking down, she saw all of the blood that had soaked her body, and then she looked up and stepped slowly toward her friends

*****

In a Los Angeles hospital room days later, Jaime opened her eyes after reliving this nightmare once again.

They had given her drugs to help her sleep, but she still dreamed of Sid's body on top of hers. She tried to shake the memory, and she let the bright, white hospital light slowly bring her back to today.

But there was someone standing over her bed, someone who must have been watching the entire time her body twitched as the nightmare plagued her body.

Could it be? No, it couldn't be him. *Could it?*

Jaime screamed.

Chapter Three

"Take a look at this," Carol Fisher told Diane Willow.

"That is the most disgusting and awesome thing I've seen this summer! How'd you do that?" Diane pulled up a chair and watched Carol's latest horror short. In the film, a young girl, clearly possessed, was spread-eagle on a bed while blood shot out from straight between her legs. Not just a little blood. Diane thought they must have had a fire hose and rusty water or something. It was a disgusting scene, and Diane hoped Carol had a good reason, other than shock value, for creating this.

"One of the students in my group has an older brother that works in one of the major lots. They showed us how they filmed the original *Nightmare on Elm Street*. You know the scene where Johnny Depp's character is sucked into the bed and then a fountain of blood shoots out?"

Diane nodded.

"Did you know they have a rotating room that just turned the bed upside down? So, in reality, the blood was pouring straight down, but in the movie, it looks like it's shooting up. How crazy is that?" Carol smiled and turned her attention back to the short film she and her group had been developing.

Diane knew that trivia about the original *Nightmare*. It sounded like something right out of JB's playbook, with such disturbing special effects.

"How's it going with your group?" Carol asked. For as much time as Carol spent in front of a computer, she had gotten pretty fit. Her blonde hair was pulled back tight. She seemed to have lost some weight in her hips but not her chest. It made Diane a bit jealous.

Diane shrugged. She'd gotten stuck with a bunch of introverts who stared at one another and had no original ideas. "I don't know if we're gonna make the deadline."

Carol jumped up. "Diane! You've got to! The winner of this short film fest—"

"I know," Diane interrupted. "I just don't know how we're gonna—"

Their dorm room door swung open. Diane gave a half wave, got up from the chair, and threw herself face down in bed. Her dark hair had really grown out over the past few months, and she ate a mouthful of curls when she plopped herself on the bed. It was all right, though. She'd gag one way or another in just a second.

"Hey, babe." Then there was the smacking, sucking sound of two mouths slobbering on one another. Yep, Diane would much rather eat her own hair than see that. Even listening to it was just about as gross as a possessed girl shooting a fountain of blood out from between her legs.

"Hi, Dan," Carol finally said after a long minute of face-sucking. Diane slowly rolled over. Of course, Carol would get the boyfriend. She was gorgeous. Beautiful, blond hair and a bangin' rack to match. Diane was genuinely surprised that Carol hadn't been convinced to take her shirt off for someone's film.

"'Sup, Diane?"

She nodded a little less enthusiastically than she had waved, sighed again, and threw her face back into the tiny twin mattress supplied by the University of California Los Angeles.

Daniel fucking Lloyd, she thought. How the hell did those two hook up? She rolled her face over just enough to see if it was safe to look. *Nope!* Their faces stuck together like *The Human Centipede*. Diane didn't know which was actually grosser.

Daniel. Here was a guy that manipulated every situation he'd ever been in. No one really trusted him at Rabbit in Red. And he had even tried to trick Carol last year! Diane got up and walked out of the room. She couldn't be there any longer.

Still, she couldn't erase the memory of what had happened. During their time together at Rabbit in Red, Carol had been JB's number one fan. Daniel saw that, too. In an attempt to ruin JB''s credibility, Daniel made every effort possible to turn Carol against him. No, Daniel wasn't actually a crazy killer. That was Sid Malcolm, the brother of the JB's assistant, Chester, who'd disguised himself as a student named Ricky. So what was Daniel exactly?

Diane glanced back at them one more time as she stepped out of the room. Daniel was just a hormonal teenager, she thought. That was it, really. And Carol was gorgeous, too. Diane took out her phone and used it as a mirror. Her hair had grown, and while some might like natural curls it was a mess, always a mess. She didn't have time to take care of it. And unlike Carol, who apparently didn't have to do anything to lose weight, Diane had been trying to walk and exercise more, but she noticed her legs were just getting bigger. She looked down at her thighs and shut off the phone. *Tree trunks*, she thought. *Well, not yet, but getting there.* She shook those thoughts away and looked back toward her room, thinking of Daniel and Carol.

She had heard stories from the first years that he was a bully. That didn't surprise Diane. Then she saw how Daniel used jealousy and anger and whatever other problems he had going on inside of him. When he was hurt, he took it out on other people.

Diane didn't trust him one bit.

And now? So now the jealousy and the anger and whatever else goes on in a teenage boy's mind like his was replaced with other hormonal emotions. Maybe he just wanted to get laid.

But Diane couldn't help but worry that he was using Carol.

This summer short film contest at UCLA was a *contest*, after all. And she knew not to trust him when it came to competition.

Diane sat in the lounge and browsed the pictures in her phone. She had reason not to trust people, of course. She had been burned, literally, in the Hellfire challenges at Rabbit in Red. But what confused her now was that Daniel had once tried to convince Carol that it was all JB's fault.

JB sure had his faults. But it was Sid who had burned her. Sid—a monster of a man who wanted to take down JB, Rabbit in Red, and everything inside of it. And why?

She supposed it was because they locked him up and hurt his feelings. That was the story she had been told anyway, and that was her problem with Daniel, too. Take away an unstable boy's toys, and he may just try to kill you.

She survived the burning—luckily, it was minor—and she returned to Rabbit in Red more determined than ever. It was she who had first really seen what Ricky/Sid was capable of. He had shoved her and tried to hurt her when they were competing in Hellfire. She had thought he just really wanted to win. Turned out, he really wanted to lock her and everyone else up in Hellfire and burn them alive.

But he'd failed. Well . . . not entirely.

She looked at the pictures on her phone. There was Bill— Diane liked Bill. He was the kind of guy who kept calm when others went crazy. He got shit done.

And there was Jaime. Diane thought of everything Jaime must have been through these last few months. They weren't close, exactly, but Diane always thought Jaime liked her. Diane was good at solving the riddles and tough at competition. She sensed that Jaime respected that.

She scrolled through and saw a picture of Wes and Rose. Oh, poor Rose. She was so beautiful. She and Wes were always together. There was something so sweet about them. Not like Daniel and Carol back in her dorm room. Rose and Wes may have been young, but Diane always thought what they had was true love.

Then there was a picture of JB, talking to them back in the *Candyman* commons. He always looked a bit like Frankenstein's monster. So big. So powerful. She had thought, and to be honest they had all thought . . . he was invincible.

She wiped a tear and closed her eyes.

She let the memory take her back.

Back to JB's funeral.

*****

They had all gathered back at the grounds that had once been Rabbit in Red. Well, almost all of them.

It had been a month since the destruction of the building, but it still felt like there was ash in the air. Diane's parents had talked about 9/11 this way. Her mom said that after terrorists attacked the Twin Towers in New York City that there was ash in the air for months.

Chester Malcom had gathered the rabbiteers together, the first years and the new recruits, all who would and could come, anyway.

"I don't know if this is what JB would have wanted," Chester said. "But it's what I want. What you want, too, I know. We need a proper good-bye."

He lowered his head, and so did everyone else.

"There's so much to tell you all. So much. But what I must express is this: JB loved you all as if you were his own children."

Diane swallowed hard and looked up front as Jaime reached out and held Bill's hand. Diane was surprised Jaime was here. But then again, Jaime never would have missed this.

"We've lost more than JB. We mourn for all our losses. Friends. Family. Loved ones. But I mean what I say. To JB, you were his children. He loved sharing his passions with you. Bringing to life what no one else could ever have done. He had a great vision, one that was much bigger than any of you even experienced. You all saw the tip of the iceberg." Chester coughed and wiped away tears. "He had so much more planned for you, and in the end . . ." He couldn't finish.

Annie started sobbing. She stood close to Diane, and Annie's tears started a chain reaction. Diane watched Carol cry, then Venus, then some of the boys. Kent and Leroy lowered their heads. Even Brandis looked like he let the tears escape freely.

Diane felt her body shake, but she didn't cry.

Not until she saw Bill wrap his arm around Wes. Bill's long arm wrapped around Wes's shoulders, and Wes leaned against him.

Wes had started shaking. Diane could tell he was trying to hold back the tears, but then he leaned forward and let out a sob.

And when he cried, Diane could hold back no longer.

Everyone cried.

After a few moments, Chester coughed to get their attention. "I've been left in charge of JB's estate, temporarily. There's more that he is going to ask of you." He tried to smile. "You know that, right? That crazy son-of-a-bitch will have challenges for you even from beyond the grave."

They all smiled a bit at that.

"But for now, we grieve together. No matter where you all go, we will always be a family. We will always be rabbiteers."

He took a great big breath. "What words can I share with you to ease your pain?" Chester asked. He wiped at his eyes, took another deep breath, and continued. "What bonds us, no matter our differences, is that we will all die. Our breaths are limited."

His voice cracked, and he reached for a bottle of water. After a sip, he said, "It doesn't seem real, does it? How can a warm hand, a fast-beating heart, a powerful voice—how can all that be gone? I feel . . . empty. I know some of you do, too."

Chester swallowed hard, and took another sip of water. "JB will live in all of you now. He will be in your hearts and your memories. It may be a terrible condolence to know that that's all you have, but you will always have that." He looked everyone in the eye and nodded.

"Now, please hold one another's hands." Chester waited a minute. They all formed a giant circle. Diane held on to Carol's hand on her left and Jimmy's hand on her right. In front of her, she watched as Jaime, Bill, and Wes held on tight to one another.

She tried not to cry, but she failed.

Then Chester sang. "Aaahh-maazing grace, how sweeeeet the sound . . ."

They all joined in. It was the most beautiful singing she had ever heard.

*****

"Hey, what are you doing?" Carol asked and shook Diane on the shoulders.

Diane looked around. She was still in the lobby. "Shit, I must have fallen asleep."

"Well, we've got another interview request. This time with some horror podcasters. Yes or no?"

"No. I'm so tired of interviews." Diane stood up and stretched. "I think I'll take a nap."

"Uh, didn't you—"

"Shut it. I'm tired." Diane walked past Carol and back into their dorm room. They had become sort of celebrities since Rabbit in Red burned down. National and local news networks bombarded them with interview requests.

All the new recruits had managed to finish high school and graduate. After so many students nearly got killed, most high schools were flexible enough to allow for a combination of online classes, tutoring, and home-schooling. It was Carol who had texted Diane about a summer film camp at UCLA. Diane wanted to get back to her passions. She'd had months of parents and teachers asking if she was okay, and she realized the only way she'd ever really be okay was if she got back to being active. If she got back to *creating*.

Would she ever see the others from Rabbit in Red again? The group hadn't been together since JB's funeral. Diane thought it would just be her and Carol, which was fine. Carol knew her horror, and when she wasn't sucking face with Daniel, Carol and Diane had great conversations.

She had missed that.

That might have been the best thing about Rabbit in Red. She was surrounded by people with similar passions. That was what she had hoped to get out of this summer film camp. But the students here were just like the media. They drooled around her, literally sometimes, to learn JB's secrets, to learn what had really happened.

Did you really get set on fire?

How many people were killed?

Did the Rabbit's Eye really make you feel pain? What was it like?

Will there ever be another Hellfire?

Do you know anything about JB's will? He had to be loaded!

The questions never ended, and Diane didn't want to talk about them. She wanted to be here so she could be on a team again and work together on projects.

But this was nothing like Rabbit in Red.

She went into her dorm room and put on some PJs, even though it was still daylight. She'd just read until she fell asleep.

That was when she saw a package on her bed. There was one on Carol's, too.

"Hey, Carol!"

Diane turned around and jumped. Carol had been standing right behind her.

"What's this?" Diane asked, pointing at the boxes.

"Those just arrived. That's what I wanted to tell you."

"They have—"

"The Rabbit in Red logo on them, I know! How exciting!" Carol smiled, but Diane's stomach dropped. What could this be?

"Open yours first," Carol said. "Do it!"

Diane moved slowly, one step at a time to the box. She picked it up and shook it. It weighed maybe a couple of pounds, and there was a mysterious rattle. The box had her name and the college address on it. The entire front of the box had one of the most recent Rabbit in Red logos on it. She remembered JB playing with several new designs last year. This one had a skull with rabbit's ears and a virtual reality headset—the Rabbit's Eye they had worn in Hellfire.

She looked back at Carol, who nodded encouragingly. Then Diane ripped open the box.

The first thing she saw inside the box was a tiny movie projector. It had an old-fashioned design, one with movie reels and a big lens. It wasn't as big as a coffee mug.

Diane examined it closely and saw that it had a small play button. When she pressed it, an image popped out and she gasped.

It was JB.

She placed the small camera on her desk and a hologram version of JB appeared on their dorm room wall.

"Hello, my old friends." The voice was his. No computer simulation, Diane thought. That was the real JB, and it sent chills down her spine.

"I've missed you," he continued. "Nothing should surprise you at this point, yes? You've done so much, but it's time to do more. I'll explain everything once you're all back together. In this package, you'll have also received a special ticket. Hold on to that closely. It will get you on any plane for any destination for the rest of this year. It's quite valuable."

He smiled, the mischievous grin they all had loved so much. "Use it to get to your first destination. See you there."

JB's image vanished. Then the rabbit popped out of the projector. It sneered and danced, shooting out images of blood. Diane looked back at Carol. They were both smiling.

The rabbit announced its message.

Follow the Rabbit. Follow the Rabbit in Red.
You've got so much to gain. No, geen.
We all wear many faces, alive or dead.
Go to his fire, his chains, to so much more unseen.

Diane smiled, and when she opened her mouth, Carol jumped in before she could even get out a word.

"I think I know where we're supposed to go!" Carol yelled.

"Me, too." Diane smiled.

"What are we waiting for?"

"Let's call the others. I'll start with Bill. You call Jaime. I hope we can get them all back together."

Carol nodded, and Diane took out her phone and called Bill Wise.

While the phone rang, she looked at the shiny plastic card inside the box.

It was a golden ticket. Just like in *Willy Wonka*.

Chapter Four

Bill Wise tripped over the step and stumbled into the front door of his house. "Dammit," he mumbled. If his mom caught him like this, she'd literally kick his ass.

Bill was drunk.

Falcor greeted him with kisses and a vigorous wag of the tail. Bill bent over to give the pup some love. Dogs never judged, and he loved that. He had been more than happy to take Falcor after Rabbit in Red burned down, but now he felt a sharp pain of guilt. He'd been gone a lot and hadn't been paying much attention to him.

It was near one in the morning on a humid June night. Some friends had invited him over. He wasn't used to having a lot of friends, but since he had returned home, he had received a surprising number of Snapchat follows.

Earlier tonight, he had attended a party hosted by kids he graduated with but never hung out with. Never. But they wanted to hear all his stories. They drank Jack Daniels and Coors Light, and although there had been a time in his life when he swore he'd never touch a drop of liquor, that had all changed this summer.

In fact, he'd been drunk every night this week.

"William Stephen Wise, you sit your ass down on this chair." Sally Wise, his mother, stood tall in the kitchen and pulled out a chair.

Bill sighed. This wasn't the first time this summer that she had pulled out the kitchen chair and lectured him.

"What the fuck do you think you're doing?" Sally asked.

"Mom!" Bill was used to her cussing, but not at him.

"Don't 'Mom' me. *Sit*."

Bill shuffled into the kitchen and plopped himself onto the chair.

"Now, talk," she said.

"Huh?" Bill scratched the top of his head.

"I need to know what's going on with you. *Talk*." She put her elbows on the table and folded her hands as if she were praying.

"What do you want me to talk about?" Bill felt drool spill out of his mouth and he wiped his cheek.

"How do we move forward? I know life sucks. JB is gone. Rabbit in Red is gone. Everyone is back home and you're away from them all. But we have got to move forward." She stared at him and didn't blink once.

Bill just shrugged.

"You're not living, Bill. You're alive, but you're not living."

He didn't say anything. The words sobered him up, but he couldn't speak. He took out his phone and looked at his text messages.

"Bill!" He looked up at his mom. "Talk to me."

"I don't know how to explain it," he finally said. "I feel . . . I feel like there's nothing to be excited about. That's all."

His mom placed her hands flat on the table and nodded.

"A bright, young man like you has hundreds of opportunities! Don't you know that?"

He looked at her with puffy eyes. Drunk eyes.

Sally took a deep breath. "When you're young, like you, and you get excited about something big, like Rabbit in Red . . . nothing else compares. Not at first. But it will, Bill. You'll see that." She reached for his hand. "I'm not gonna be that hypocrite mother. Lord knows how much I used to drink. It was you who helped me then." She squeezed his hand. "Let me help you now."

Bill pulled away his hand. He looked into her eyes but turned away quickly. She could say whatever she wanted, but he saw the disappointment in her eyes.

"I'll be okay. Just need to sleep it off."

She grabbed his arm as he stood up. "You won't want to hear this, but you have to. You've got an obsessive personality. I know because I have one, too. You throw yourself into that horror shit, and that was fine until people started getting hurt." She pulled him closer. "Someone with an obsessive personality will jump from that to booze in no time. Before you know it, you've got a real problem." She let go of him, and Bill looked up at her slowly. "You sleep it off, but don't think for one second that we don't have more to talk about later."

He turned around walked upstairs to his bedroom and felt her eyes on his back the entire time. Falcor ran up the stairs behind him, his tail still wagging, oblivious and happy.

Up in his room, Bill kicked unopened Horror Block boxes out of his way. He scanned Netflix for new horror films he hadn't seen. When he found one called *Hush*, he pressed play and watched it till he fell asleep. He liked the description. The main character was deaf—couldn't hear and couldn't speak—and she had to battle a home intruder.

*****

In the morning, he reached for his running shoes and thought he'd jog through the cemetery to clear his mind. But as soon as he bent over, a pain in his head told him that wasn't going to happen today. Instead, he reached under his bed and grabbed a different kind of shoe box.

This one had pictures of his father, Arnold Wise.

Arnie, as he was known to his friends, looked like Bill. Tall, but not as thin. His hair was a darker blonde, too, but there was no missing the resemblance. Looking at pictures of Arnie felt like looking at a future Bill. Weird.

His favorite pictures were the ones with both of his parents and the old family dog, Sparky. Bill sat on the floor with the pictures spread out all around him and checked his phone. He had several missed calls from Diane. She had called yesterday, but he never heard the phone ring. *Too much liquor,* he thought, as he rubbed his head. Looking at his text messages, he kept wishing for a reply from Jaime.

It had been weeks since he had heard from her.

He had visited her in the hospital for as long as he could, but eventually Bill's mom made him fly home. He texted her daily, just asking how she was feeling and whatnot. At first, he got brief messages.

I'm okay.

Just tired.

Then they got shorter and shorter.

Okay. Or *tired.*

She never asked how he was doing. Then a few weeks ago, she stopped texting altogether.

It made Bill sick to his stomach.

He had tried messaging Tara, Jaime's little sister, too. He got a few brief updates from her, and then he received a terrible message.

Mom's making me do a tech blackout. That's what she's calling it. No phone, no social media. She's still scared someone may be after Jaime. Or me.

Bill didn't like it, but he understood. Last year, Tara had been kidnapped and set on fire. Well, only her hair, but it had scared everyone, that was for sure. When Tara's hair grew back, she buzzed a rabbit outline on the side of her head. Many of the other first years followed suit.

JB had tried to protect Tara by bringing her to Rabbit in Red. He brought Janet Stein, too, Tara and Jaime's mom. But obviously, he didn't protect them. Sid Malcolm had managed to sabotage Rabbit in Red from the inside.

He hurt Jaime and burned down the studios. He killed people.

And the worst thing?

He was missing. No one knew where Sid Malcolm was.

Jaime had told the police that she had killed him, or thought she had. She told Bill the same thing when he visited her.

But they never found his body. Sid Malcolm was still missing after all these months. *That's why the Steins are all on edge,* Bill thought. He just wished he could be with Jaime. With all of them.

Instead, Bill Wise spent the hot summer days alone in his bedroom and the hot summer nights out drinking with so-called new friends.

He put the old pictures back in the shoebox and slid it back under his bed. Then he took a swig out of a half empty old water bottle that was sitting on his desk. Sitting down at his computer, he searched for a name on Google.

Jason Lamb.

Jason Lamb was the man who murdered his father. Through his creative resources, JB had managed to find Jason Lamb. At the end of the first Halloween weekend, JB had showed news footage of Lamb getting arrested and had given Bill a file with the details. Bill had looked at the files before, but they never really sunk in. There was always something else to look forward to. Talks with Jaime, the summer and new school year at Rabbit in Red . . . until all that went to hell.

Last year, his mother had said something to Bill when he was home on winter break. He recalled the conversation, a question Bill had on his mind.

"How did the intruder—uh, Jason Lamb—how did he know that I was here? Do you remember? He asked you where I was. He said 'your son.' He clearly knew you had a boy. He didn't ask about anything else. How did he know?"

"Oh, for heaven's sake, how would I know?" Sally shook her head and rubbed her eyes.

"Doesn't it seem weird to you? Was he watching the house? Or did he know us somehow?"

"I guess you could ask him," she stated matter-of-factly.

When Lamb had entered their home on that fateful night, he wanted to know where Bill was. His parents had quickly said that Bill was spending the night at a friend's house. It had bothered Bill that the intruder knew about them, that perhaps it wasn't random at all.

So when he had asked his mother about it and she said, "I guess you could ask him," Bill's stomach turned upside down. He hadn't ever thought about it, but now—with absolutely nothing else to do—the thought consumed him.

Could he find the courage to go see Jason Lamb in prison?

Bill had asked Lamb once that dreadful question. "Why?"

Lamb had answered, "Sometimes there is no why."

But not knowing had always bothered Bill. For more than a decade, Bill could only guess. At some point—probably around the same time he had watched *The Strangers*—he had settled on the idea that maybe it was random, that maybe there was no answer to why.

Now Bill had a feeling there was an answer, and he was determined to find out.

So he searched for the arrest record of Jason Lamb to find where he had been imprisoned. With a couple of clicks of the mouse, Bill learned that Lamb was less than two hours away.

He shut down his computer, ran downstairs, and picked up his mom's car keys. It was a Saturday morning, and she appeared to still be asleep.

Bill looked at his phone to check the time. Just as he did, another call came from Diane. He hit decline and ran out of the house. He stumbled over a small box on the front porch, but he didn't even bother to look at it. His mind was completely focused on getting the answer to a question he had asked over ten years ago.

*****

From her bedroom window, Sally Wise watched her son leave in her car.

"He could have at least asked," she said to no one.

Shaking her head, she sat back down in bed. She hadn't slept very well. It was one of those nights where she could have used a drink. But no, no more drinking. She had been sober now for 380 days. She thanked God for each one. It was near this time last summer that she had promised Bill she'd quit.

She quit drinking, but had started smoking. *It's what addicts do,* she tried to rationalize in the way only addicts understand. *Better for me to smoke than drink, right?* She opened one of the bedroom windows and lit up. Maybe she'd have to try vaping. That was what all the cool kids seemed to do these days.

She rolled her eyes at the thought.

When she knew Bill was gone, she opened her dresser drawer, the one where she kept bras and underwear. In other words, the one drawer she knew Bill would never intentionally open.

She reached in underneath all her undergarments and searched for a special item.

When she removed her arm from the drawer, she held on to one VHS tape. It was labeled, *For Sally—you deserve to know. And for Bill—when you think he's ready.*

It had come in the mail just before Rabbit in Red had burned down. The return label listed Jay Bell as the sender.

That made sense to Sally, since the video was all about JB.

She watched it from beginning to end multiple times.

First, it showed JB as a little boy with a female friend. They re-enacted a scene from *The Exorcist*. Some people may have found it cute, but Sally had said, "No wonder he's fucked up," when she first saw it.

The next scene, though, was truly disturbing. JB was older, maybe junior high age, Sally had guessed. He said that he was going to "hang those who shame."

He had recorded a skit where he played himself and some kids who had been picking on him, kids who took his Halloween candy. These kids kept calling him "Smell Slime" over and over. Sally didn't understand the nick name, but she jumped out of bed when JB put a rope around his throat and pretended to hang these imaginary children.

He kept repeating, "Hang those who shame."

Sally had held her hand hard against her mouth when she saw the next video. JB was in high school. He had brought his camcorder with him, and she saw kids tease and ridicule him at a high school dance. She didn't see what happened at the end of this scene because JB had dropped the camera. Apparently, he had had enough. One by one, each one of them dropped as if JB was beating them up. She heard screams and the sounds of bones crunching. At the end, she heard JB say, "I should kill you all."

She had stopped watching the video then, and for a moment, she genuinely contemplated flying directly to Rabbit in Red and dragging Bill out of there. She paced the house for a bit, cell phone in hand, and minutes later had decided to finish what was on the tape before making any decision.

In the next scene, JB was in college. He had a girl in his dorm room, and he paid her to beat him.

He talked about needing to know what pain felt like. Real pain.

Then in another scene, a man came into JB's dorm room. JB choked this guy until the man almost passed out. He paid the guy, and Sally's jaw about hit the floor as they seemed to set up another appointment for an afternoon of torture.

JB was a bit older in the next scene, and Sally couldn't tell where it had been filmed. It was a different room, not the dorm room where he had filmed the others.

JB talked about falling in love with a woman.

Today, on this summer Saturday after Bill left the house, she replayed that particular scene.

When JB spoke into the camera, his voice was nervous. "I've done something unforgivable," he confessed. "Someday I'll show you this video and you'll understand. I hope. That's why I need to record this. I fell in love with the most beautiful woman. She took away my pain. I felt nothing but pleasure when with her. She took away my desire to learn about pain."

JB shifted and cracked his neck. "We had many great years together, you and I. But I realized I need to feel that pain. I can't create without it, and for a few years now, I've been unable to create anything. I lost a part of me when I found you. I have to find that part again, or I'll go through life like a zombie. I don't want dinner served at six or a routine date night. I need to experience the world, all of its sights and sounds. All of its emotions too, including the pain of leaving you."

He stood up and looked in a mirror. "I don't recognize myself." He took scissors and started cutting his hair. He turned it into an uneven mess.

He looked straight into the camera. "I can use the monster in me to create. Or I can let the monster die and do nothing at all. The latter is not an option. I'm sorry. I hope one day you'll forgive me." He picked up a long, sharp butcher knife. He faced a direction off-camera. Then he lifted his arm high up over his head, and just when he was about to bring the knife down, the video feed became disoriented. Lines squiggled throughout, and the sound cut off. Then the screen went to black.

JB came back on.

"That's the last thing Bill and the others saw," JB said. Now it was the JB she recognized.

"These tapes were clearly planted so that the kids would turn against me. But I want you to know that I love these kids as if they were my own."

He was speaking at the commons in Rabbit in Red. Sally had been there once before.

"This particular video was edited so that they couldn't see what I really did. I had a lot of home movies. Tons. I had as many home movies as the old video stores had rentals. Someone stole these and edited them the way they wanted the kids to see me." JB, almost always large and powerful, sat down and looked defeated.

"So I made my own video tape that shows the real ending. The real ending and more. It's time you all know the truth about my past."

The new scene began, and Sally watched JB pick up the long, sharp butcher knife once again.

The first time she saw what happened next, Sally Wise screamed.

Today she re-watched the rest of the video quietly and thought about what was happening to her son. Maybe it was time she showed this to him.

He needed to know who JB really was.

Chapter Five

For Wes Pike, the first half of this year had been the hardest, most challenging months of his life. He sat on an oddly cool summer day at a park in New Orleans. Enjoying the fresh air, he flipped through his Instagram feed.

He followed nearly everyone at Rabbit in Red, and Venus Bowers had just posted a picture of the first years from the original Halloween contest. Wes didn't interact a whole lot with Venus—let's face it, he'd spent most of his time at Rabbit in Red glued to Rose Dawn—but Venus was cool. Her ideas largely inspired Hellfire, Wes remembered.

Clicking on the picture, Wes zoomed in to get a closer image of Rose. Rose was so beautiful. That red hair, the fire in her cheeks and her in words. She didn't always say a lot, but when she did speak, it was powerful. Rose's purse hung from her shoulder, and Wes could make out the purple stitching of her favorite quote: "Speak only if it improves upon the silence."

Wes leaned back on the park bench, turned off his phone, and closed his eyes. He'd give almost anything to go back to that time at Rabbit in Red. Oh, he remembered being angry, mostly angry that JB had designed a contest where Rose had been kidnapped. But it turned out to be only a game, and Rose had wanted to go back. Wes, of course, wanted to go wherever Rose went.

A cool breeze glided across Wes's face, and he sighed.

He had relived the final moments at Rabbit in Red over and over again in his mind. They rushed to get out, he, Rose, and some others, and Rose went back for Lester and Falcor. The rabbit and the dog. The studios were crumbling under the flames, and Rose ran back for the animals! Wes should have stopped her. He knew that, and he had berated himself every single day since that terrible night.

But he also knew that he couldn't have stopped her. It was what he loved and hated about her all at the same time—her determination.

They got both animals to safety, but right after Rose passed Lester to Wes from the *Alien*-themed bedrooms above the commons, the ceiling collapsed on Rose. The flames and smoke engulfed the studios, and Wes and company had no choice but to leave or die.

What a terrible, terrible night that had been.

"One cherry snow cone for you. Blue raspberry for me."

Wes opened his eyes.

"Thank you," he said and reached for the treat.

"Even on this cool day, it tastes great, don't you think? I just had to have a snow cone. It's not summer without them, especially in New Orleans."

Wes nodded and smiled.

He licked the outside of the snow cone, and he felt more tears prick at his eyelids. He tried to shake them away. He always felt so stupid when the tears would just come out of nowhere. Here, they were just trying to enjoy a day in the park, and then just like a little kid, not the man he was supposed to be, he started to cry.

She reached for his hand and squeezed.

He knew she was used to these outburst from him. He loved her all the more for it.

He squeezed her hand back. "I'm sorry."

"Please. It's okay."

"No, I'm sorry. I just . . . I was looking at an old picture. Thinking about what happened. I don't know. I get so mad and so grateful all at once. You know?" Wes sniffed hard and blinked back the tears and turned to her.

"I know. Me, too."

"I think about all we've gone through this year." He swallowed and tasted his tears, then licked the snow cone to erase that taste.

41

He looked at her, closer than he had since her last surgery.

"Oh, Rose, I just love you so much." He put his arm around her on the park bench and kissed her. He tasted her blue raspberry flavor, and when he pulled away, he smiled.

"I love you, too," Rose said.

To Wes, Rose would always be beautiful. She had scars that covered nearly two-thirds of her face now, and her chest, back, and legs had all been burned, too. The paramedics found Rose in the burning Rabbit in Red studios, and when they had pulled her out on a stretcher, Wes thought for sure that she was dead.

But she wasn't.

Somehow, she survived. She had the worst burns on her body that Wes could ever imagine, but she had survived.

He stayed at the hospital with her as long as the nurses would let him. He had refused to go home. Getting a hotel in L.A., Wes spent the next couple of weeks with Rose. At that time, no one was confident she would survive.

But she did.

It had turned out the burns looked significantly worse than they actually were. Damaging the skin, Wes had learned, wasn't too hard, and burning could do significant and permanent damage quite quickly. Rose's burns looked terrible, but somehow they didn't penetrate deep enough to do serious internal damage. The doctors had called it a miracle over and over again—no one, they claimed, should have survived what Rose had.

Wes smiled at the thought. He knew how tough she really was.

Rose eventually went to a hospital in her hometown, here in New Orleans. No one—*no one*—could convince Wes not to go. Rose's parents let Wes stay at their house, and Wes spent every day at the hospital with her. She went through several surgeries, but now she was completely independent.

And somehow, Wes thought, she was stronger than ever.

He wondered what she saw when she looked in the mirror. Her hair had grown back, but it looked short and messy, like she had just been in a wrestling match. He was grateful for the cool days in the hot South because she typically wore long sleeves and jeans, as her legs and arms were scarred, too.

The one place that was the same was the left side of her face. She must have fallen on that side. Her cheek, her eye, and even a bit of her forehead had been completely unharmed. The rest of her face—well, the surgeries did the best they could. From a distance, she looked old, like she just had a bunch of wrinkles. Up close, the skin was still rough and healing, like marshmallow over fire right before it bursts into flame.

Wes didn't care. He loved her. They sat in the park and ate their snow cones, and that was all he needed.

Hand in hand, they walked the park, then later that day hopped on a bus to head back to Rose's parents' house, where they both stayed. They made Wes sleep in the guest room, but every night he had snuck out to cuddle with Rose.

They hadn't been intimate since the fire. Rose let him cuddle with her, but nothing else. Wes had tried more, but she'd just say that she couldn't and "Would it be okay if you just held me?"

It was and it would be, for as long as she needed, Wes had told her. He thought he understood. Under the long pajamas she wore to bed wasn't the same body Wes had seen the first time they were intimate. He just wished she knew that it didn't matter to him. He was in love with her. With her mind, her soul, her heart. He loved her body, too, but it didn't matter.

When they got back home, there were two packages waiting for them on the front porch. Wes felt his heart leap into his throat. Somehow, he knew. He knew this wasn't over. He just wanted to spend the days with his girl. No way in hell did he want to spend any more time with *anything* related to Rabbit in Red.

One package was addressed to Rose, and the other to Wes.

They opened them without speaking.

Inside each, a small, old style recording camera waited for them. When they pressed play, JB spoke.

Wes had chills. He listened to the message and the riddle. He saw the golden ticket in the package. The first thought in his mind: Destroy it. Destroy it now.

But then he looked at Rose and saw something he hadn't seen since . . . since before.

Excitement? Maybe. A purpose? That was closer. Wes saw in her eyes that she'd want to solve the riddle and find out what JB wanted from them.

They listened to the riddle again.

Follow the Rabbit. Follow the Rabbit in Red.
You've got so much to gain. No, geen.
We all wear many faces, alive or dead.
Go to his fire, his chains, to so much more unseen.

Rose's eyes lit up. Wes thought he knew the answer, too.

"Do you want to go?" Wes asked.

Rose smiled. It was the biggest smile he'd seen on her face this summer. "I do. Are you okay with that?"

Wes inhaled deeply and held his breath. *No, not really,* he thought. But he said, "Wherever you go, I go. But this time, I bury the fuckin' rabbit. There has to be an ending."

"Bury the rabbit," Rose repeated. "I like that."

*****

Rose Dawn packed a bag. Excitement pulsed through every vein in her body. She wondered what other people would think, and she laughed out loud.

They'd think she was crazy, and maybe she was. She had spent months in and out of operating rooms where doctors tried to make her look as normal as possible. For months, she didn't enjoy a single damn thing about life. It was all about doctors and nurses and looking in the mirror. Oh, there had been lots of time to look in the mirror and wonder who the hell was staring back.

"That cannot be me," she had said out loud.

But it was.

She loved Wes, loved him more than anyone or anything in the world, but she worried about him, too. She couldn't tell him that. Taking care of her had been his world, and that was what worried her.

There has to be more to our lives.

So when this riddle and message from JB showed up, it was a miracle. They needed to get out, to do something, to find a purpose again. Solving the riddle would be good. Finding out some answers to the million questions she had would be better.

What was on the final video tape? She knew there was more to see.

And where the hell is Sid Malcom? She knew that no one had found his body, even though she had been told that Jaime attempted to kill him. Sid was responsible for this, she thought and felt her face. She needed to talk to Jaime. Maybe the two of them—Rose and Jaime together—could find Sid. Bury the rabbit, Wes had said. Rose smiled. If there was one thing that needed to be buried, it was Sid Malcom.

Since JB is dead, who is organizing these riddles and deliveries and golden tickets? That had to be Chester, right? Rose hadn't been able to attend JB's funeral, as she was still in the hospital, but Wes had told her that Chester said JB still had more planned for all of them and that they'd find out when the time was right.

Was this what he meant?

So, we've got a scavenger hunt across the country, Rose thought. Then she repeated the riddle to herself. *And we start in Wisconsin?* She thought she knew the answer to the riddle, but Wisconsin seemed like an odd place to begin.

Well, the place doesn't matter. I'll get to see everyone again. I need to talk to Bill and Jaime. There's so much more to discuss.

She ran downstairs to feed Lester. Bill had taken Falcor, but Wes had kept Lester for Rose. The bunny hopped when he saw Rose, as if he knew he was about to get a special treat.

Rose couldn't wait to go, and she wasn't going to tell her parents until the last minute. Of course, they'd refuse and do everything in their power to keep Rose in the house. But Rose wasn't a kid, and she was going to do what she wanted. She'd tell them they were going to spend the night at Louisiana State and tour the campus or something. That would make them happy, she supposed. But really they'd sprint right to the airport and figure out which flight would get them to Wisconsin with their golden ticket.

She checked on Wes, and he had a bag packed. She heard the shower running in the guest bathroom and figured Wes must be cleaning up before they left.

She ran outside to stretch her legs. No way she could sit still and wait, so she paced the backyard.

That was when a man leapt out at her.

He grabbed her by the shoulders, spun her around, and put a hand over her mouth.

"Scream, and I'll kill your fat ass boyfriend and your parents while you watch. Got it?"

She wanted to bite his hand and kick him in the crotch as hard as possible, but she nodded instead.

"Good girl. Now, where are your golden tickets?"

The man had been wearing a baseball cap to cover his eyes, but Rose would recognize that voice anywhere.

She wanted to tell him to fuck off.

But he squeezed harder and repeated, "Where are your golden tickets?"

It was Dexter Lange.

Chapter Six

Bill Wise sat face to face with the man who murdered his father. Whatever hangover or memories of the morning lingered in his mind vanished the moment he saw Jason Lamb.

He couldn't remember how he got to the prison or how he asked to visit Lamb. There was a moment where he was sure the prison staff would just laugh at him, but no, here he was, several minutes later, facing Jason Lamb with nothing but a piece of glass separating them.

Lamb looked into Bill's eyes, and Bill instantly thought of Dr. Loomis in *Halloween*, and what Loomis said about Michael Myers: "He has the darkest eyes. The devil's eyes."

It was true, too, about Jason Lamb. Lamb looked his age, forty-two or forty-three if Bill remembered correctly from his research. His head was buzzed, but stubbly black hairs had already sprouted all over his scalp. His face was clean-shaven, but those eyes, they were the darkest eyes he had seen.

Next to Michael Myers, he supposed. Or—no—Dexter had the same kind of eyes, too. He remembered thinking that when he first saw Dexter Lange on a TV interview that he had psycho, dark eyes.

Bill froze. What was he even going to say? He couldn't believe he was here, and now that he was here, he lost all sense of thought.

Lamb motioned at the telephone. Bill looked dumbly at the old-fashioned telephone receiver attached to the wall near the glass. Oh, yeah. He had seen this in plenty of movies, but his brain wasn't working at all today.

He picked up the phone. So did Jason Lamb.

"Hi, Bill," Lamb said.

Bill's throat felt like he just swallowed a whole apple. *How does he know my name?*

Lamb's eyes narrowed, and he looked intensely at Bill as if he had been waiting for this moment his entire life.

"Whether it stars men or women or marshmallow men, the most fun part of this movie is when the green little ghost does what?"

Is he asking me a riddle? What the hell?

"When he slimes you," Bill said. Somehow, thinking about Ghostbusters made him focus a little. Maybe that was Lamb's objective, but Bill sure wondered what Lamb was up to.

"Slime is the answer. Wish I had a prize to give you." He smiled, and Bill wanted to vomit. *This guy's just playing games with me,* he thought. *This is the fucking guy who murdered my father! Focus, Bill. Get what you want out of him and then get the hell out of here.*

"How do you know me?" Bill asked, and Lamb's smile grew bigger.

"We have a mutual friend."

Who the hell would that be? *I was like eight years old the day you ruined my family forever!* Bill held his breath.

"Who—"

"No, my turn," Lamb interrupted. He licked his lips and then said, "Fill in the blank. The house BLANK musty and damp, and a little sweet, as if it were haunted by the ghosts of long-dead cookies."

Bill squinted and turned his head to the side. *What is that all about? Lamb is reading Neil Gaiman in prison? I don't get it,* he thought. But he answered, "Smelled."

"Smell, smell, smell. How I miss that smell." Lamb laughed.

"So, who is the mutual friend?" Bill asked. He felt sweat drip down his back and his forehead, but he refused to move. He felt like he was in a staring contest with Jason Lamb. Maybe it sounded ridiculous, but Bill thought he had to win. He had to prove to Lamb that he was tough, that he wasn't a child.

Lamb moved closer to the window, the phone tightly pressed against his ear.

"What do the two riddles have in common?"

"Enough of your *questions*." Bill didn't want to give him the credit of calling his stupid questions riddles. Riddles were creative. This guy was just psychotic. But Lamb didn't retreat. He smiled again.

"Put the answers together."

Bill didn't understand what Lamb was trying to accomplish. Slime and smell. Those were the two answers. He wanted to shrug, he wanted to yell, but he held still.

As if sensing his dilemma, Lamb repeated, "Put the answers together."

Bill breathed hard out of his nose, and without blinking, moved the phone receiver from his left hand to his right. "Slime and smell," he said out loud without confidence.

And then it hit him.

"Smell slime," Bill said. He blinked then, and felt another apple in his throat. "Smell Slime" was the cruel name the kids had called JB on the VHS tapes. Bill had never understood the nickname, but that was beside the point. How the hell did Lamb know this? Bill blinked again and sweat rolled down his cheek.

No, it's more than that, too! How the hell does he know that I know about the Smell Slime nickname? That would mean that somehow Jason Lamb not only knew JB, but knew that Bill would learn about the nickname and JB's past. How was this possible?

Bill thought it might be better to not reveal everything. This wasn't an interview. It was a poker game, and right now Lamb held all the good cards. But Bill wanted to do everything possible to not reveal his hand.

"Why?" Bill asked.

Lamb pulled back a bit and shifted in his chair. "Are you referring to the why that you asked me the night I killed your father?"

Bill nodded.

"I already answered that once."

Sometimes there is no why, Bill recalled. But that wasn't good enough. There had to be a reason, and that was why Bill was here.

"You knew about me. It wasn't random. You asked my parents if I was home. Why did you do that?"

Lamb cocked his head to the side the way Michael Myers did when he examined a kill. Goosebumps popped up on Bill's arms.

"Kid, I scoped out the house. I knew how many people lived there. I just didn't want a surprise." But Lamb looked away when he said this. Bill had won the staring contest. Lamb was hiding something, but what was it?

"How do you know JB?" Bill asked. This time he leaned in toward the glass.

"Finish watching those video tapes. You'll understand." Lamb started to stand up, but Bill leapt to his feet first.

"No, look, you don't get to play games in there!" Bill lost his cool. "You . . . you have no idea what you did to my family, do you? I lost my father. My dad! I have nothing but the memories of an eight-year-old. No dad to teach me things. Not even a mom, really, because you drove her into alcoholism, and I had nothing but . . . but fucking books and movies. You don't get to play games! Tell me why. Why my family? *Why?*"

Bill wiped his sweaty forehead. A guard stood up and approached.

"Watch the video tapes," Lamb said again. He hung up the phone and walked away.

Bill threw his phone at the glass and slammed his fist against it. He went to hit the glass a second time, but a guard grabbed him and escorted him out.

I've got to see what was on the rest of those fucking tapes, Bill thought. But how?

*****

"You are NOT going!" Janet Stein yelled at her daughter Tara, who was holding a gold-colored plastic card in her right hand.

"JB sent one to Jaime and to me," Tara snapped back. Jaime thought she sounded more and more adult every day. What had happened to her kid sister? "That means I'm meant to go."

"That lunatic?" Janet turned her head from Tara to Jaime. "I thought you were crazy for even liking this horror shit. Then look at all that's happened to you." She looked back at Tara. "To both of you."

Janet wiped away tears of anger. "To us, Mom. You're right. A lot has happened to *us*," Jaime said and stood up. They were gathered around the kitchen table. Moments before, a knock at the door alerted them to a delivery. Jaime and Tara had each received a package from JB, with a riddle and a golden ticket.

"What does that mean?" Janet asked, slamming her hands on the kitchen table.

"It means we need to go." Jaime looked at her mother hard. Her mom flinched. Jaime knew the changes she had experienced. She had been nearly raped and killed. A couple of years ago, the worst thing she had ever experienced was Uncle Tim's suicide. Uncle Tim was like a father to her. Her own father had left them years ago. With the exception of an occasional e-mail or a bad Skype session—he was always in some part of the world without good internet, it seemed—she never heard from her dad. When Uncle Tim died, it was like losing a father.

Then Tara had been kidnapped and hurt. Then her friends. Then she, and then JB was actually murdered.

Jaime had stayed in a variety of hospital rooms, and the last string had been for mental challenges. When she first woke up in the hospital after the attack, she had sworn to all of the nurses that Sid Malcom was standing over her bed.

She had seen him many times since that night. He watched over her while she slept. He hid in her closet. When he got tired, he'd sleep under her bed and grab at Jaime's foot if she dangled it over the edge. Sid Malcolm hung out in her back yard, behind the bushes. He walked dark alleys late at night, hoping to grab her.

Jaime saw Sid everywhere she went, and that was why her mom kept forcing her to talk to doctor after doctor.

After so many therapy sessions and a few different prescriptions, Jaime worried she wouldn't be able to tell when the real Sid Malcolm showed up. And he would show up, she knew. He would want to finish the job he started. Why wouldn't he?

"Mom," Jaime continued, "I'm going. I have to. You didn't know JB like I did. There's an end to this story. There's an end that was always meant to be, and it wasn't some filthy psycho feeling me up in the back of a van!" She turned and marched out of the kitchen.

"Wait for me," Tara said and followed.

"No!" Janet yelled. "Jaime, I may not be able to control you, but Tara stays. She's too young." She jumped up from the kitchen table, grabbed Tara by the shoulder, and spun her around. "There's no way you're going!"

Jaime sighed. "You two figure it out. I'm getting my bag." She ran upstairs to her bedroom, taking two steps at a time. Grabbing a suitcase, she started to pack some clothes. How long would she be gone? And why Wisconsin? She knew the solution of the riddle, but would have to explain it to Tara.

After filling up her suitcase with clothes, she sat at her computer desk. She touched the mouse pad to see if the computer was on, so she could shut it off before leaving. She had written so many short stories at this computer, but this entire year she had yet to write one. She hadn't written anything, including a text message to Bill or Brandis, both of whom sent her plenty.

They wanted to make sure she was okay, and they asked question after question. Didn't they realize she didn't want to fucking talk about it? She knew they meant well, but she wanted to try to go a day without thinking about what had happened to her. And if she got close—if she managed to spend an entire day with her nose in the book and not think about Sid—then Bill or Brandis would text and ruin the whole thing.

She had considered blocking them, blocking everyone from Rabbit in Red. Then today, the box showed up, and like a light switch, her attitude changed. It scared her to think about how quickly her feelings changed on the subject. For months, she wanted to be in her room and have no contact with the outside world. Then this package arrived.

She didn't understand it completely, but it offered . . . hope. *That's what this is about. Hope,* she thought. Hope that everything happened for a reason. Hope that there was a purpose to all of this. Hope that people didn't kill themselves, or get hurt, or get murdered without a fucking good reason.

Slow down, Jaime, slow down, she told herself. Her chest heaved, and she realized she had been breathing extraordinarily hard.

Refocusing, she went to shut down her computer. That was when she saw an email. It was from her dad.

The inbox sender listed J. Stein to recipient J. Stein. The subject read: *Finish it, and move on.*

How does he know? That's what he means, right? My dad, who hasn't been a part of my life since I was able to retain memory, must know about Rabbit in Red, right? Finish it, and move on. And today of all days? It's like he knows about the riddle and the golden ticket. But how?

She hovered over the e-mail, wondering what the message inside would be. Rubbing her forehead, she closed her eyes and breathed hard out her nose.

Sitting up straight, she opened her eyes and deleted his e-mail without even opening it.

Fuck him, she thought. *You don't get to be a part of my life via e-mail. Not today.*

She shut down the computer, grabbed her suitcase, and ran downstairs. Her mom stood standing with arms crossed at the bottom.

"Jaime, please don't do this."

Dropping her suitcase, she grabbed her mom with both arms and hugged her hard. No matter what disagreements they may have had, at least her mother was always there for her.

"I love you, Mom." Jaime held on for several more seconds. "I don't want to fight. I understand, and I love you, but I have to go. This is the only way for me to . . ." *Finish it, and move on.* "I just have to do this," she said. "I'll call you every day."

She let go of her mother, picked up her suitcase, and ran out the front door.

She never looked back.

When she got to the airport, she looked in the backseat and screamed.

At first, she swore it was Sid Malcom hiding in her backseat.

But it turned out to be her little sister, Tara, who was still holding on to her golden ticket.

Jaime smiled at her sister. "Let's go."

Chapter Seven

The first thing Diane Willow decided that she needed to do was get together all the other people in her little class, the new recruits as they had been called last year. Since they had a golden ticket, she had the idea that they could all meet up together in L.A.—close to their old Rabbit in Red home—and then fly together to Wisconsin.

Diane paced her dorm room while waiting for them to arrive. Today was the day. They'd reunite here on campus, which had plenty of guest dorms open during the summer session, and Carol had reserved several rooms for everyone. She had probably reserved a special one just for her and Daniel, which made Diane puke a bit in her mouth and celebrate at the same time. At least she'd have the dorm room to herself tonight.

Trying to distract herself, she jumped on the Fitz of Horror Facebook page, browsing through the latest horror film recommendations, but she couldn't focus. Then a knock on the door got her attention.

"Diane?" It was Brandis Dern. Behind him stood Jimmy Cyphers and Kent Callahan, both looking anxious.

When he called her name, Diane understood why Jaime had fallen for him. He was tall, strong, and confident—he reminded Diane a little of how Johnny Depp used to look, before he got all gross and creepy—teenage Johnny Depp from the original *A Nightmare on Elm Street*. How could you not crush a little on him?

"Brandis, hi!" She felt her face warm and then looked at the others. "Jimmy, Kent. Hey."

"Hey," Kent said. He looked taller than she remembered, but he still rocked the corn rows in his hair. Jimmy nodded, and Diane thought he looked good, too. Somehow his jaw was bigger or something. More masculine than she had remembered.

She hugged each of them, and it felt both nice and awkward. Diane never felt as if she had made best friends, not in the way Jaime and Bill had, although she supposed Jaime and Bill had a whole lot of other stuff going on. But seeing the guys felt good. Sure, she had been hurt, nearly killed, but she came back with a vengeance to win—to beat whatever Rabbit in Red had in store for her. Now, bored out of her mind at the summer film camp, she couldn't wait to get on a plane and do something.

Brandis sat on her bed, and Diane felt a tingling sensation in her stomach that surprised her. "So where's everyone else?" Brandis asked.

"Carol's here, of course. She's been my roommate. And Daniel." She rolled her eyes, but she saw Jimmy's eyes light up at the mention of Daniel's name. "They're dating, can you believe that?"

Brandis laughed, and Jimmy looked like he just got hit in the stomach. She laughed a little. She just didn't understand why anyone would like Daniel.

"Anyway," Diane continued, "the rest should arrive tonight. Then we can fly out together to Wisconsin."

"It's a good idea," Brandis said. "After everything that happened, we should stick together. As much as possible. For all we know, someone's waiting at that location in Wisconsin and they'll just pick us off one at a time, horror movie style."

Kent nodded. "True. Sucks what happened, sucks bad. JB was cray, but he didn't deserve that. And Rose. Man, I hope she's better. But you know what? I want to finish this, whatever it is. Fuckin' Ricky last year, or Sid or whatever his name is, ruined everything." His pants were hanging bit loose, and Kent pulled them up and then sat down next to Brandis. Diane didn't understand why anyone wore shorts like that, but whatever. Kent was right.

"We never got a real chance," Diane said, "at whatever Rabbit in Red was going to become. We were students, or auditioning to be students. You know? And then what? What was it all for? A horror college? Sure, that's what the first years were told, but what happens *next*? It's the next I always wanted to know. This could have changed our lives, and it was stolen from us."

She took a deep breath and stared out the dorm window. From the distance, she saw Daniel and Carol walking this way hand in hand. There were plenty of times she wished she could be distracted by a boy. Glancing over her shoulder, she looked at Brandis. He'd most certainly do, she thought, if there was time.

She squeezed her hands into fists.

There was a *next*. There had to be! What would JB have done for them after two or four years of his horror education? They'd have been making a living in horror movies, their dreams come true. Money never would have been an issue. They'd be set for life.

All those dreams burned down with the rabbit.

Diane wanted her dreams back.

She turned and faced the guys. "JB was a genius, right? I mean, he filmed that riddle and message before he died. He must have always known something like this could happen." She paused and saw the hunger in their eyes for answers. "There's more to the story. There's always been more. And we're gonna get what we deserve."

Brandis smiled at her, and she liked the way that made her feel. Jimmy and Kent nodded.

They were back. The new recruits from last year, who never really had their chance to get what was theirs from Rabbit in Red. Well, now was their chance. And nothing was going to get in their way.

*****

Dexter Lange threw Rose Dawn in the back of a rental car and took off straight to the Louis Armstrong International Airport. *You can get anything with a fake ID and a credit card*, he thought. He had been prepping for this day far longer than Rose and any of her friends had realized. Little things like proper identification weren't going to get in his way.

"What do you want?" Rose yelled from the back seat.

He had tied her hands together behind her back, but she never cried. Dexter respected her for that. In fact, her eyes turned almost as red as her hair, pure fire. She was angry, and Dexter liked that.

"You and me are gonna have some fun together," he told her, starting the car.

"Wherever you think you're taking me, I'll just scream and yell. You'll never get anywhere with those tickets!" She kicked at the back of his seat, and he smiled. *She is a fiery one*, he thought.

"Oh, I don't need those. I just wanted to make it more difficult for your little boyfriend." He laughed and drove even faster.

"Where are we going?" Rose kicked at him again.

"Stop that."

Dexter thought about JB's conversation with him, the private conversation no one had heard. It infuriated Dexter that he wasn't invited back to Rabbit in Red. He played their stupid games, and so what if he turned to violence to win, even after the fact.

Horror movies were violent. No one should have been surprised, least of all JB.

Dexter replayed the conversation with JB in his mind as he left New Orleans and headed north on the highway. Rose still kicked at his back seat. When he glanced in the rear view mirror, he saw such fury in her eyes, but he just smiled back at her. That made her kick harder, and in turn he smiled bigger. That was the current game they were playing. He didn't mind.

"Dexter, have a seat," JB had said that day.

Dexter did as JB instructed. They were back in his monitoring station, just past the game chambers. JB sat in his huge chair, which was almost comical in the way it resembled a villain's chair. This was where JB watched them all play through their simulations, re-enacting and then interacting with famous movie scenes to demonstrate their horror movie knowledge. That part was too easy. Dexter knew something more had been planned.

When he had left with Daniel—who Dexter only used because he knew the kid was sneaky and jealous and would do whatever it took to win the games—to explore the studio rooms beyond the game chambers, Dexter had thought that this was the real game.

He would show JB that he had what it took to overcome evil. Dexter was sure the maniac lady with the sledgehammer in studio room one was real, and he had pushed her hard out of his way. He was also sure the gunshots in studio room two were real, and he ran past the shooter fast without looking back. In the end, Dexter thought he'd win the games by showing JB that he was the only one who had what it took to really fight. All these other kids, well . . . that was what they were, just kids. He could fight.

And he did.

But it had turned out that he was tricked. He was supposed to help these kids? Not fight them? And in the end JB just talked some bullshit about working together and overcoming fear.

Whatever.

Dexter looked at JB hard in the eyes. He knew he had that power—to look at someone hard enough and get them to do whatever he wanted.

Except it didn't seem to work on JB.

"My boy," JB started. "What were you thinking?"

He's calling me boy on purpose, Dexter thought. *I'm no kid.* He tried to stare even harder at JB, trying to scare him, and said nothing.

"I know that look," JB continued, "because I had it once, too. I did something a long time ago, something big, something to . . . to change who I was."

So what? Dexter wanted to shout. He didn't want to hear some lame story.

"You have great potential, my boy," JB said and reached out and touched Dexter's shoulder. Dexter jumped.

"I'm not going to hurt you," JB told him.

Yeah, well, I might hurt you.

"Listen to me carefully. I'm going to ask you do something, just you. Not the others. Not every challenge is inside these walls." JB gestured and lowered his voice.

"When you do this, I won't have to invite you back." He pointed out beyond the game chambers, back to the commons.

"Here's what I want you to do. First—"

"WHERE ARE YOU TAKING ME?"

Rose must have been screaming the entire time Dexter drifted away. He drifted away quite often these days, but she had screamed loud enough to get his attention.

He looked in the rear view mirror and smiled at her.

"I need to pick up a friend," he told her, and his smile grew even bigger.

*****

Back at the dorm, Diane watched as everyone finally arrived. Everyone hugged one another and talked as if they hadn't seen each other in years. Did they also forget that they were almost all killed?

They were a strange bunch, Diane thought. All of them willing to finish whatever JB had planned for them. All of them willing to take such a risk just to see how the story ended.

So why do you care? The voice inside Diane's head surprised her. *Because!* She only said it inside her mind, and she shook her head at her childish response.

Diane closed her eyes. *Because someone set out to hurt me. To hurt all of us, but—except for JB—they attacked all the girls. I want to do whatever it takes to get back at Sid and to take what's mine. Plus, I deserve a win, too, you know. JB may have had his favorites in Bill and Jaime, but the rest of us count, too!*

Diane opened her eyes, shook away the thoughts, and put on a smile. Then she walked over and hugged Julie Clarke and Amelia Davis. Samuel Roach, Morgan Rima, and Cameron Ryan seemed to be very close to one another. Brandis talked to everyone. In some ways, Brandis was this group's Bill. They had been a group of eleven, and ten of them were here today. The only one missing was Ricky Thomas, but of course there never was a Ricky Thomas.

Daniel held Carol's hand in the corner of the room and they talked to Julie and Amelia. Diane supposed that Daniel had taken Ricky's place, so they were still lucky number eleven.

Or unlucky number eleven.

All in all, it was a nice evening. They asked about Rose, but no one knew how she was. They asked about Bill and Jaime, and Diane didn't like that Brandis perked up to listen to any gossip on that. Eventually, they fell in to talking about their favorite subject. How great was *The Conjuring 2*, and don't you wish all sequels were that good? Do you really think they're doing another *Gremlins*? Rob Zombie's *31*—bad ass or just disgusting gore?

They formed a circle on the floor, and Diane sat next to Brandis. She liked it when his knee touched hers. Daniel managed to score some Summer Shandy, the only beer Diane liked, and they drank and played spin the bottle.

Diane felt like a real teenager again, and for just a moment, the memories of Rabbit in Red drifted away. She held her breath as the bottle spun and spun and slowed down, oh so close to . . . nope, it landed on Jimmy.

Jimmy laughed and jumped up and said, "Well, if I'm gonna kiss a girl, I can't think of a braver or more beautiful one than you." She kissed him on the lips, gently, no more than a peck really. Was that Brandis now who looked a bit jealous? Maybe this summer would turn out to be a good one, after all.

It was Jimmy's turn to spin the bottle, and the entire group laughed when it landed on Daniel.

Daniel's eyes popped out of his head. "Fuck you, man, no way!"

Jimmy said, "Rules are rules," and he reached for Daniel, who jumped up and ran out of the room, knocking over a bottle of Shandy on his way.

"Alcohol abuse!" Kent yelled. Everyone laughed. Even Jimmy. Even Diane.

She had forgotten what being a college kid was supposed to feel like. It wasn't supposed to be about death and destruction. She had almost been burned alive, nothing like Rose—nothing at all like poor Rose—but still, it was scary. And did she really want to return to that?

"I need another beer," Diane said and walked to the cooler Daniel had brought. Next to the cooler was Carol's dresser, where a few people had tossed keys and phones.

Just as she opened the cooler for a beer, she saw one of the phones light up with a new text message.

It read: *Meet you tomorrow as planned. I've got the girl.*

The sender's name was Dexter Lange.

Chapter Eight

Bill rushed to get home. After the meeting with Jason Lamb in prison, he felt like a kid who needed his mother. He also needed a drink. He hid some liquor in a Freddy flask in his bedroom. Just a couple sips would help right now. He also had to tell his mom more about JB, tell her about those video tapes they saw last year, and then tell her about Lamb. Something was on those tapes that JB wanted them to see, right? But how did Lamb know what was on those tapes? And how would Bill ever find a copy, anyway?

He cranked the music in his car—Terribly Happy, of course. The energetic songs from their album *Wanchu* shook the windows, and it took Bill several moments to realize his cell phone had been ringing.

Glancing at his phone, he saw he had four missed calls from Wes. As the phone rang again, Bill turned down the music, switched on his blue-tooth device, and answered.

"What's up, Wes?"

"Bill! Bill, it's bad. It's really bad!" Wes's voice shook so much the words "Bill" and "bad" almost sounded the same.

"Take a deep breath. What's happening?" Bill turned the radio completely off and picked up the speed in his mom's car to eighty miles per hour. He had a feeling he needed to get home even quicker.

"Rose is gone. She's gone! She's not answering her phone or anything, and the tickets are gone. Both of them!"

"What tickets? What are you talking about?"

"Didn't you get the tickets? JB's riddle?" At the mention of the name of his old mentor, Bill felt a lump in his throat.

"I didn't get anything." Was that jealousy he felt?

"You've got to have one, man," Wes said. "It's like a final challenge or something. Remember what Chester said at the funeral?

65

There's more. But that's not the point!" Bill heard things crash, as if Wes were throwing things or running into walls or something.

"Rose is gone! Both tickets are gone! That has to mean—"

Bill interrupted him. "Someone took her?"

"Yes!"

"And the tickets?"

"Yes!"

"Who?" Bill sped up to eighty-five.

"Sid, right? I mean, Sid nearly killed her once, and you know we always worried he'd be back to finish the job. He's got her and the tickets so they can get to Wisconsin before anyone else, I bet."

"Wisconsin?" Bill asked.

"Ugh, you'll see when you listen to the damn riddle!" Wes's voice went up several octaves. "What do I do?"

Bill pushed the speed to ninety. "We go after her."

"Yeah, okay, of course, but how?" Bill could picture Wes squeezing the old clown nose ball, if he hadn't ditched it after the first Halloween.

"What's this ticket?"

Wes briefly told Bill about the riddle and the golden ticket.

"Okay, wow." Bill took a deep breath. "So, can you get a car?"

"I'm at Rose's house now. Her parents are gone. I haven't even been able to tell them!"

Bill tried to think and squeezed the steering wheel hard as he drove. "Okay, listen. You tell Rose's parents what's going on, and you get one of their cars. Make them give it to you, steal it, whatever you have to do. They can get the police out looking for Rose. In the meantime, I'll run home, get this ticket, and fly straight down to you. You pick me up at the airport, and we'll drive where we need to go. Okay?"

"Don't you live in Illinois?" Wes asked.

"Yeah."

"I may not have the golden ticket, but I've got a credit card. I'll fly to you, you pick me up, then it's just a hop to Wisconsin, right?" Wes's voice was calmer. Why didn't Bill think of that?

"Duh, yeah. That makes total sense. I'm closer to Midway than O'Hare." Bill slowed down. Somewhere in the back of his mind, a voice said he sure didn't need the cops pulling him over.

"What about your ticket? I'm sure JB's package was delivered, and you just missed it."

"I can always get that later. Right now, I'm turning around to get to the airport. You get your ass on the next flight to Midway, okay?"

Wes sighed. It sounded like relief. "Thanks, man." He heard Wes breathing. "Bill?"

"Yeah?" Bill recognized that voice. It was the voice of the boy who wore baggy sweatshirts. It was the voice of the boy Bill shared a room with two Halloweens ago. It wasn't the Wes he knew today.

"I don't know if I can do this again, Bill."

Bill nodded, thinking the same, even though Wes couldn't see him. "I know."

"No, I mean, I can't take . . . I can't think about Rose getting hurt again. Or . . ." Bill heard Wes gulp. "Or worse. I can't think about that."

Bill sighed this time, a sigh of sadness. "Don't think, Wes. Just do. Go now. Everything will be okay, but we have to act now."

Wes breathed hard. "Okay, Bill. I trust you. I always have."

Bill heard the click of the call disconnecting. He took the next exit off the highway, and put the airport in his phone's GPS.

Would everything be okay?

Bill's hands shook as he entered his destination. Siri then told him where to go, and Bill got back on the highway. He'd have to worry about Jason Lamb and the video tapes and all of that later. Right now, he had to help his friends. His best friends.

If only he could shake this terrible feeling that things were only going to get worse, so much worse.

*****

Their phones buzzed repeatedly in their pockets, and Jaime thought for sure that her mom would call airport security. Whether she did or not, Jaime never knew, but they boarded a plane that took them to Madison, Wisconsin. Jaime hadn't thought about how she'd get from the airport to the next location, but it turned out to be no problem at all with the golden ticket. A car had been provided for her, and there wasn't a single form to fill out. Good thing, as most rental companies didn't rent out cars to teenagers. JB must have taken care of all of that.

The agent swiped the card and smiled. Somehow, the ticket included all the necessary information because no questions were asked. Just, "Here you go, miss. All has been taken care off."

JB's money and connections must have been limitless.

With Tara in the passenger seat, they drove north. It wouldn't be long now until they arrived at the solution to JB's first riddle.

"Tell me about the first Halloween again," Tara said. "Before all the crazy happened."

Jaime glanced at her little sister. Not so little now, it seemed, and in more than one way. She had grown up fast, faster maybe than Jaime. If Jaime had to pick a defining moment in her youth, one that made her leap toward adulthood, it would be Uncle Tim's suicide. If she had to pick such a moment for Tara, it would be the poor girl nearly getting burned alive by that sicko Sid Malcom.

What about what Sid did to you?

The voice would often come out of nowhere, just like images of the psycho. She even caught herself checking the backseat through the rear view mirror. She didn't want to think she was crazy. Anything was possible, and she knew it.

"When we first went through it, we thought it was the most twisted thing. Looking back, doesn't it seem so simple? So . . . basic?" Jaime bit at her lip as she drove. "Everyone was acting. The people who went missing. They acted like something was wrong, just as JB told them to. But nothing was ever actually wrong. That's what I miss. It's like . . . ." She thought for a moment and settled a bit more comfortably into the driver's seat. "It's like a haunted house. Everyone's screaming. But none of it's real."

"That's why people like horror?" Tara asked.

Jaime nodded. "They get to live out primal fears, think about what it would be like to be chased or hunted or possessed or whatever. But at the end of a two-hour movie or a ten-minute haunted house, they get to return to normal."

"We'll never return to normal." This time it was a statement and not a question. Tara turned her head and looked out the window.

Jaime didn't need to reply. She knew they had been through too much.

They drove in silence for a bit, and then Tara spoke up again. "What about you and Bill?"

Jaime had gotten sick of these questions. When she didn't answer, Tara followed up.

"I've seen your phone light up with his texts. But you never reply. Why?"

Did Jaime still have feelings for Bill? Of course she did. He was her best friend. She always thought he was meant to be something more. But those were normal thoughts. The thoughts someone had who hadn't been . . .

She pictured Sid's body on top of hers. Her body shuddered, and her eyes glanced at the backseat again. Just double-checking.

"I'm sure we'll see Bill soon." Jaime rubbed her forehead and realized she was sweating. She turned up the car's AC and the car's radio.

Tara turned the radio down.

"What will you say to him when he asks why you never return his texts?"

"Tara—"

"No excuses, Jaime. I might be younger, but I'm not dumb." Tara crossed her arms. "He's going to ask, and he just cares about you. We all do."

"I know." Jaime sighed. "I just needed time. It hasn't been easy." She paused and looked in the rear view mirror. She didn't recognize the face that looked back at her. Darkness under her eyes, messy hair. She used to feel both pretty and strong. Now she wasn't sure if she was either. But she forced a smile for her sister. "I'll talk to him. I promise."

Tara smiled then. It was always nice to see her light up. Her smile brought out her youth, and she looked ten all over again. She had the same brownish-hair as Jaime, but it was longer and much better styled. It would be good to have Tara by her side, Jaime thought, and this time the smile that formed on her face was real.

"Okay, good. I'm gonna text and see where he's at." Tara took out her phone, and Jaime didn't try to stop her.

It had been long enough. She needed to talk to Bill. The thing was . . . no matter how many counselors or nurses asked her questions, no matter how many times her mom and Tara had asked her about that night . . . Jaime always found a way to keep some of those details and feelings to herself. Since that night, she had become a caged bird.

The truth about Bill was that she knew that when and if she talked to him, she wouldn't be able to hold back the way she had with others.

The cage doors would fly open.

And she'd scream.

*****

Bill stood outside of Chicago's Midway airport. He wished he had taken that flask with him. God, he could use a drink right about not. But finally, Wes Pike's plane had landed. Wes ran to his old friend as the hot summer sun shot down on them like flames from a fire.

They hugged, two friends not caring about image or stereotypes, no bro-hug with a single or even double pat.

"I'm parked over here," Bill said, not wasting any time, and they ran to his car. All things considered, Bill thought Wes looked good. He had continued to slim down, but would always have that look of being a bit bigger. No baggy sweatshirts, at least. Wes wore a *Gremlins* t-shirt, and that made Bill smile. It was his favorite Christmas movie, one he used to watch with both his parents, before Jason Lamb entered their lives and took that away from him.

"How long will it take to get there?" Wes asked.

"GPS says four hours. I'll get there in three." They hopped in the car, and Bill sped out of the airport like he was in a *Fast and Furious* movie.

"I hope she's there." Wes kept clenching his hands into fists, and Bill again thought of the old clown nose stress ball.

"Whoever took her took her golden ticket and yours. That means they're after the same thing. They'll be there." Bill talked confidently, but on the inside, he wasn't so sure. There were too many unanswered questions. How did this kidnapper even know about the riddle and the golden ticket? Why did he (or she) take Rose in the first place?

Bill sped out of the city, and Wes and he were mostly quiet. They hadn't seen each other since JB's funeral. Under other circumstances, he would have enjoyed talking to Wes about the new *It* movie—who was the better Pennywise?—but today wasn't the time for that.

After a while, Bill asked, "How's she doing? How was she doing, anyway?" That was a poor choice of words, he berated himself.

But Wes seemed to understand. "Okay. She's had a lot of surgeries. We had been going out more and more. Mostly just to parks for walks and stuff. We were going to take some online classes together, just to keep moving forward, you know?" Bill nodded. "She's still . . . the fire didn't just burn away at her skin, it burned away at everything else. You know?"

"I can imagine." He pictured his mom. When Bill's father died, his mom lost a lot more than a husband. Bill had lost a lot more than a father. Madness takes its toll.

Bill pushed the speed limits, but not too much. Eighty at the most, and he slowed down whenever he thought he saw a cop car. They drove into the night, and darkness engulfed the highway.

He had turned onto rural roads, two-lane, dark highways that required the car's bright lights. For a moment, he thought he should have called his mom, and he nearly laughed out loud. *Oh shit, she's gotta be pissed.* He had turned his phone on silent since picking up Wes, and God knew how many missed calls he had. But he tried to push that from his mind.

They slowed down as Siri told them they were approaching. "Your destination will be on your right," she said. Of course, on their right was nothing but land. Just a large, empty field.

A place where a home had once stood, but had been burned down, just like Rabbit in Red.

Bill never heard the riddle directly from the video JB sent to everyone, supposedly, but Wes repeated it for him.

Follow the Rabbit. Follow the Rabbit in Red.
You've got so much to gain. No, geen.
We all wear many faces, alive or dead.
Go to his fire, his chains, to so much more unseen.

Bill drove carefully through this patch of land. The grass was tall, and he was surrounded by cut-down trees. Wishing his bright lights could shine just a bit brighter, he drove into the field itself and carefully through a rusty, old gate.

"Creepy, isn't it?" Wes asked.

"I . . . I don't know how to feel," Bill said. "You know," he continued, speaking softly, as if something outside would hear him, "it's one thing to be in a movie studio, but to be out here, where terrible things happened . . ."

"Look!" Wes nearly shouted.

It was another car. They weren't the first to arrive. Bill could make out two people in the car, but they shielded their eyes from bright lights. He turned the lights down, parked, and stepped out.

The two passengers from the other car stepped out, too.

"Jaime," Bill said, and his heart beat tripled. How long had it been? How much had she gone through? She was still just as beautiful to him—more so, even—and he wanted nothing more but to run and hug her. But it had been so long, and she never did reply to his messages, so he stood there, waiting for her to say something.

Then Tara ran to him. She didn't hesitate to wrap her arms around him and squeeze as hard as she could. "Bill!" she cheered, and then she ran to Wes and hugged him, too.

"So good to see you," Bill said, but he was looking at Jaime. Jaime nodded, but didn't say it back.

"How creepy is this place?" Bill kept talking.

"It's about to get creepier," Tara said. "Jaime—tell them. Tell them what we found!"

Jaime opened up the back seat of her car and pulled out a box. She opened the box for all to see. "It's our Rabbit's Eye. The ones we designed for Hellfire."

Bill felt a lump in his throat. In Hellfire, they had designed a haunted house that was enhanced by the virtual reality technology of the Rabbit's Eye—anything could happen in Hellfire, and not just images and sound. The Rabbit's Eye had neurological technologies, too. It could make you feel pain.

Swallowing hard, Bill said, "Jesus, are we gonna have to do what I think we are gonna have to do?"

Jaime nodded and took a deep breath.

"Ed Gein," Wes said. "We have so much to *geen*. I can't believe it."

"Ed Gein was the serial murderer who inspired *The Texas Chainsaw Massacre*," Jaime said to Tara.

"But we're in Wisconsin?" Tara asked.

"Yeah," Bill said. "A Wisconsin serial killer is the true Leatherface and inspiration behind *Texas Chainsaw*. A fact JB would have no doubt loved and expected us to know."

"You know Gein made chairs and shit out of his victims' skin," Wes said. "And kept their skulls and put them on his bedposts." He shuddered.

"He had belts made out of nipples," Bill added. "And he took the skin off women to make a woman's suit. He actually wore the damn thing. To pretend to be his mother."

"Yep," Jaime said. Did Bill just see her smile a bit? "Gein didn't just inspire *Texas Chainsaw*. He also inspired *Psycho*."

74

Bill gulped and looked at the box full of Rabbit's Eyes.

"Have you put them on yet?" Bill asked.

"Hell no," Tara said. "We aren't doing this alone."

Bill nodded. He knew the history and the legends about Gein. He knew the locals had burned down his property, burned it down because he was a madman, and there were certainly too many ghosts here. It deserved to be burned to the ground.

And he knew exactly what JB had planned for them.

They were going to have to put on the Rabbit's Eye and re-live the terrors that took place on the very ground where they stood.

Chapter Nine

Rose opened her eyes to pure darkness. She must have fallen asleep. How did that even happen? Stress, perhaps. Maybe stress could just knock you out the way a baseball bat to the head could. Thinking about that, she looked around for a weapon. Still in the backseat of Dexter's car, she tried to make sense of the situation. It would be best not to let Dexter know she was awake, so her movements were very small.

Wes!

The thought of him struck her mind like lightning. The poor guy must be crazy worried, and she had no way to contact him, since Dexter had taken her cell phone. *I wonder what he's doing right now.* She pictured him at a police station with both of her parents. Nervously pacing the halls, he wouldn't be able to sleep. Hopefully he reached out to Bill. Bill used to have a way of calming Wes down.

Where am I and what the hell does Dexter want? Since Dexter didn't give her any real answers, she needed to figure this out on her own. But underneath those questions, a more dangerous one lingered.

Would Dexter hurt me? Would he kill me?

She had seen what he could do once before, at Rabbit in Red. She had been taken by actors dressed as witches, put in a giant crib, and made the baby of a strange *Rosemary's Baby* re-enactment of sorts. Dexter had stabbed JB over and over again that day. They were all locked in a room, JB had dressed up as Daniel's father—and Dexter grabbed a knife and stabbed him.

Of course, nothing was real that first year, it seemed.

Nothing except Dexter's craziness.

When JB took off the hoodie he was wearing, he had congratulated everyone for overcoming fear, for winning his contest.

A witch had held on to Rose the entire time, keeping her from moving. It turned out the witch was the assistant who dressed as Samara, the assistant whose real name was Donnie Chase. And Donnie was murdered last year by Sid Malcolm.

That was sure real.

Donnie had seen Dexter's wrath, too. After JB announced the contest was over, Dexter slugged her in the face. Rose wasn't even sure why, or she just couldn't remember. Dexter, she thought, was mad that it wasn't real. After Dexter punched Donnie, JB had grabbed him and easily overpowered him. At the very end of the weekend, when JB had explained everything, all Rose remembered about Dexter was that JB wanted to talk to him privately. None of them had seen Dexter again, although he was certainly the prime suspect for everything that happened last year.

She tried to piece together the puzzle. The missing pieces stretched out over two years.

What was Dexter doing all of last year?

What was his purpose now?

Rose hadn't thought about him in a long time, and she tried to remember all those details to answer the more urgent of her questions: Would Dexter hurt her?

She wished she hadn't tried to remember because every bone in her body said that he would. Yes, he would very much hurt her. Maybe worse.

Paying attention to the road signs, Rose saw they were entering St. Louis. They had driven quite a distance from New Orleans. Dexter drove into the city, and Rose carefully looked up into the rear view mirror.

He had the darkest eyes. The lights from the dash barely brightened his face, but somehow those eyes had depths that frightened Rose.

Don't they say the devil has dark eyes, too?

Just as she thought that, Dexter slowed his vehicle in front of a two-story, brick colonial-style home. The house looked familiar to Rose, like something she had seen on a *Ghost Hunters* episode or something, but she couldn't quite place it.

Dexter didn't quite stop. He drove around the block, but again slowed in front of this home. Rose searched for a street sign and saw that they were on Roanoke Drive, but still nothing clicked.

"Good morning." His voice chilled her. Quiet and raspy, he spoke in a haunted whisper.

His eyes caught hers and she looked away.

"Do you recognize the house?"

She refused to answer. He grinned at her and drove around the block again.

Rose sat up straight in the back seat. A few other thoughts shot through her mind. Maybe she used to be shy, but JB had helped her gain confidence. Maybe she used to be afraid of people like Dexter, but she'd also nearly been killed before. *Once you've survived,* she thought, *you get a little stronger*.

"I want to know what you're doing. What the fuck do you want?" She cracked her knuckles as she spoke.

Dexter laughed. "Little girl, shut up. When I need you, you'll know."

They drove by the house a third time, and when Dexter slowed down near the brick house, Rose threw herself back and kicked at the window. She screamed with all her might, hoping that in a quiet neighborhood that she'd get someone's attention.

Dexter instantly sped up at her screams and bolted down the street. He parked at a dark corner, and Rose still yelped and kicked from the back seat. He got out of the front seat, opened the back door, and pulled at her hair.

Then he hit her.

"Shut up, you bitch! Shut up!" He clenched his fist and punched her in the stomach. She bent over in pain, but refusing to give up she kicked him as hard as she could in the groin. Dexter was the one to bend over this time, and she kneed him in the face. Then Rose sprinted down the street, screaming for help. Her hands were still tied behind her back, but she wiggled as hard as she could to free herself as she ran and yelled.

Within a few seconds, she was in front of the brick house that Dexter kept driving past. She yelled as loud as she could, and a porch light came on at the brick house. *Should I go there?* She looked behind, just for a second, and Dexter was nearly on top of her.

Rose darted to the brick house, just as the front door opened.

A large man stepped outside the front door, and Rose sprinted wildly, crashing into him. He grabbed her, and when Rose looked up, she screamed again.

It was JB.

*****

A noise woke Diane up. She opened her eyes and let them adjust to the dark. There was something about all the horror movies she had seen that kept her from leaping right out of bed. *First, let the eyes adjust. Don't move. Because whoever is in the room will know you're awake, and you don't want that.*

Cautiously, she blinked. Then she turned her head ever so slowly and looked over at Carol's side of the room. She heard light snoring—that was Julie. Carol left to stay with Daniel, so Julie had claimed this room. Diane felt a chill just looking at the art on Carol's side. She had purchased a painting of Valak—the creepy, demonic nun from *The Conjuring 2*—and hung that on their wall. What a great thing to stare at in the middle of the night.

No one else appeared to be in the room, and Diane sat up slowly. What had she heard?

Boom!

There it was again, but it was coming from outside her dorm room. It sounded like someone had crashed into a wall.

Swiftly, she moved from her bed to the door, and opened it just a crack to see what was going on outside.

She smiled at who she saw. It was Brandis, but he looked a bit drunk.

"Oh, hey!" Brandis called from outside. Diane quickly walked toward him, her finger by her mouth, making a *shh* sign.

"You're gonna wake everyone up, drunk-o," Diane told him.

"Old Danny got some more when we left, and the boys may have had a bit too much." He hiccupped, and she found it adorable. That soft, dark hair, those lovable puppy eyes.

"I can see that," she said. "You're gonna love the flight tomorrow."

"Phhhff! We be wonderfine." Brandis mumbled his words together, and Diane giggled. *Yeah, I'm sure you won't, but whatever you say,* she thought. Los Angeles to Madison, Wisconsin would take a few hours, and she couldn't imagine wanting to be stuck in uncomfortable seats with a hangover.

"Can I sleeps with you?" He smiled, showing a mouthful of perfect white teeth, and how could Diane say no.

"Come on, crazy." She grabbed his hand and pulled him into her room. They'd have to sleep close in her small dorm bed, but that would be okay. He still smelled nice.

They slipped into bed, and he put his arm around her. She rolled the opposite way. She was the little spoon, and he was the big. This couldn't hurt, could it? What would he think in the morning? Eh, she'd worry about that then.

The snores from Julie over in Carol's bed continued, and Diane felt a bit jealous at how easy some people slept. Then she felt a rhythmic breathing on the back of her head and realized Brandis had fallen asleep, too. She closed her eyes, even though she didn't want to sleep just yet. It had been two years since she had had a boyfriend, and she really couldn't count that, could she? He had taken her to homecoming and kissed her at the end of the night. They went on a few dates and held hands, but he had broken up with her to go out with one of the school sluts.

After everything that had happened to her, she didn't mind the idea of someone's arms wrapped around her in the middle of the night. She was strong, sure, and she wouldn't let anyone else say otherwise. It was her own decision to return to Rabbit in Red after getting literally burned because she wanted to kick some ass, and she didn't need anyone's help to do it.

But now . . . they lost people for real last year, including JB. They almost lost Rose. Maybe life was too short to try to be this tough. Being independent was one thing, but if something could happen to her at any time, then dammit, maybe she'd try to enjoy it a little more in the company of others.

Especially in the company of cute others like Brandis.

Sleep was close now—Diane could feel it. That was also when she felt Brandis's cell phone vibrating near her lower back.

His rhythmic breathing had developed a bit of a snore, too, and so—out of sheer curiosity—Diane reached her hand behind her back and felt for his cell phone. Her hand brushed something else of Brandis's on the way to his phone, and even in the dark she was sure her face turned instantly red when that happened. But she kept going, and pulled out his phone.

He had a missed call, and several unread texts, and Diane realized this was the phone she had seen earlier—the phone that was left unattended near all those drinks. Brandis must have been hitting the liquor hard all day long.

The missed call and the unread texts were all from the same person: Dexter Lange.

Diane had heard storied about Dexter, and of course she had researched Rabbit in Red before going there herself. She had learned that Dexter was one of the original nineteen, but that he turned out to be a pretty bad guy—a violent guy. He hadn't been invited back, and Diane had never met him.

So why was he texting Brandis?

Diane listened for a moment to make sure Brandis was still asleep, and then she scrolled through his texts messages with Dexter.

She sighed as she read, and just thought, *damn!*

She finally liked a guy, and he seemed to maybe actually like her, and what the hell was all of this?

Dexter: Meet you tomorrow as planned. I've got the girl.

Brandis: K, dude.

Dexter: Pair up with the best, and get through Gein's house as quickly as you can.

Brandis: Diane is prob the smartest. I'll work with her.

Dexter: Alright. If anyone else gets there before you, they'll be in for a surprise.

Brandis: LOL what do u have planned?

Dexter: I've got a friend waiting for them there, too. And he ain't virtual.

Brandis: LOL okay. Why can't I just go straight to St. Louis?

Dexter: Everyone goes through everything. No short cuts.

Brandis: Whatever, okay.

Diane kept reading, and realized this was when Brandis must have been getting really drunk. Dexter had texted several times in a row, with no replies.

Dexter: I'm here now. The Roanoke location.
Dexter: Jesus, the bitch almost got away.
Dexter: You there?
Dexter: We got her though. Man, was she surprised. LOL.
Dexter: Where you at?
Dexter: ???
Dexter: Don't mess this up. I wasn't fucking around when I warned you. I'll do it if you fuck things up.

Then a few missed calls. Whatever Brandis and Dexter had planned together, Dexter was sure worried about it, it seemed. Diane started to scroll back to as far as she could in their conversations when Brandis moved behind her. She quickly shut off the phone and held her breath, listening. His breathing had changed, and Diane wasn't sure if he was fully asleep.

What did Dexter have planned? Who did he have?

What did he want from Brandis? And what was his warning?

She'd just ask Brandis. She'd tell him his phone slipped out and she saw the messages. No harm in that, right?

She needed to know more. She scrolled as far back as she could, wanting to know everything Dexter and Brandis had ever talked about. Listening for a moment to make sure Brandis was still asleep, Diane dove deeper into his text history.

One text caught her attention.

Dexter: I've said it before, and I'll say it again. Jaime's a bitch, bro. You deserve better.

Diane didn't know how much time had passed, but before long, she felt like she knew so much more about Brandis.

One conversation in particular stood out from about a month ago.

Dexter: You up?

Brandis: Yup.

Dexter: Tell me you're not thinking about her.

Brandis: I wish I could.

Dexter: There's only one way to get back at her. You know that, right?

Brandis: I guess so

Dexter: No fuckin' guess. Dude, I can tell you some things about JB. Things he only told me. The guy was fucked up. But you know what? Next to Jaime, JB looks normal.

Brandis: Whatever

Dexter: Bill's even worse. You know they both played you, right? JB, too. They used you and the new recruits as their guinea pigs. Bill and Jaime were the teacher's pets. You were the teacher's pet's pets. You know that right?

Brandis: Fuck them.

Dexter: Exactly. Fuck them all. I told you what they did to me, right?

Brandis: They made it sound like you were fucked up.

Dexter: I had to be. You see how JB always favored them. You've got to take it up a notch.

Brandis: Yeah, okay.

Dexter: I mean it. This next contest—I helped JB with parts of it. You'll see. But I need an inside guy. That's you. Let's get back at the fuckers that betrayed us. Jaime. JB. Bill. Get back at them all. Take what's ours.

Brandis: I want it all.

Dexter: That's the attitude. Let's take exactly what we want.

Diane clicked the phone screen off and listened to Brandis. His breathing sounded rhythmic, and she knew he was still sleeping. Diane slipped his phone back into his pocket. No, not there. I need to make sure he knows it slipped out. She put it in between them, brushing his front again. Brandis felt excited, literally. Diane felt embarrassed, at first, but then she pressed harder against him, spooning him tighter, feeling his hardness against her lower back.

Dexter was right. Jaime and the others had manipulated Brandis and the other new recruits. Diane thought of the fires. She had experienced her own burns, but she returned even more determined to win.

And what did she get for her trouble? Nothing.

Well, nothing yet. She couldn't let Bill and Jaime take all the winnings, definitely not. And it sounded like Brandis might do just about anything to keep them from winning, too.

She liked that. And she liked the way he felt against her. Perhaps she could get used to this. Certainly, she could get used to winning.

It was time for a new leading lady, Diane thought. And maybe a new leading man, too.

She smiled and fell asleep.

Chapter Ten

Bill Wise put on the Rabbit's Eye and stepped onto the land that had once belonged to Ed Gein—a notorious murderer and grave robber who had inspired some of horror's best films.

The Silence of the Lambs, Bill remembered. That was the other one Gein inspired. *Psycho, The Texas Chainsaw Massacre,* and *The Silence of the Lambs.* If you were the inspiration behind those stories, you just had to be all kinds of fucked up, he thought.

"Fifty kinds of fucked up," Bill could hear his mother say.

Wes stood on Bill's left, and Jaime and Tara stood on his right. When Tara had picked up the virtual reality headset, Bill wondered if Jaime was going to stop her.

"We're safer together," Jaime said. "Never leave one behind. We've learned that after all these movies, right?"

Bill nodded reluctantly. *If something is gonna go wrong though, it's gonna be with these things on,* he thought. *That's the way it always happens.*

But another part of him thought they'd have strength in numbers, and he wanted to know what this was really all about. JB's message, according to Wes, was pretty vague. There was more to the story, of course, and maybe once they finished this first simulation, they'd be that much closer to knowing what this was all about.

The four of them stood outside of a cheap, low-hanging wired fence with the words NO TRESPASSING written in bold letters on it. Once the Rabbit's Eye was activated, the words changed to ENTER HERE IF YOU DARE.

There are those moments in life, Bill thought, *that change everything.* Good and bad moments. His father's murder. Meeting Jaime online. That first weekend of Rabbit in Red. He felt a premonition that this—right here in the middle of nowhere Wisconsin—was another one of those moments.

He looked over at Wes, who nodded. Then to Jaime and Tara. Bill took a deep breath and reached out his hand to Jaime.

She left it hanging there for a moment, and Bill's heart beat hard. His mind swung somewhere in between "we have to be a team" to "hold my hand I love you dammit" and he reached a bit further, brushing against her arm.

Jaime reached out and held his hand. Bill's heart skipped a beat. He felt electric, and they took the first step together, beyond the NO TRESPASSING sign.

The wide-open space of the land quickly transformed through the Rabbit's Eye into what could have been an episode of Hoarders. If this was what Gein's house had looked like, it was ridiculous: shit was everywhere. Boxes, magazines, desks, chairs . . . Bill and team walked carefully through. Virtual reality or not, the point of the Rabbit's Eye was to pay attention to all of the details and not just walk on top of shit, just like any video game, really.

"Do you smell that?" Tara asked. "How is that possible?"

"It smells like rotten flesh," Wes said. He looked at Tara. "This device, it changes things. It's not just virtual reality. It changes your neurological responses. Just remember. What you feel isn't necessarily real. If we took these off, the smell would go away. So if it gets too much, take it off. Okay?"

She nodded and wriggled her nose at the smell.

"Look!" Jaime said. There was a string made up of human ears hanging across the room. The chairs appeared to be made of human flesh. Various sized skulls—that must be a child's skull, Bill thought in horror—were spread throughout the space.

"How could anyone live like this?" Bill asked.

"You'd have to be mad," Jaime said. Bill wondered what Sid Malcolm's home looked like. Did he live like this?

"Okay, so we're here," Wes said. "What do we do now?"

"JB always wanted us to learn something, right?" Bill replied. "Whether it was overcoming fear, looking through the eyes of a killer, or experiencing pain, there was always something we were supposed to learn. Something to help us better understand horror. So, what do you think that is?"

They walked into what must have been the kitchen, and the smell of rot intensified. Spoiled food and dirty dishes had piled up everywhere.

"Get out!" Ed Gein walked in next to the pantry and pointed a small pistol at them. "Get out of my house!" He shot, and Bill ducked. He felt the bullet whiz by his ear. Again, he knew he wouldn't really get shot, but the Rabbit's Eye could make you feel that pain, and he wanted to avoid it.

He released Jaime's hand, then turned and ran upstairs.

"Why the hell are you going upstairs and not out the front door?" Tara asked.

"This isn't a movie, Tara," Bill shouted as he ran. "It's a challenge. We have to figure out what that is, so we explore."

He must have entered Gein's bedroom, but how Gein slept here, Bill sure didn't understand. A guitar sat on the floor next to a cluttered rocking chair. *What are we looking for?*

A half dozen old calendars from the 1950s hung above the bed. How lazy must you be to not get rid of old calendars? Bill looked around, and then he saw something that sent chills down his spine.

Gein walked in the room with the pistol pointed right at him. Just then, he heard the others enter the room from behind him.

Bill bent over, picked up the guitar, and threw it at Gein. Gein dodged it, and pointed the gun at Bill.

"I like your face," Gein said. "I could wear that face. Oh, yes." He shot, but Bill dove onto the mattress. It hurt when he fell, and he had to remind himself he was literally outside in a field. There was no mattress to fall on, just ground.

Tara screamed, and Bill jumped right back up.

"No!" Bill cried, as Gein turned the pistol and pointed it right at Tara. He ran forward and tackled the simulation, but he dived right through it, landing hard on the ground.

"What do we do?" Bill shouted back at Jaime.

She ran forward and swung her fist at Gein's face. The simulation simply laughed. Gein lowered the gun and hit Jaime back. She fell backwards and held her hand tight against her face. Then Gein raced toward Tara. Bill brushed at his legs, wiping dirt off his knees, and then shot off toward Tara.

But he wasn't fast enough. Gein kicked Tara in the face, and she flipped backwards, landing hard on the ground. She cried out, and it was Wes this time who ran right through Gein trying to tackle him.

Wes tossed his arms up in the air. "I don't understand," he yelled.

Bill ran for Tara and pulled her up. She moaned, and Gein laughed at them.

"Are you okay?" Jaime asked.

Tara nodded, but she held her leg and winced as Bill pulled her up.

"I think I understand," Jaime said and stepped closer to Gein. "Take your best shot."

"Jaime, no!" Bill shouted, and Wes ran to push her out of the way. Tara yelled, too, but Jaime kept marching close to Gein.

"No!" Jaime snapped her head back at Bill and Wes. "Don't you see? We can't fight it. Just like the old fear simulations. Except this time, we've got to be able to take the pain." Jaime adjusted the Rabbit's Eye. "I hope that's it, anyway," she said again. A small smile formed on her face, and then she faced Gein.

"Do it, fucker. Shoot me!" Jaime yelled.

Gein laughed, pointed the gun right at Jaime, and fired. The bullet struck in her the head. She didn't scream, though. Wouldn't the Rabbit's Eye make her feel the pain like it had when she was hit?

But Gein vanished, and in his spot, an item appeared. It looked like a small, old-fashioned video camera.

"It's just like the first one we got!" Tara cried.

Jaime picked it up and faced them. "We've experienced pain and fear and everything in between," she started. "I think now we have to experience death. First hand, and not in a studio, but out here. In a real world enhanced by the technology only JB could create. If we can face our death, then that's how we move on. Don't you think?"

Bill shrugged, but it seemed to have worked, at least here. "Are you okay? Did it hurt?"

She shook her head. "Maybe it only hurts when we're not doing it right."

Bill nodded. "Okay. What's next then?"

"We watch this," Jaime said and pressed a button on the small camera. The camera wasn't a real object either, but a virtual piece—like a reward in a video game. From it, JB appeared. The sight of him made Bill hold his breath. He never got to see the first riddle, and the last time he had seen JB . . . JB was imprisoned in a wicker man cage, and then he burned to death inside his own studios.

"Congratulations, friends, you've made it through the first challenge. I hope you're all safely back together." Bill felt like he was punched in the gut just hearing JB's voice. It was really his voice! He must have recorded these before his death. *Jesus, he really thought of everything, didn't he?*

"I wanted to give you all opportunities to be leaders at Rabbit in Red. But fate made our time short. So, let's get right to the point.

Starting now, this is a race. The first to finish—whether it's one of you or all of you—will be given the keys to my estate."

He smiled, and Bill looked over to Jaime, who wasn't smiling. She looked almost . . . angry?

"I always have had a plan B, and this is the plan I created if anything happened to me and Rabbit in Red. So sadly, I must no longer be there in person, and neither is my home. But we all will live on, in your memories. In spirit."

Where was JB recording this? And when? His smile disappeared, and JB looked sadder than Bill had ever seen him look. Did he somehow know what was going to happen?

"Physically, there's much more than the studios. The deeds to all my land are yours, along with the remaining funds in my bank accounts, which should be enough for all of you—and all of your families—to be happily set for life. But to get that, you must finish my final challenge."

Bill wished JB were alive more than ever in this moment. He wished JB were standing in the commons of Rabbit in Red with fake blood rushing towards them and eerie sound effects playing throughout. But instead, what was left of JB was only a hologram, an image, a memory.

Death destroyed anything that would be fun here.

"And so, my final challenge is for you to explore the world as I did. To get a taste of real horror that inspired all the stories we love. But we love some things based on terrible tragedies. Remember that. We must always remember that evil is real, and you must learn to face those real evils, should you inherit the Rabbit in Red estate. Do you understand?"

It wouldn't do any good to reply, but Bill nodded. He loved the movies that Ed Gein had inspired, but here—in the virtual memories of this creepy dwelling—Bill felt something even bigger. He felt . . . horror. Not the jumpy-scary-fun horror of a haunted house or a movie. But genuine horror. The kind that comes from murderers and psychos and people who would literally skin you alive.

"So, I'll see you again at the end, my friends. Your journey is long, but worthwhile. Follow the rabbit." With those final words, JB's image disappeared, and the image of the rabbit that they knew so well hopped out of the virtual projector.

It spun, it danced, and it snarled. Finally, it spoke:

Follow the Rabbit. Follow the Rabbit in Red.
Heads will spin, and vomit will spew.
A legendary exorcism became widespread.
Go not there but to where the evil came through.

Bill gulped at the thought of where they had to go next, and the rabbit disappeared.

He was about to take off the Rabbit's Eye, but then they heard the sound of a chainsaw.

The sound came from downstairs, and it was getting closer.

And it sounded all too real.

Chapter Eleven

Rose looked up at the man who grabbed her outside this eerie two story brick house in St. Louis.

"Jay . . . JB?" Rose asked.

The man cackled, and Rose tilted her head. That laugh? That wasn't the haunting, deep laugh she knew so well. It sounded nothing like JB's. But this man—his appearance—it was striking how much he looked just like JB.

"You're not the first to tell me of the striking similarities, but I assure you, we are not even related." The man let her go, and Dexter approached, breathing heavily.

Confused, Rose looked from Dexter to this older man, then down the street. She could keep running. Maybe someone else would come out to help her. Even though she felt like she was in danger, she couldn't help but be curious about the man standing outside this Roanoke home.

"Who are you?" Rose took a step away from Dexter, who was now right behind her.

"Come inside, dear. You must be exhausted after that run down the street in the middle of the night. It was amusing, though, I'll tell you that." He laughed again, a high, effeminate giggle.

Once inside, the man faced both Rose and Dexter, and pointed to some chairs in the living room. "Have a seat, dear. You too, boy. A quick chat, and then some shut-eye. That's what we need. I expect we'll have several visitors in the coming day."

Rose scanned the house, searching for answers and options. Would it be easier to run out the front door? Was there a back exit? Why did Dexter bring her here to this JB look-alike?

"Would you like some hot tea?" The man sat on a reclining chair in the corner and crossed his legs. *No,* Rose, thought, *I'd like some fucking answers and I'd like them now!*

Instead of saying exactly what she thought, she shook her head. "What's going on? Who are you and why am I here?"

"Oh, so direct and to the point. I thought you were a Southerner? No time for conversation, eh?" The man pulled at the dark blue bath robe he was wearing, straightening the bottom, and then continued. "JB had a fascination with doppelgangers," he said with a creepy smile. "Do you remember the original announcement for Rabbit in Red?"

It had been ages, but she nodded.

"In his announcement about the original Fright Fest, JB said that that contest was limited to young adults. But he added, however, that older fans of horror would get their turn, too. In short, I'm part of that contest." The man grinned, and Rose wished she could give him a toothbrush. His teeth were stained yellow, like a heavy coffee drinker and smoker.

"What other contest?" Rose asked.

The man giggled. "Y'all were so focused on your own thing, that you didn't even browse the website for other news?" He shook his head. "JB had started a horror doppelganger contest for adults. Initially, it was meant to be of famous villains. You didn't even need to look exactly like them, but you had to be able to get creative with appearances. He was recruiting new assistants, see? The original ones looked like Captain Spaulding, Samara, Pumpkinhead, and . . . who was the fourth?"

"Sam from *Trick R Treat*." It was Dexter who spoke up, and his voice gave Rose chills.

"That's right, that's right," the man said and took out a pipe. *That explains the teeth,* Rose thought. He lit the pipe, and Rose covered her nose. "I'm a long-time horror fan, too, dear. You should be able to tell by this residence, if nothing else. I bought this house. I live here. And JB, in part, hired me for this part of the final

94

contest." He coughed and then said, "Allow me to formally introduce myself. My name is Boris. Boris Clarke.

Rose sat up a little straighter. "What do you know about the final contest?"

"Only that whoever wins it will inherit JB's large estate. Millions if not billions of dollars, and the rights to Rabbit in Red. Even in ashes, that Hollywood land is worth more than you could ever imagine." The man took a long inhale of his pipe and looked at Dexter. "That's why we're going to make sure we take it all."

Rose bit her tongue. She wanted to cuss at him. How dare he—some outsider with the crazy, psycho sidekick—think he was going to take control of JB's estate.

"Why am I here?" Rose asked, trying to show her temper.

The man giggled again. "Well, my dear, Dexter and I tried to crack JB's code. You see, whenever you finish one of these challenges, you get the next riddle. We know the basic plan. Whoever finishes all the riddles and contests will take ownership of Rabbit in Red's key, and JB's estate. But JB was smart. Damn smart." He paused and took another puff on his pipe. "That Rabbit's Eye you have to wear to complete the challenge is programmed to know who completed it. But more than that . . ." He paused and coughed hard. "More than that, not just anyone can wear the Rabbit's Eye. JB must have programmed them so that only those he invited—his rabbiteers—can actually wear them. Dexter and I both tried, but they don't work for us."

Rose looked over at Dexter. "How did the two of you start working together?"

"Enough," Dexter said and stood up. "I think that's enough."

The older man sucked on his pipe and didn't respond.

So, they planned on using her to help them win the contest? *Hell, no. I won't help. I won't do it! And if the Rabbit's Eye is programmed to know who wins, then how exactly would they be able to steal that, anyway?*

Rose hoped that Dexter and this other man didn't have this planned out too well. But then she saw the way the man looked at her as he smoked his pipe. She felt a chill. They were up to something, something more than they were letting on, that was for sure.

I need to warn the others. But how?

"Lock her in the room as planned," the man told Dexter. "Try to get some sleep tonight, dear. You're going to need it."

Dexter grabbed her and Rose moaned out in pain. His hands gripped her arm violently, and his fingers dug into her skin—and then he grinned. He enjoyed this, and that scared her all the more.

"Oh, dear, one more thing," the man called out to her. "Don't pray tonight, if you're the religious kind. It really pisses off the demons in this house." The man cackled until he coughed, and then he just smiled at her.

Dexter pulled her across the house, up a flight of stairs, and tossed her into a bedroom. She heard the door lock from the outside.

When she turned around, she swore she saw a ghost.

*****

As Diane had suspected, Brandis was hungover. He squinted at the morning sunshine, closed his eyes on the ride to LAX, tried to sleep on the entire flight, and rubbed his forehead again—hours later—as they arrived in Wisconsin. Diane wanted to ask Brandis about the texts, but she worried Brandis was too hung over to give her the answers she really wanted.

Instead, she asked him another question.

"What were your biggest fears?"

"Huh?" Brandis rubbed his forehead.

"You know, JB had all those tests. Tests about personal fears, too. Not just monsters under the bed." She thought about holding his hand, but instead, she turned and leaned into his shoulder. "My fear," she started, "my fear was always being betrayed." It was a lie, but she had a feeling it might get Brandis to open up.

He cleared his throat. "Really?"

She nodded. "What's yours?"

"The same, actually." He looked her closely in the eyes. "Weird."

"What happened? I mean—had you ever been betrayed?"

"Yeah. Oh, yeah. When I was a kid. A bunch of things, really."

Diane pressed for more. "Like what?"

"My father left my mom when I was little. He had a big affair, I guess. But it was my best friend when I was like fourteen that was the hardest."

"What happened?" Diane asked.

"I had my first real crush then. Was gonna ask this girl to homecoming. He knew it, too. But he didn't care. He asked her out then completely stopped hanging out with me." Brandis leaned back and closed his eyes. "I got over it, eventually, I guess. But then last year, I caught my girlfriend cheating on me. That's a whole 'nother story. But yeah. One backstabbing after another." He turned to look at her. "I guess you could say I have a hard time trusting people."

Diane tried not to blink or swallow. Was he challenging her? After a moment, Brandis looked away, and Diane played on her phone until the plane landed.

The golden tickets JB had given them were like magic—she couldn't believe the car rental people hadn't asked for anything else. Everything had been taken care of, and the employees literally looked the other way, as if Diane and her friends were celebrities, and the staff had been warned that she didn't like eye contact.

Maybe that was exactly how JB had set this whole thing up.

The entire team of Hellfire recruits plus Daniel drove to Plainsfield, Wisconsin, the site of the legendary Ed Gein's house. Diane wondered if they would be the first to arrive, or if some of the first years had already been there.

She got her answer when they pulled up to the vacant field that had once been Gein's home.

There was a box full of the Rabbit's Eyes. They were stashed inside a giant cattle truck. The virtual reality headsets stuck out through the spaces reserved for the cattle's heads, just like the meat truck in *The Texas Chainsaw Massacre*, she knew.

"How do we open it?" Carol asked.

Daniel took out his golden ticket. "Try this," he suggested. "It's worked for everything else."

He slid his golden ticket around the outside of the back of truck, and as if the vehicle had some sort of scanner, the backside opened.

Others had been here. The Rabbit's Eyes headsets in the box were bloody.

Not virtual blood. Real blood.

"What happened here?" Brandis asked.

"I think it's a question of what happened there," Jimmy said and pointed to something out in the field. There was a series of bushes, but they had been trampled on, bled on. The bushes looked like demonic Christmas trees—so much red over so much green.

"Look around," Daniel suggested. "See if you notice anything else unusual." He took Carol's hand and moved forward. Diane thought of grabbing Brandis's hand for a moment, but instead she put her hands in her pocket and moved forward.

It was obvious that at least a few people had been here. Besides the blood, there were several footprints, the dirt had clearly been stomped on, and several patches of grass and bushes had been uprooted or smashed.

"Shit, look at this!" It was Kent shouting from Diane's left.

"What is it?" Julie asked.

"Hair. Long, dark hair." Kent looked straight at Brandis, then to Daniel.

"That's Jaime's hair," Brandis said, stepping closer to Kent. He touched it, and Diane couldn't tell if that was sweet or creepy. Either way, she didn't much care for it.

"So, looks like Jaime was here," Daniel said, "Which means we can assume Bill was, too."

Diane didn't like the twitch in Brandis's face at Bill's name. Was he jealous? Were there still feelings for Jaime?

"And it looks like they were hurt," Carol added. "But they're obviously not here now."

"So, we put on the Rabbit's Eyes, see what they saw, and get to the next location," Daniel said.

They all nodded and ran quickly to the cattle truck full of Rabbit's Eyes.

But just as they started to put on the headsets, several other cars pulled up.

Chapter Twelve

Before the sun came up that day, before anyone else had arrived at the Gein location, Jaime, Bill, Wes, and Tara took off their Rabbit's Eyes and listened to the sound of a chainsaw.

Jaime had heard it from downstairs, but downstairs was no longer down. They were in a field that became the old Gein house, thanks to the technology in the Rabbit's Eye, but now they were back on land, back in reality.

Jaime needed to know if the sound was real. They had already received the second clue. JB had even spoken to them, told them of his plans. Those who finished this final challenge—however long that would be—would get the keys to Rabbit in Red and JB's fortune.

When Jaime had first heard that, the only thing she wanted to do was win. Not for the money. For the rights to Rabbit in Red.

As she threw off the Rabbit's Eye though, the image in front of her was very real.

"No way," Wes mumbled. "No way!"

"Jaime, whaaa . . . what's going on?" It was her sister. Tara had taken off her headset, too.

A man stood about twenty feet across from them. He held a chainsaw, and it roared. Jaime had no time to answer. The man sprinted right at them.

"Jesus!" Bill yelled. He grabbed Jaime, and they ran toward their cars. Her heart beat harder than it ever had—harder than in Hellfire, harder than in Gein's house just then, harder than—

No, not harder than that, she thought. Sid Malcolm had haunted her dreams since that terrible night, and now she was sure Sid Malcolm had sent someone here to finish her once and for all.

She pulled away from Bill and turned around.

"Jaime, what are you doing?" Bill shouted.

Jaime stood there as the man charged right at her, his chainsaw above his head.

Bill called out again. "No!" Then he dived at Jaime just as the Leatherface-wannabe brought the chainsaw down. He missed, and the weight of the tool kept his momentum moving forward.

"What are you doing?" Bill asked. Jaime had never seen such panic in his eyes.

"Stopping this," she said and stood up. She heard Bill gasp as she sprinted at the man's back. In seconds, she jumped on top of him, and the man fell to the ground, almost landing on the chainsaw. The chainsaw rolled to the side, and Jaime wrapped both of her arms around the man's neck, choking him as hard as she could.

Bill and Wes darted toward the chainsaw.

Before they could reach it, the man stood up. It made Jaime feel like a child. He easily threw her off his back, as if he were a giant and she only a kitten. She landed hard on her back.

"Jaime!" Bill yelled and ran for her. He pulled her off the ground, and Jaime moaned. She opened her eyes wide when she saw that Wes had just reached the chainsaw. But the man turned quickly and back-handed Wes across the face. Then he kicked him, and Wes went tumbling backwards.

The man picked up the chainsaw, turned, and charged at Bill and Jaime.

Jaime couldn't really see his face, but now she knew it had to be the actual Sid, coming once and for all to end her after having failed in the back of his stupid van.

Bill threw a soccer-mom arm around her, as if that would stop a chainsaw. The man brought the weapon down, and they rolled to the side, but a warm spray hit Jaime's face.

She felt a great pain then, not for herself, but for what was happening. Her eyes wide, she looked at Bill. The chainsaw had cut into the arm he had used to try and protect her.

"Arggh!" The cry from his mouth brought a vengeful tear to her eye, and Jaime turned to face the man.

Before she could see his face, he pulled at her hair, and she fell back and cried out loud as several of the hairs came right out of her head.

She felt the warm spray of blood again. Bill was still bleeding, and it didn't look good. He held onto the cut arm and tried to stand up.

"Ugh!" The man made an ugly adult cry and shot his hands up to cover his head. Behind him, Jaime saw Tara with a handful of bricks. She had launched one straight at the man's head. Then she tossed another. The man dropped the chainsaw. Jaime jumped at it, but it took both arms and an adrenalin-charged yelp to pick it up. Wes joined Tara, and they threw brick after brick until he fell to the ground.

Jaime lifted the chainsaw up to her waist just as the man finally stopped moving. Bill walked over to Jaime, putting his good arm around her.

"Are you okay?" he asked.

Her eyes grew wide again. *Am I okay? He's asking me, while his arm is pouring out blood. Shit, he could be bleeding to death!*

"I'm . . . yeah," she said, looking into Bill's eyes. It was as if she were seeing him for the first time.

"How are you guys?" Bill asked Tara and Wes.

"Fine, man, but what about your arm?" Wes cried.

Bill looked down at it and managed a smile. "It's only a flesh wound."

Jaime couldn't stop the laugh from coming out, and they all laughed, awkwardly, for a moment. Then the laugh turned into a sob. A hard sob, a cry that had been bottled up inside of her for many months. She dropped the weapon and the let tears flow down her face.

Bill held her and didn't say a word. Jaime glanced up at the man on the ground, who had started to move.

She walked over to him.

"No, Jaime, don't," Bill said and held on tighter, but she forced her way out of his hold.

She grabbed another brick and squeezed it hard. She'd smash someone in the face if needed. "We have to know who it is, don't we?" Jaime looked from Bill, to Wes, to Tara. Tara looked too shocked to speak, but Wes nodded.

Wes walked with Jaime, and he reached out for her hand. Tara ran to Bill and put her arms around him.

She was sure it would be Sid Malcom. She had seen Sid in her nightmares and in the corner of every dark room for months. And now, he had finally decided to come out of the shadows and hurt them. No, he wanted to kill her, she was sure of that. Kill them all, too. That made her angry. Her sister was here! Bill and Wes—they had already gone through too much! When would it end?

Jaime felt the rage grow, and Wes must have sensed it also because she felt his grip tighten on her hand. She tried to steady her breathing and her step. She would do what needed to be done.

With her left hand in Wes's, she used her right to take out her cell phone and turn on its flashlight.

She shone it at the man's face. He blinked and started to wiggle.

Jaime gasped at what she saw. It wasn't Sid Malcolm.

It wasn't a man at all.

It was a woman. A large, strong woman—and she was waking up.

*****

Dexter paced back and forth across the formal living room in the Roanoke, St. Louis home. Now was the waiting game, and they would arrive soon.

He didn't just need the Rabbit's Eye. The old man was right about this—they needed their brains. Dexter snickered at the thought. It was like a modern-day zombie story. *Just need your brains, fuckers. More brains!*

The plan was simple. Wes, Bill, Jaime, and crew would agree on the spot—as soon as they arrived—to give all the money they'd win over to him. Or he'd kill Rose and "JB."

He was ready to kill Rose, too. There were all sorts of special rooms in this house, but Rose's room was the ultimate project. The old man had helped him design it like a gas chamber.

They fussed at all, and Dexter would turn on the gas and they'd all watch Rose suffocate and die.

Wouldn't that be fun?

Of course, he also couldn't wait to see the looks on their faces when they learned that "JB" was here and alive.

That will be a nice *fuck you* for not having him back at Rabbit in Red. The ultimate payback.

Once they agreed, he'd let JB out on good faith, and the crew would have to sign some papers. The old man just happened to be a lawyer in his former life, and they'd take the money from those fuckers before they even got it. As for Rabbit in Red, Dexter had no interest—it didn't exist anymore.

Dexter would have to share some with the old man, and he knew that. The old dude was easy to manipulate, though. He had always wanted fame and fortune—that was why he tried to contact JB and become his doppelganger in the first place.

Looking out behind the corner of the curtains for the hundredth time, Dexter still didn't see anything. He sat down on a chair, and he let his thoughts return to his last night at Rabbit in Red.

"Listen to me carefully," JB had said. "I'm going to ask you do something, just you. Not the others. Not every challenge is inside these walls." JB gestured and lowered his voice.

"When you do this, I won't have to invite you back." He pointed out beyond the game chambers, back to the commons.

"Here's what I want you to do. First—"

Dexter cracked his knuckles and closed his eyes.

"First, if you want to be a part of this empire, then here's what you need to do." JB had leaned closer to Dexter and appeared to wait for Dexter to give some kind of nod of approval. Dexter was angry, and now JB wanted a favor? Fuck him.

But curiosity got the best of him, and he had nodded, ever so slightly.

"After everything that happened, it's best if you take some time away from Rabbit in Red. See things from a new perspective. I'm giving you a list of locations to travel to, and I'm covering all the travel expenses, so don't worry." JB sat up a bit straighter. "I want you to see what real horror is. These are locations that will come into play in a later challenge. For now, you're to research them. What happened at each place? What pain did the victims experience? You're to write all of this down and report back to me. You've got a smart eye, no doubt, and you'll help me more than you can know. We'll be using your research in future simulations."

Dexter had frowned. It sounded like work with no reward, like he would just become JB's lapdog. He didn't much care for that.

"We'll get you out of school, get your degree online, no problem. You'll need to do this research now, and finish up by summer." JB paused and took a deep breath. "I'm trusting you, Dexter, with a rather large and important project. This is how you earn your trust back. Do you understand?"

Dexter hadn't known what to make of the situation. Would he be some kind of outside employee for Rabbit in Red? Was JB just using him, or was this really a chance to become a part of the industry after all?

Dexter blinked, and evidently JB took that as a yes.

"Good," JB said. "Your research will contribute to more than you can possibly know. If all of this goes well, come next Halloween—if you want—I'll re-introduce you to the team. Do we have an agreement?"

Dexter had thought about it. He'd get out of school. That was definitely a plus. He'd spend the year researching various locations that he could only assume had something to do with horror. Definite plus. So Dexter put out his hand. JB shook it, and Dexter said, "Agreed."

Dexter stood up in the Roanoke, St. Louis, house and looked out the curtains again. Still no one.

The biggest advantage Dexter had was that he knew all of the places they'd be travelling to during this final adventure. After all, he had researched every one. He gave JB lots of first-hand information, video, and research. Although he didn't know it at the time, Dexter's work helped put the final contest together.

He could have been back in JB's good graces. He could have been back at Rabbit in Red, competing right now, legitimately, for JB's estate.

Instead, last summer, he had watched as Sid Malcolm kidnapped Tara Stein.

Dexter had been determined to do more than research horror locations. When he had left Rabbit in Red, the first thing he did was take notes on each person. He didn't want to forget who his competition was or who worked behind the scenes.

He had a special file devoted to Chester and Sid Malcolm. Dexter had been learning as much about Sid as he could from the internet and horror chat rooms. Even though Sid was an adult and not a student, the other adults treated him differently. Hell, his own brother had locked him up! Sid had been exiled from Rabbit in Red that Halloween weekend, and then Dexter had been kicked out.

Although he'd never admit that he needed help, Dexter thought he might find a partnership with Sid that could be mutually beneficial.

So in between on-location research, Dexter learned as much about Sid as he could. One weekend in Boston, in fact, Dexter had found him and had decided to follow him.

Dexter watched as Sid took Tara to some hotel and set her hair on fire.

Dexter rubbed his forehead at the memories. He could have stopped all of that. He could have told JB everything. He really could have gotten in JB's good graces by calling the master that very weekend. But it was the first time he had seen Sid Malcolm in person. Dexter knew he could learn something from Sid, but he didn't know he'd get this much—his first encounter and the crazy dude kidnaps and tortures a girl.

Did JB know that Dexter had seen this? Dexter had wondered that, too. JB seemed to know so much.

Dexter sat down after another glance out the window. He had saved his final conversation with JB on his phone, an e-mail that he wouldn't forget. There were many things Dexter wanted to do, but he had decided helping JB wasn't one of them.

He had had enough of JB's research. He wanted to spend his time following Sid and learning from him instead.

JB couldn't have been telling him everything. *I'm not going to be an errand boy. I'm not going to spend my time protecting the weak when it's the strong who should be rewarded. JB had this entire game upside down. Fuck teamwork, fuck friends, and most of all fuck you, JB.*

Dexter had smiled when he knew Tara was getting hurt, and he had decided to let JB know what he had seen.

Dexter: You should see what I see.

JB: What do you see?

Dexter: It just so happens I'm outside a certain hotel room, watching things . . . go up in flames.

JB: WHERE ARE YOU?

But Dexter didn't respond. Lots of texts, calls, and e-mails came . . . more every single day.

Dexter simply smiled. He had waited for Sid to finish doing whatever he was going to do to Tara. *Let the girl die. That's fine. I won't protect the weak and hurt the strong. It's this man I should be watching and following. He could be my mentor. Not JB, and definitely not these stupid girls.*

Dexter was chuckling at his own thoughts when Sid ran out of the hotel room. Dexter saw the glowing light of fire inside. He didn't look in the room because he didn't care.

Instead, he followed Sid.

JB sent an e-mail again later that night. It was the last time Dexter would hear from him.

JB: I gave you a chance, boy. Only a coward hurts people. Don't you see that? Only a coward needs to hide his face. Weak people need to hurt others to be strong. A strong person helps others. Don't you see the difference?

Dexter read it but didn't reply. It was eerie, though. It felt like JB was reading his thoughts. Dexter thought Sid was strong, and JB goes on a rant calling Sid weak? Dexter shook that thought from his mind and turned off his phone. He followed Sid out of the city. Then he waited for Sid to park and get out of his car. They were now at another motel outside the Boston area.

Dexter had waited some more—this time for Sid to check in. When a few minutes had passed, Dexter thought it was time to make an introduction.

He knocked on the motel room door.

Sid opened, clearly surprised.

Dexter put out his hand. "My name is Dexter Lange, and I would like to meet you. I think we have something in common. Something we hate, to be more specific."

Sid had grinned and shook his hand.

Chapter Thirteen

Sitting at the Gein property, Diane waved at the others as they got out of their cars. It looked like Annie, Leroy, and Venus had ridden together, and more flooded out of three other cars. She looked around for Jaime, Bill, Wes, and Rose, but they weren't here. Diane frowned. Typical that the four of them would go off on their own.

Not with us.

After several greetings, they put on the Rabbit's Eyes and explored the Gein property. When JB spoke at the end about his inheritance and the keys to Rabbit in Red, Diane's chest tightened.

Sure, she'd had a feeling that was what this was all about, but it also explained why their "leaders" were off on their own. Diane felt her skin warm and she brushed up against Brandis. Should she let him know she'd do whatever it took to win?

An annoying voice in her head asked, *What about the others? What about all these people who showed up to work together?*

She felt bold and she reached for Brandis's hand. He took it and smiled at her.

"What do you think that blood is from?" Carol asked. Diane had nearly forgotten about the blood they had seen on the ground. This blood was no simulation.

"There's more going on than we realize, guys," Daniel said. He dropped to one knee and took a closer look at the blood. "We better get a move on it. And fast."

They agreed to move forward as quickly as possible. If it were just a race, they were already losing. But if it was more than a race—and surely it was—then she wanted to find the answers to everything else, too.

Brandis and Diane rode with Carol and Daniel, and they wasted no time driving as quickly as possible. They could catch a flight in Madison and get to St. Louis in no time at all.

Diane put her head on Brandis's shoulder in the back seat. Was now a good time to ask about those texts with Dexter? Didn't she hear that Dexter and Daniel had a confrontation before? She looked at Daniel, who was focused behind the steering wheel.

This could get very interesting, she thought and smiled.

"So, hey, Brand," she started, "What do you know about Dexter?"

As she had suspected, Daniel's face twisted and his eyes darted to the back seat.

"Who?" Brandis coughed and shuffled in his seat. *So that's how we're playing this, huh?*

Diane sat up and looked at Daniel through the rear view mirror. "He was the first year who never returned, right, Daniel? Didn't he actually hurt someone?"

Daniel nodded. "He's an asshole. Basically used me the first year to get ahead, but he never seemed to realize this was a game. Yeah, he hit Bill pretty hard and threw Jaime even harder." He looked over at Carol, and Diane wondered how much shoving and punching Daniel was responsible for. "The worst thing was, though, he tried to stab someone. Turned out to be a movie prop and not a real knife. But he would have killed JB if it were real." His face contorted into something darker that Diane didn't understand. "The weird thing, though, is that he thought he was stabbing *my* father."

Carol turned in the passenger seat and faced him. "Your father?"

"You've all heard the stories. We had to face our fears." Daniel swallowed hard. "JB dressed up like my father to scare me. And Dexter tried to kill him."

"That's messed up," Brandis said. "Then what happened?" Diane wondered if he was simply trying to avoid the question she had asked him.

"We both got kicked out," Daniel told them. "I got a second chance, though. JB left it up to the rest of the students to give me that second chance." He frowned. "I was pretty pissed at first. I think they only invited me back because they thought I may have been the dude responsible for everything that happened last year."

He looked forward and accelerated. Diane followed his gaze.

"And Dexter?" Carol asked.

"All I remember," Daniel said, "was that JB needed to talk with him privately. Dexter was not given a second chance. At least not as far as we all know. No one knows what they talked about in private."

Diane looked at Brandis and wondered if that was true. They rode in silence for a minute, and then Diane asked, "Do you think Dexter is a part of this final game? He was an original part of Rabbit in Red. Would JB have included him?"

Daniel shrugged, and his face told her that he hadn't considered this possibility.

"I bet he is," Diane said. "It makes sense. It would add to the competition." She let the words sink in and watched as Brandis shuffled uncomfortably in his seat.

Carol spoke up. "Do you think we should work together? I mean, there's so many of us. We can't all possibly win, can we?"

Daniel sighed. "Let me tell you, knowing JB, anything is possible."

"Carol's idea is good," Diane said and nodded. She wanted to make sure to compliment Carol, to make sure the others knew this was Carol's idea, after all. "This is gonna become a race, if it's not already. Bill, Jaime, Wes, and Rose—they're our leaders, right? And where are they?" Diane sat up straighter in the back seat and leaned toward the front. "This should be for all of us," she continued. "Not just for some of us."

"What are you saying?" Brandis asked.

"The four of us—we stick together. When we win, we'll know what's fair and we'll do what's right." She leaned back against her seat and took a deep breath. "I like everyone, you know. I just don't know if I trust everyone."

She looked at Brandis, and he nodded, but there was something in his eyes. He had no doubt opened up to her more now that he had told her his stories of betrayal. Still, there was something else, she was sure of it, a story she hadn't heard yet.

But she wanted to know it, and she wanted him on her side. She smiled and reached for his hand.

He took it and smiled back.

*****

"Absolutely not," Bill said through clenched teeth. "Hospitals ask questions." He held a hand against his shoulder, and although the words that came out of his mouth sounded tough, there was a little boy on the inside shivering and frightened.

"Besides," Bill continued, "we have no time to waste."

Jaime drove, but shook her head. "We'll find a twenty-four hour drug store and wrap you up. But if the bleeding continues, we'll have no choice." She looked at him through the rear-view mirror. Slumped against the passenger side of the back seat, Bill bit his lip and nodded.

"It's not as bad as I thought. But a little Jack Daniels would sure help right about now" Bill said. Tara shifted in the passenger front seat so she could see him. Bill locked eyes with her and said, "I promise I'm okay."

But it sure was the first time he had ever really been attacked. He had been punched a couple of times—by Dexter and by Brandis about a year apart from one another—but he had never been cut, not like this.

Was she trying to kill him? Really kill him?

This time her weapon of choice was no sledgehammer. It was a genuine chainsaw, and she sure looked like she was out to kill them all.

Bill first knew her as Annie—a character from Stephen King's *Misery*—that they had encountered during the initial Rabbit in Red challenges. Back in studio room one, Annie had attacked Bill, Jaime, and Wes nearly two years ago. But she had turned out to be a well-trained actress.

She had continued to help JB last year, and her real name was Bonnie Villa, Bill remembered.

And now she had taken a bit of Bill's arm.

As if reading his thoughts, Wes asked, "Why did Bonnie do this?"

Bill shook his head. "Everything we've ever done—none of it caused real pain." He sat up a bit and then winced at the pain in his arm. "Think about it. The first year—just actors. The second year—some neurological technology to make us think we felt pain."

"Exactly," Jaime said from the front seat. "JB never wanted to hurt us." Her face twisted with anger. "It was always someone else who wanted to hurt us."

"Then why did Bonnie attack us?" Tara asked.

"I don't know," Bill said. "The simulation at the Gein house was over. We had the next clue. JB spoke to us. I think that was the end, anyway. Right?" He took a deep breath through his nose. "She couldn't have been a part of JB's plan. She's a part of something else."

"Someone else's plan," Wes mumbled, and Bill saw his face flash with fear. "Or her own." He looked at Bill. "We'd be stupid to think that we're the only ones in this *game*, or whatever you wanna call it." At the word "game," he made quotation marks with his fingers. "Shit, you guys, think about it!"

"What?" Bill asked, sitting up straighter.

Wes rubbed his forehead. "JB has had help from God knows how many people. We saw dozens of assistants, helpers. Then there's the hundreds of actors we rarely saw. How many others?" He looked down and shook his head. Then quietly, as if someone else would hear, he whispered, "But he chose us to inherit his estate and Rabbit in Red. *Us.*"

Bill felt a chill. "That's gonna piss a lot of people off."

"A *lot*," Wes said and looked out the window on his side of the car.

Bill looked up at Jaime through the rear-view mirror, and she looked back with worried eyes.

This wasn't going to be as easy as solving some riddles and playing with some simulations. If Wes was right and Bonnie was after them out of spite or jealousy, then there'd be even more people after them.

Right?

And who else?

This wasn't a game. That was a real person—a very big, strong person with an actual chainsaw—who wanted to kill them.

They had left her unconscious, but she wasn't dead. She'd be after them again. She and who knew how many others.

"Jaime, can you drive any faster?" Bill asked.

She didn't reply, but Bill heard the car accelerate. The sound of the engine and its speed provided a little comfort. But then he realized they'd just arrive at their next destination quicker, and a new layer of fear covered the ever so brief comfort.

Wes looked back over at Bill. "I wish I knew where she was." Bill tried to smile at his friend, who had his cell phone out. He had taken it out to text and call Rose, and he was relentless. Unfortunately, there had been no replies.

They had no clue or information about Rose at Gein's house. Bonnie had provided a distraction from their missing Rose, but now that things were calmer, Bill knew she must be on Wes's mind.

"Keep trying to reach her," Bill said, but it felt discouraging. "I think all we can do is move forward. Oh-right? And quickly. Wherever she is—whoever has her—it's a part of all of this. Do you feel it?"

Wes nodded and rubbed his eyes. "The last time she was taken," Wes said and looked straight at Bill, "it was a part of the game where people with weapons weren't actually out to hurt us. This time . . ." Wes sighed and didn't finish. He didn't need to. Bill understood and worried about that, too.

They drove through the night, only stopping twice. Once for gas and once to get a first-aid kit for Bill. Thankfully, the bleeding had stopped. The chainsaw could have removed his entire arm, and luckily, it had grazed him, barely touching him, but enough to still cause quite a cut. He kept thinking he'd need a tetanus shot and that this was going to leave one hell of scar.

Now the sun had risen, and Bill rubbed his eyes. Did he sleep at all? He didn't think so. He didn't think any of them had slept.

When they entered St. Louis, Bill broke the silence. "Hey. Find a park or something. We've gotta try to close our eyes for a bit. You, especially."

Jaime looked as tired as he felt—little bags had formed under her eyes. Bill wondered how many sleepless nights she had experienced. She had driven all night without complaint. Maybe she had gotten used to it.

"We'll be no good," he continued, "if we have to fight like this. A couple hours, even if we don't sleep." She looked too tired to argue, and Wes and Tara simply nodded.

Jaime exited the highway and drove until they saw a tiny park next to an elementary school. They pulled in the parking lot, rolled down the windows to try and enjoy any kind of breeze, and closed their eyes.

He didn't think it was possible, but Bill did fall asleep. Maybe it was an hour, maybe two. He didn't look at the time.

When he woke up, his head was heavy—like he had taken too long of a nap—and then he felt worse. A sense of dread fell upon him. They'd have to go through the second simulation today, and he had a terrible feeling that things were going to get worse.

Maybe Bonnie and her chainsaw would be back. Who else would they have to deal with this time?

Bill cracked his neck and sat up. Wes was still sleeping, and Bill looked into the front seat.

Tara was still asleep, but Jaime had woken up. She turned to Bill. "It's time. Let's go."

Chapter Fourteen

Diane let go of Brandis's hand as they pulled up on Roanoke Street in St. Louis. They had driven through the night without sleeping, but they had rotated drivers every couple hours.

As they pulled up, Carol said, "Let's read the clue again. Just to prepare, you know?" Daniel nodded, and he spoke from memory.

"Follow the Rabbit. Follow the Rabbit in Red.
Heads will spin, and vomit will spew.
A legendary exorcism became widespread.
Go not there but to where the evil came through."

"Do you believe in all of that?" Carol asked. She had pulled her blonde hair into a pony tail, and it made her look twelve years old.

Diane shrugged. "I don't know. So many movies claim to be based on true stories."

Brandis stretched his arms and sat up. "Look at where we just came from. A dude in Wisconsin inspired *The Texas Chainsaw Massacre*."

"But this seems . . . darker," Carol said. "We're at the home where supposedly the actual possession occurred that inspired *The Exorcist*. The real deal." She shuddered.

"Plenty of people would say this is real," Daniel added. He parked the car and rubbed his eyes. "If God exists, then doesn't Satan?"

"I don't know about that," Brandis told them. "But there's gonna be evil in that house. One way or another."

Diane felt a chill when he said that. Was he implying something else? She wished she could get in his head.

"Hey, look!" Carol pointed at a car across the street. "Look who it is!"

"Well, how nice of them to join us," Daniel snapped. Diane looked out the window. It was Bill, Jaime, Wes, and Tara. The other cars pulled up behind them, and Diane realized this would be the first time they had all been together since JB's funeral.

Except where was Rose?

Daniel got out of the car, and the others followed.

"Hey, guys," Wes said. He was the first to get out of the other car.

"Hey, yourself. Why didn't you wait for us?" Daniel asked and crossed his arms.

Wes shook his head. "They got Rose. They took her. Whoever 'they' are. We couldn't wait."

Diane watched as Daniel's arms relaxed. Too bad. She had a feeling he'd be at his best if he were angry.

Bill exited the back seat, and Diane noticed the bandages on his arm. "What happened to you?" she asked.

"We need to talk," Bill said and walked closer. "Before we go in there." He looked tired, but then the smallest of smiles formed across his face. "I'm glad you guys are here."

"Me, too," Jaime said and put an arm around Tara, who stood by her side.

They gathered in the middle of the street and waited for everyone to get out of their cars and join them. Diane thought they must look foolish. This was a residential street, and here—early in the morning—a bunch of teens just standing around.

"There's something very important we need to tell you," Bill said to everyone. He held onto his bandaged arm, and everyone got a little closer. Bill opened his mouth to speak, but then the front door of the Roanoke house opened.

Diane gasped. They all did. It was an eerie echo that boomed on the quiet road. Was that JB? How could that be? No, impossible. But there he was! He stood in the doorway and grinned, his lips nearly touching his ears. He wore a black suit and gestured at them to come in.

"What the—" Tara started to say.

"It can't be," Jaime said, her jaw hanging low.

Bill ran forward. Wes reached out for him. "Bill, no!" Wes cried. But Bill didn't listen.

Diane looked at Brandis, who shrugged, and in seconds, they were all running to the house. It was a total stampede, but they shot directly at the front door, halting just feet away from the entrance.

"The answers are inside," JB whispered. His voice sounded different, like he had a cold. They stared at JB then to one another in surprise and confusion. *Should they go inside?*

Then Bill, as if hearing her thoughts, stepped forward. Diane sighed. She knew the group well enough to know that all it took was the lure of possible answers to get them to move forward, and so they did. One by one, slowly, they each walked into the house.

What was Bill going to tell them? The question left Diane's mind the moment she slammed into the back of Brandis. Then she heard a door slamming from behind them. The room darkened, and JB stood at the top of the stairs. He pointed to a screen in the living room. The screen turned on.

It showed Rose tied to a bed. "No!" Wes shouted. "You son-of-a-bitch!" He tried to move, but they were all squished together. Then a voice came on the screen.

The voice was not JB's or anyone else Diane recognized.

"Listen carefully," the voice said. "I'm only gonna give you instructions once."

Diane looked around, but everyone was glued to the screen. JB remained by the doorway. Along with the dark suit, he wore an evil grin. She felt her skin pop with goosebumps.

"Our master host has a new contract for you to sign. You will sign it. There's no time to read the fine print. Your rights to all money won in this contest are being turned over to us."

Dead silence covered the room. The quiet haunted Diane even more.

"You will also finish the contest. If you fail to do either of these things, we will kill Rose, and then we will kill you. No fucking around."

Diane looked at Wes, and he seemed to be shaking, almost convulsing.

"Now, sign the papers. Now!" JB grabbed a briefcase and passed around the papers and pens. One for each of them. Diane didn't know what to feel, and she tried to listen to Wes who whispered something to Bill.

She struggled to grasp a paper in her shaky hands. Then someone roared and she dropped the pen she had been holding.

Wes Pike had charged at JB, and Bill and Jaime followed. Wes tackled JB to the floor, and yelled, "You let her go right now! How could you! How could you! We . . . we thought you were . . ." Wes cried and punched JB in the face.

Diane stood still, too stunned to move, but she saw Brandis leave the room by the other side. *Where is he going?*

"I warned you!" It was the voice from the screen, and then the next thing they heard was Rose's scream. Wes jumped off of JB and charged up the stairs. Diane heard pounding.

Then Wes flew backwards, back down the stairs, crashing into Bill and Jaime. They held him up, and the three of them looked fiercer than she had ever seen them.

What have I been doing? Diane took a deep breath and stepped forward. *What did I really want? To win this game, to humor some jealousy?*

That's a team. That's a friendship and a bond, she thought, watching the three stand side-by-side. Tara joined them next, and then the others approached.

JB stood up, and the voice on the monitor spoke again. "Pass in the contracts. Now, or I hurt her again!"

Diane noticed that Wes was hunched over, but he signed and threw a contract at JB. Diane passed hers up, as well.

Diane felt a fire rise in her chest. She wanted to fight, yes, and she would. This was not all right. Perhaps it started as a game, something she wanted to win because of ego or whatever, but forget all of that. *We have to fight, don't we?*

"There!" Wes yelled. "You have the damn papers. You can keep the damn money! We don't care. Let Rose go!"

JB counted the contracts and then smiled. When he spoke, they all gasped.

"Thank you, losers. Thank you very much."

That was not JB's voice. Not even close. The voice on the monitor laughed.

"I'd like you to meet JB's doppelganger, Boris Clarke," it said. Dexter walked out from upstairs and joined Boris. He held a voice-changer in his hand, and the rest of the group gasped at the sight of him.

"Now, we have a very serious game to play." Dexter put the voice-changer in his pocket. *This is the guy Brandis has been texting and working with?* She saw hate in Dexter's eyes, something darker than she had ever seen in Brandis. Sure, Brandis had betrayal and maybe jealousy, not hate like that. *Did he?*

"You fucker!" Wes shouted, and Dexter just laughed.

"Shut up. If you don't shut up and listen, I'll hurt her again. Ahh, hell." He reached in his pocket, pulled out another device, and hit a button. Then they heard Rose scream again.

Wes and Bill started to move, but the man they'd thought was JB took out a gun and pointed it at both of them.

"This is no game," he said. "These are not blanks. These will kill you. You listen to what Dexter has to say." He grinned at them, and the resemblance between this man and JB gave Diane more chills.

Dexter returned. "It was just an electrical shock," he said. "If you talk out of turn again, I'll shock her again. And if you don't follow my instructions, I will fucking kill her. Got it?"

Diane's chest hurt. Jaime, Bill, and Wes all looked like they wanted to attack, but there was nothing they could do. Not with that gun pointed at them.

"Here are the rules. You each will put on the Rabbit's Eye. You will complete the simulation and move to the next. My friend here and I will be joining you to make sure everyone completes the challenges, and that no one does anything stupid."

Dexter laughed, and Diane swore his eyes grew darker.

"If you do something stupid," he continued, "then one of you will have to pay the price. To illustrate what that price is, please look behind you."

Diane watched as Jaime, Bill, and Wes slowly turned their heads around. Diane was both scared to look behind her and scared to break eye contact with Dexter. She had never felt her heart beat so hard. Not in Hellfire, not in anything.

I'm too young for a heart attack, right?

First, she felt fingers stab into her left shoulder harder than she had ever been gripped. A hand pulled her back, and she gasped at a burning pain like she had never experienced.

It was a sharp pain in her chest, and her hands flew up over her heart.

Diane coughed, and blood projected from her mouth. She felt her lungs burn. Literally, she felt like she had been gutted. Diane made eye contact with Jaime, whose eyes grew wider than Diane had ever thought possible. Then she saw Bill's mouth open wide, too, but she didn't hear any words come out.

Diane pulled her hands away from her chest, still feeling an unbearable amount of pain. She looked at her hands.

They were soaked with blood. It poured out from her like a powerful faucet.

Painfully, she looked over her shoulder. Brandis Dern faced her. He held a long knife in his right hand, and blood dripped from it. He wore no smile. His lips were pressed tightly together, and the look in his eyes—what was that look?

Diane thought for a second that maybe it was regret or sadness, but the thoughts were mixed with such terrible pain. Why would Brandis do this to her?

She tried to open her mouth to speak, but no words came out. Just blood. Blood shot from her mouth, and when she tried to speak again, she coughed.

She collapsed on the floor and looked up at Brandis. She blinked several times, tears rolling down her face. A terrible sadness coalesced with the sharp pain. It was so unfair. She felt hot, a terrible burning all throughout. She wished it would all go away. *Take away the pain, take away the sadness, just take it all away.*

Then she closed her eyes and felt her heart beat slowdown. Just before her heart completely stopped, she realized she'd never open her eyes again.

Part Two:

Bloody Rabbit

"I met this six-year-old child, with this blank, pale, emotionless face, and the blackest eyes... the devil's eyes. I spent eight years trying to reach him, and then another seven trying to keep him locked up because I realized that what was living behind that boy's eyes was purely and simply... evil."

— Dr. Loomis, *Halloween*

"People are strange creatures. You can't always convince them that safety is in their best interest."

— Howard, *10 Cloverfield Lane*

"Never leave a friend behind. Friends are all we have to get us through this life—and they are the only things from this world that we could hope to see in the next."

— Dean Koontz, *Fear Nothing*

Chapter Fifteen

Panic.

Screams. Cries. Moans. Then thunder.

Bill Wise covered his ears at the sound of gun shots.

He turned around slowly, and the man who looked so much like JB stood at the top of the stairs and with the gun raised. *Have I been shot? Who did he shoot?* His body felt numb. He looked down and patted himself. Still in one piece, for now. When Bill looked up, he saw that the gun must have been fired into the ceiling. A shot to shut up everyone.

It worked. Quiet filled the room. The silence was palpable, an uncomfortable blanket on a hot summer morning.

Brandis just stabbed and killed Diane. That really happened. Right in front of him. Right in front of them all.

"Put on the Rabbit's Eyes," Dexter commanded. "Now." JB's lookalike extended the arm that held the gun to emphasize Dexter's point.

Where were the Rabbit's Eyes? Did we bring them in? What day is it? I can't even remember what day it is. Bill rubbed his forehead. *Am I sure I didn't get shot?*

Someone handed him a Rabbit's Eye. He held it and looked over at Jaime. "Jaime! Are you okay?" Bill shouted the words, and Jaime flinched.

"Shut up, Bill," Dexter snapped.

Jaime nodded, but Bill didn't like the look on her face. She looked different from how he felt. She put on the Rabbit's Eye, and she looked like a soldier getting ready to fight.

Tara! Wes! Are they okay? Bill managed to keep the thoughts inside his head this time. *Oh no, Tara!* Bill could tell she was crying, and he stepped over to her. Wrapping an arm around her shoulder, he whispered, "It's gonna be all right. Oh-right?" She looked up at him, her eyes red and wet.

"I said, shut up, Bill!" Dexter marched down the stairs, grabbed Bill by his t-shirt and threw him against the wall.

Bill's back hit some kind of knob, and he moaned.

"But—"

Dexter back-handed him across the face before he could speak. "You will shut up. You will put on the Rabbit's Eye. You will complete this challenge and move to the next. No talking. Or Tara will be next." Dexter looked over at Brandis, and Brandis grabbed Tara and pulled her back.

"You mother fucker!" It was Jaime. She turned around and sprinted right at Brandis. Brandis swung the knife at her, but she dodged it. She spread out her fingers like they were claws and she gouged him right in the eye.

"Owww!" Brandis cried and dropped the knife. Jaime picked it up, brought the knife over her head, and then Bill had to cover his ears again—another gun shot.

"Jaime!" Bill yelled. But Jaime was okay. The gun had fired into the ceiling again.

"There will be order or there will be more death."

Bill hated that man's voice. He hated that he looked like JB. He hated that the man had a gun pointed right at Jaime and that he didn't know what to do about it.

Dexter walked back up the stairs. Even he didn't want to face Jaime, it seemed. "You will put on the Rabbit's Eye now. You will also drop your cell phones in this box." Dexter bent over and picked up a cardboard box that he must have brought out with him. "You will finish the challenge and meet behind the house when you're finished. That's all you need to know. Now, let's begin."

Bill looked from Tara, who was still crying, to Jaime, who looked more vicious than ever. She gave Bill a small nod, and he put on his Rabbit's Eye.

He had so many questions, but he didn't have time for them now. The house had changed with the Rabbit's Eye on, and it felt like the foundation had started to shake. Objects flew off the walls. Bill dodged pictures, crucifixes, figurines. Anything that had previously been on display now flew at their faces. A few hit Bill, and the Rabbit's Eye made him feel pain, but he didn't care.

Under semi-ordinary circumstances, perhaps he would have explored the house. He would have laughed at the scares. But now he just wanted to finish the simulation. The sooner he did that, the sooner he could grab his friends and get the hell out of here.

But he had to find Rose first. He looked for Wes, who turned out to be right behind him. Could he talk to Wes without Dexter hearing? No, too risky, probably. One look on Wes's face, and Bill knew that Wes only had one thing on his mind.

There were four rooms upstairs. The first appeared to be the master bedroom. Plenty of spirits and demons cursed at them and threw things at them. Bill shut the door and moved to the next room.

This second room looked like an office, but one thing caught Bill's eye. Knowing what this house was all about, Bill picked it up—a Bible. Then they went into the third room.

Jaime was right behind them now, and she held hands with Tara. Bill noticed the others were coming upstairs, too. Several were now exploring the master bedroom and the office. Maybe they didn't know exactly what they were looking for, but Bill did.

Remembering the true story that inspired *The Exorcist*, Bill knew that it was about a thirteen-year-old boy. The boy had lived in the Washington, D.C. area. That was where most horror seekers visited: the boy's childhood home or the famous stairway from the movie. But when the boy became ill, his family took him to his uncle's house.

This house.

It was here in this very bedroom that his demon first met an exorcism. Bill had read stories about the bed shaking—this very bed, perhaps that he was staring at. The family had reported all sorts of strange noises in the house, noises that the boy had claimed to hear days before anyone else did. Welts formed on the child's body, and he spoke in another voice, cursing at the priests.

The events in the movie were inspired by the events that took place here, in this house, in this very room.

Bill, Wes, Jaime, and Tara entered the bedroom.

The door slammed shut behind them, and a boy appeared. He sat in his underwear, and across his chest, a series of scratches and welts formed.

"Go to hell you dirty sons-of-bitches. You dirty assholes!" The boy snarled at them, and Bill held out the Bible, to which the boy's body began twisting.

"Go to hell!" The boy shouted again, this time in a deeper voice.

"Where is Rose?" Wes asked, looking around the room. He opened the closet door, but she wasn't there.

Jaime ignored the cursing child and looked under the bed. "She has to be here somewhere," Jaime said. "When we heard her scream, it came from up."

"Are you guys okay?" It was a voice from outside. Bill thought it sounded like Carol.

"Yeah, just fighting a demon," Tara told her.

"Keep looking for Rose," Wes yelled.

"Okay," Carol said.

The possessed boy threw things at them. Bill felt more annoyed than anything else. There was no time for this game. They needed to get Rose and figure out what the hell they were going to do. But where was she?

Jaime sighed. "Let's just finish this simulation and see what happens. She has to be here somewhere."

"How?" Tara asked. "How do you beat it?"

The possessed child barked and cursed at them.

"Assholes! You will never beat me! Dirty assholes!"

Wes shut the closet door and faced the bed. "We say what the priest said in the movie. Remember any line you can. That's how we'll beat this thing. What do you think?"

Bill nodded. "That's how JB would have programmed it. No doubt."

"Shove a stick up your ass!" The boy cursed again.

Jaime started. "The power of Christ compels you!" She looked over at Tara and nodded encouragingly.

"The power of Christ compels you!" Tara said.

Bill added, "Be gone! In the name of the Father, and the Son, and the Holy Spirit!"

The child roared and twisted. Then it floated above the bed and spun. It turned upside down, looked at all four of them, and vomited.

The Rabbit's Eye made Bill's skin feel warm, almost sticky, as if this were real.

"Dirty fucking assholes!"

"The power of Christ compels you!" All four said it together this time. "Be gone! In the name of the Father, the Son, and the Holy Spirit, be gone! The power of Christ compels you!"

The child crashed into the bed. Then a new image appeared.

It was JB. The real JB.

Bill felt a pain in his chest at the sight. On one hand, everything about this room and this event would have been beyond fantastic, under normal circumstances. They would have laughed and sprinted through each challenge with an adrenaline-charged spirit. Plus—to see JB again, the real JB—he felt this way sometimes when he looked at old pictures of his father. Like his dad, though, JB was really gone. And they were in so much trouble—there was no time to enjoy it, and that pissed him off, too. Bill would have given anything to speak with the real JB right now.

"Congratulations, my friends," JB said. It was really his voice, too. Not that annoying voice from the man outside this room.

"You're one step closer to the end. Two challenges down. How many more will you have? That's an easy number. The first number." JB grinned, and Jaime grabbed Bill's hand. She must have felt what Bill was feeling.

"As I record each of these messages, I can't help but already miss you. I wish I could see your faces. I always loved seeing your reactions." JB's smile went away, and he took a deep breath. "I'll see you at the next one."

JB vanished and the rabbit appeared. It did its bloody dance for them.

Then it announced the third riddle:

Follow the Rabbit. Follow the Rabbit in Red.
Go to the close encounter of the first time.
So many words, so much ink bled.
Who you gonna slime?

Chapter Sixteen

Dexter tossed Jaime into the back of a fifteen-passenger van parked behind the Roanoke house. JB's lookalike pointed his gun at some of the others. They had two such vehicles, and they forced everyone into them. Dexter got behind the wheel of the van that Jaime, Bill, Tara, and Wes were shoved into. Boris got behind the wheel of the other.

Well, not quite everyone.

Diane Willow was still lying on the floor inside, as far as Jaime knew.

And Rose?

"Where is she?" Wes yelled at Dexter.

Dexter turned his head slowly and smiled. Once everyone was in the van, he walked back to the house. Jaime was already talking about how to escape when Dexter walked back out with Rose.

Wes shot up. "Rose!"

"I wouldn't do that if I were you," Dexter said. As they approached, Jaime saw that something was tied around Rose's small neck. "Your friend is wearing something very special."

He reached into his pocket and pulled out a small black device, which must have been what he had used earlier to hurt Rose. "This is a remote," Dexter said. "Rose comes along to make sure you all do exactly what we need you to do. So sit your fat ass down, boy." Dexter glared into the van. "That goes for all your friends, too. It has a couple special features. One—I can send shocks right into her spine."

Smiling, Dexter pressed the button, and Rose screamed. Her chest shot up in the air. Wes looked equally agonized. "And two," Dexter continued, staring at Wes as if daring him to move, "it can kill her. If anyone tries anything, I click this other button, and her head explodes. Then we put my special collar on someone else. And so it goes."

Where the hell would he get such a thing? The only person who had access to such technology, Jaime thought, was JB. She didn't like the connection her mind was making.

Dexter laughed, and he threw Rose into the front passenger seat. He glared at the others sitting in the back. "Try just one thing, one of you running out of here or doing anything, and I'll press this button." Then he walked around the van and hopped in the driver's side.

"Are you okay?" Wes asked.

"Shut up, fat ass," Dexter snapped. But Rose turned her head around and nodded, ever so slightly. Jaime could hear Wes's breathing. It was hard, almost mechanical. She understood that rage and hoped they'd be able to use it.

"We're gonna drive all the way to New York?" Bill asked. "In this?" Bill asked. He sat close to Jaime, and she reached out for his hand.

After the demon simulation, Dexter and Boris had brought them straight out here. There was no chance to run away. No chance to escape without hurting Rose. Two vehicles monitored by two fucking psychos—three fucking psychos, actually, because Brandis sure wasn't one of the good guys—and all of them just tossed in the back like animals.

She looked over to Bill. Squeezing his hand, she let her shoulders relax the tiniest bit. There was plenty to worry about, but she took in this moment like a swimmer coming up for a gulp of air. It was brief, but refreshing, and it allowed her to concentrate harder on the moment. Yes, she would fucking kill Dexter when she had the chance. And Brandis. Whatever it took to get them out of this mess. She looked into the other vehicle, where he sat up front with that stupid doppelganger. Brandis caught her eye for a moment, and she glared at him.

She hoped her eyes said that karma was a bitch. And so was she, when she needed to be.

Turning away from Brandis, she looked over at Tara, who was sitting on the other side of Bill. Now she wished she had listened to her mother. Jaime felt like Freddy's claws were inside her chest, pressing to get out like an alien baby. How could she have let her little sister experience this horror?

If anything happened to her . . . no, Jaime wouldn't let that happen. That would never happen.

New York's not too far from home, she thought. If only there were a way to get out of here without anyone getting hurt. Jaime looked up at Rose. Rose's head was lowered, her hair a mess. Jaime looked at the scars—the scars that would forever remind her of Sid's destruction.

Speaking of destruction, where was Sid?

Jaime turned around quickly.

"Are you okay?" Bill asked. Jaime didn't answer right away. She looked at each person in this vehicle and in the other. Sid wasn't here. Surely, he had something to do with this. Right? Jaime had always thought Dexter was psycho, but would he have teamed up with Sid?

And what about Bonnie? Bonnie who had chased them with a chainsaw and cut Bill's arm? How was Bill's arm? Jaime didn't see any blood soaking through the bandages, so that was good.

I need to think clearly, she told herself. Dexter started the van's engine, and they drove down the street.

Okay, so Dexter and Boris, they want JB's money? They have us sign some papers and force us to finish these challenges until it's over. They keep Rose hostage. They're obviously willing to kill . . . and all for JB's money?

But how would they get away with it? They'd have to leave the country, she supposed. They'd sure have enough money to do it. Hell, they could probably buy a country.

Still, that left Sid Malcolm somewhere out there. That didn't explain Bonnie attacking them at the Gein property. What else was going on?

She put her head on Bill's shoulder.

"Everything's gonna be okay," he whispered.

It was nice of him to say, but she didn't believe it.

*****

They had been driving for hours, maybe ten or fifteen even. Jaime's head felt fuzzy, and she really wasn't sure how long it had been. Out of habit, she looked for her phone to see what time it was, but of course Dexter had taken all their phones.

It had to be after midnight. They had stopped twice for gas, and Dexter brought back water and gas station sandwiches.

At one gas station, he let them use the bathroom, and Jaime's jaw dropped when she saw what was on the television the gas station attendant was watching behind the counter.

It was a news report about Rabbit in Red, and it flashed through each of their pictures—Bill, Jaime, Rose, Wes, and all the others. There they were on national news. Maybe someone would recognize them—though apparently it wouldn't be the oblivious cashier. Maybe the police would find them.

But if they did, how far would Dexter go?

She returned to the van and slowly ate the sandwich Dexter had brought for them. Delicious—not so much. But they needed some energy for the third simulation.

Her mind obsessed on all the possibilities. They couldn't jump Dexter without the risk of hurting Rose, so somehow they'd have to get that remote control from him. Or maybe they could jump him and pin down his arms and legs, then grab the remote.

Who was she kidding? She looked at Bill and Wes and the others. She loved them, but they weren't trained fighters. Certainly, the police were searching for them now. Right?

Just finish the damn contest then. Finish it and this will all be over. You can bury it, once and for all.

The bright lights of New York City greeted them. Bill sat up beside her. Jaime loved New York. She didn't know if Bill had ever been. There was something about the constant lights and noise—the city that never sleeps—that energized her. Some people found it draining. Not Jaime. She took a deep breath and waited to arrive at their destination.

It was the New York City Public Library. They pulled up outside the Fifth Avenue location, and—even with all the real horror happening—it was impossible not to find the marble lions outside impressive.

This was the first ghost encounter in the original *Ghostbusters*.

So much ink bled—that line of course referred to the books. *Close encounter of the first kind*—she thought maybe that would throw some of them off track, make them think of the *Close Encounters of the Third Kind* movie, but Jaime knew better. The last line gave it away. *Who you gonna slime?* Too easy.

Surely the library was closed, but she knew that wasn't going to stop them.

"Out, now," Dexter shouted.

"It's so big," Bill said. They stepped out of the van, and Fifth Avenue still seemed busy. The other van pulled up right behind them, and Jaime glared at Brandis as he stepped out. He carried a couple of duffel bags, which must have the Rabbit's Eyes. At least they had made Brandis their bitch.

Daniel and Carol stepped out of the other van, hand in hand. Carol didn't look so good, but who could blame her? They had watched Diane die. Jaime rubbed her eyes and wondered if they were all still in shock. Daniel gave Jaime an awkward half-smile. They needed him, too. They needed to get together and figure out this situation.

Boris marched up to the library doors and used the golden ticket outside like he was scanning it over the lock. It worked. The doors opened, and they hurried everyone inside.

Dexter greeted them and had Rose by his side. "Again, let me be clear. No talking, other than solving the simulation. You get the next clue, and you return right here, right inside this lobby." He scanned the room and looked each of them in the eye. "No one leaves the building until we all do. Anything funny, Rose's head explodes. It's that simple."

He pulled at Rose, and Rose snarled. *Good*, Jaime thought. *There's still a fight inside of Rose. We're done for the moment any of us gives up.*

Jaime heard Wes's knuckles crack.

"Now," Dexter continued, "put these on." He tossed the Rabbit's Eyes at them.

The enormous library boasted table after table, shelf after shelf of books. On an ordinary day, Jaime would have been happy to have spent hours in here, but tonight was nothing ordinary.

Once on, the Rabbit's Eyes brought to life hundreds of ghosts. Screaming ghosts of all kinds, and yep—there was Slimer. There was the lady from the very beginning of the original film who shushed and scared the library patrons. In the back, Jaime swore she could see the legs of the Stay-Puft Marshmallow Man.

Then the ghosts charged at them.

Jaime heard some of the others scream. She just stood there and sighed. "What do you suppose we have to do?" she asked Bill.

It was Tara who jumped in. "Catch them, I would think? Isn't that what the Ghostbusters do?"

Jaime almost smiled a little. "Yes, that makes sense." She patted Tara's head.

"With what?" Bill asked.

"Look!" Jaime yelled and pointed at the chairs. On the wooden chairs that surrounded a center table, there were a variety of proton packs, the devices the Ghostbusters used to stun and catch the ghosts.

They ran toward them and threw them on. The Rabbit's Eye made the devices feel real and heavy. Jaime looked over her shoulder to see if everyone had joined them. Then she gasped.

"Wes is gone," she said.

"Shit," Bill replied. "What is he gonna do?"

Jaime shrugged. "I don't blame him, but I hope he doesn't do anything stupid."

"You guys got this?" Bill motioned at all the flying ghosts. Jaime nodded. "I'll look for Wes. And Dexter. You guys finish this. I'll be back." He took off, and Jaime tried not to think that he had said the three words one should never say in a horror movie.

Tara and Jaime chased down the ghosts. For a moment, she caught herself having fun, and she cursed Dexter all the more. This *should* have been fun. That was what JB wanted at the end, right? Some legit scares, sure. But it should have been a celebration of horror. A celebration of JB.

They captured the ghosts and battled Slimer and Stay-Puft at the end. Jaime wished Bill was here, too. She looked around, but he was gone. He would have enjoyed this.

At the end of the simulation, JB reappeared through the Rabbit's Eye.

"Hi, Jaime. Hi, Tara. I wish I were there with you." Jaime turned her head to look at her sister. This was the first time JB had addressed them individually after a simulation. Did he have it programmed to somehow know who it was? "Congratulations on finishing the third simulation. Here's your next clue."

Jaime wished there was more to it, especially since he addressed them by name. She missed hearing him speak.

The rabbit came out next, spinning and dancing. Then it gave them the next clue.

Follow the Rabbit. Follow the Rabbit in Red.
This one's close to home, but we have to go there.
Many of us lost a loved one; some just dropped dead.
Yours we know too well. Go to the place of his last prayer.

Jaime stood, mouth wide open, and a tear rolled down her cheek. Tara grabbed her hand.

"Does that mean what I think it means?" Tara asked.

Jaime swallowed hard and took back everything she had just thought about this being a celebration. *Fuck JB,* she thought.

She wiped away the tears from her face and looked around at all the others. How was this going to work? She needed to get to Bill and Wes. Rose, too. Would they all have different riddles? How would this play out, now that they were all hostages?

"I guess we go home," Jaime told her sister. Maybe they'd be able to get help. And now—now there was no way Dexter could follow them all. She sighed. Maybe JB knew they were going to need help. Her mom, her Aunt Megan and cousin Jennifer—maybe she'd get to see them all, get real help.

So JB was sending them to Uncle Tim's house, where he had hanged himself years ago. And what about the rest of them?

Jaime wrapped an arm around her sister and held her tightly.

Then from behind, they heard an explosion, and Jaime had only one thought: *Rose!*

*****

Several thoughts bounced around Rose Dawn's mind when Dexter pulled her toward the back of the library as the rest of her friends started the *Ghostbusters* simulation. The biggest thought was that she wanted to kill him.

Rose touched the collar Dexter had put around her neck. She felt like a dog. No, even less than a dog. Why was he doing this to her? He didn't need her like this. The rest of the rabbiteers worked persistently to finish the contest, everyone had already signed over the legal rights to anything they might win, and—as if holding her hostage and hurting her wasn't enough—he'd had one of them killed just to show he could.

Enough. She pulled at the collar, but Dexter shook his head.

"Go ahead," he said and rolled his eyes. "I warned you what would happen. But if you want to die, who am I to stop you?"

"Why are you doing this to me?" Rose let her hands drop to her hips, and Dexter tossed her into a chair. She heard the noises coming from the others fighting this simulation. They sounded—could it be?—excited.

"There doesn't always have to be a *why*, does there?" He smiled at her, and Rose hated it. Her heart beat quicker and her skin heated up. She wanted to slug him. She would resist, and she would persist. She was tired of always being the victim—she had been kidnapped during the first year's games, she had nearly died the second year, and now here she was again—Dexter's dog for the third year.

She pictured herself putting this collar around Dexter's neck and watching his head explode. With any luck, she'd get the opportunity.

Dexter turned and watched the others run around the library. Rose followed his gaze and hoped the others would finish quickly. The sooner this was over, the better.

From the corner of her eye, she spotted Wes. She held her breath. *Does Dexter see him? Please don't let Dexter see him.* A moment later, behind Wes, Bill appeared. What could they do with this damn thing around her neck? *I'll have to help them, somehow. Think, Rose, think!*

She looked at Dexter, who leaned forward, watching the action. He didn't seem to see Bill or Wes yet, which was good. But there was no way to get out of here if he still had the damn remote. Rose looked over to Bill and Wes, who hunched in the corner behind some computer. Rose shrugged at them. They'd have to find a distraction.

Dexter stood up. He turned left, the very direction Wes and Bill stood. *Oh no. Now what do I do?* Dexter took something out of his pocket and threw it over to where Wes and Bill crouched. Then he took out the remote from his pocket. Lowering his head, he appeared to examine the remote closely. He pressed a button.

Rose held her breath and thrust her hands up over her face. Then she heard it. An explosion. *This is it! I'm gone!*

But a couple of seconds passed by and she lowered her hands. She was still here. There had been an explosion, though, and it happened closer to where Bill and Wes had been. *What did Dexter do?*

"That's just a preview," Dexter said and walked over to the blown-up computer desk. "That's not even half of what the bomb in the collar around Rose's neck will do. In case you thought I was fucking around." Dexter stared at them, his face blank. "Now, go. Finish."

Bill and Wes turned around, and Rose sighed. It was both a sigh of relief that no one was hurt and a sigh of disappointment. She was still Dexter's hostage.

A couple of minutes later, Brandis appeared. "Dex, we have a problem."

Rose leaned forward.

"What is it?" Dexter snapped.

"The next destination," Brandis said, his face twisted with worry, "appears to be different for everyone."

Dexter crossed his arms. "That's not possible."

"I finished the simulation, too." Brandis broke eye contact with Dexter and stared at the floor. "I've gotta go home. The riddle is different for everyone, but as far as I can tell, everyone's going home."

Dexter started pacing back and forth. "What for?" he asked.

"Looks like JB programmed another fear simulation, something personal to everyone." Brandis wiped his sweaty forehead.

"But I researched all these locations. I didn't know the order, but JB . . . well, never mind." Dexter threw his arms up in the air. "How could he do this? What will we do now?"

Rose watched as Brandis approached hesitantly. She leaned so close she nearly fell off her chair.

"But Dex, think about it," Brandis whispered. "This could make everything easier. Keep everyone together, but have only one do the simulation." Brandis put his hands in his pocket, and Dexter unfolded his arms. "Then you only have to worry about one."

Dexter looked up and nodded. "Yes. Just one person doing the simulations. That could be easier to track and follow."

"Who should it be?" Brandis asked.

Dexter laughed. "I know just who I want to see."

Chapter Seventeen

Daniel Lloyd flew home to Southern California with Dexter Lange right by his side. Rose and Carol sat right in front of them where Dexter could keep an eye on them. The rest of the crew had been left behind, under the supervision of Boris and Brandis. If anyone back in New York tried anything, Dexter could hurt Rose right here. And if Daniel tried anything, Dexter would hurt Rose and Carol.

Daniel had no choice but to move forward. He had to finish JB's game. He repeated the riddle he had received at the end of the *Ghostbusters* simulation.

> *Follow the Rabbit. Follow the Rabbit in Red.*
> *To where she left you, we must go there.*
> *Many of us lost a loved one, some dropped dead.*
> *Yours left you behind with a father who didn't care.*

Thinking about the riddle, Daniel's arms felt heavy and cold. He sat them on his lap and looked out the window of the airplane. The other first year Rabbit in Red students all knew about Daniel's fear: his own father. It was what tricked him, what he couldn't overcome, during the first Halloween contest. He had failed the original fear simulation, and then at the end, his father had appeared in the flesh. It had turned out, of course, to be the master host, and that was when Dexter tried to kill JB.

All the while, Daniel had stood frozen. He had failed to overcome his fears.

What the rest of the group didn't know—not even Carol, he hadn't gotten that deep with her yet—was that what had kept him up late at night as a teen wasn't worrying if his father was going to come home drunk, wake him up, and beat him in the middle of the night. That had happened plenty of times. His dad would come home too inebriated to talk, but he sure could hit. And Daniel was his favorite punching bag.

No, what kept Daniel up late at night was wondering where his mother had gone.

His mom had left him and his father. He remembered his mother's final words and actions as if they had happened only yesterday. She had said good-bye to him one night when he was only fourteen years old, and he hadn't seen her since.

"He doesn't love me anymore, Danny," she had said, "and I can't watch what he does to you." She stood up, evidently ready to depart at that exact moment.

"Wait! Why can't you take me with you?" Daniel had nearly fallen out of bed.

"You're too young to understand. I'm too old to tell you. One day, when you get out of this house, I'll find you, okay?"

"Where are you going?" His voice was hoarse now, shaky with tears.

"I can't tell you. If you don't know, he can't beat it out of you."

"But he'll try. You know he'll try anyway." His face was stone, but his mom's was harder.

He hadn't recognized her. Her emotionless features made her more like an alien than a parent he had lived with for the last fourteen years. She placed a hand on the bedroom doorknob and turned around. The sun was now beginning to rise, sharp blades of light stinging the room.

"You have to stand up to him, Danny. I can't take watching you cower in fear any more than I can take him." She snapped her head back to the door then, took a step outside, and without looking around again, she said, "Good-bye."

144

Somehow, all along, JB must have known about that, too. How was that even possible? Daniel knew that JB did some pretty creepy cyberstalking on all of them—Bill had told them all how JB originally discovered their fears. When they first played the riddles, before even coming to Rabbit in Red, they had to accept his Rabbit in Red app terms of agreement. Legally, JB's app had given him a world of info. He could legally see their texts, listen to their phone calls, even see their pictures.

Daniel thought about some of the selfies he took alone in his room and shuddered at the thought.

But he had never talked to anyone about his mom! He had been thinking about how JB knew about his mother since that riddle. Glancing up at Carol and Rose, he supposed he should be concerned for his life, but it was this mystery that bothered him even more.

In high school, he'd texted plenty of friends about what a dick his dad was. He even took pictures of his bruises, just in case the cops showed up someday or in case he ever grew the balls to call them himself.

They never did show up. And neither did his mother. Daniel had spent many sleepless nights thinking about her. How did JB know?

He rested his head against the airplane window and closed his eyes. He told himself he needed to think about Dexter and how to stop him. *Yes, focus, you asshole. He picked you!* Daniel breathed hard. Out of all of rabbiteers, Dexter had picked him. That meant Dexter wanted to see his fears, wanted to fuck with him some more. *Why not Bill or Wes? Why me?*

Daniel flexed the muscles under his shirt. *I can take him,* he thought. *I'm bigger than him. I should be able to take him.*

But how? How can I take him without risking Rose's or Carol's life?

He opened his eyes and stared out of the window again.

And what is JB going to make me do once I get home?

*****

Amazed again at what JB's golden tickets granted them, Daniel got in the back seat of a car Dexter had been able to rent. Rose sat in the front, and Carol joined Daniel in the back. He reached for her hand.

Daniel had never really had a girlfriend. He'd had dates to school dances, but never someone he felt close to. Carol was his first, in many ways.

Last year, he had gotten close to her because she was obsessed with JB. He remembered thinking not only did Carol look like a cheerleader—gorgeous blonde hair and a hell of a rack—but she supported JB like she was his number one fan. The Annie to his Paul.

Daniel had wanted one thing last year, and that was to ruin JB's reputation. He could admit now that it was pure jealousy. Jealous that everyone else was closer. Still angry that JB had tricked him. When Daniel saw Carol's enthusiasm, he thought that if he could manipulate her, then he'd win. He'd get her to distrust, maybe even hate JB. That was his big plan—turn them all against JB, one at a time.

But it had turned out someone else had much darker plans. Plans of murder and destruction.

Since Rabbit in Red had burned down, he had felt guilty. These stupid emotions, they blinded him to what was really going on.

He squeezed Carol's hand. Maybe their relationship had started with manipulation, but it turned into something real. When he was with Carol, he didn't feel like he had to be better than someone else. She calmed him.

And now Dexter was ruining that. JB, too. Even beyond the grave, JB had managed to come up with some kind of plan that was sure to haunt him. He felt goosebumps on his arms as they neared his San Diego home. Would his father be there?

Jesus, would his mother?

No, that's not possible. JB couldn't know that. But what did the old nut have up his sleeve?

"It's gonna be okay," Carol whispered in his ear and kissed his cheek.

"Shut up," Dexter snapped from the front. "No talking."

Daniel glared at him and wished he had Carrie's powers or that the Force was really a thing. He'd set him on fire with his eyes.

They turned into the subdivision where Daniel lived. His stomach twisted, and he thought he'd be sick. He had to swallow a couple of times, and even his saliva tasted bad.

The car pulled right up in Daniel's driveway. He took a deep breath, and Dexter swung his head around and faced him.

"Do whatever you need for the next riddle. No fucking around. Got it?" Dexter's eyes were cold and black, and Daniel nodded slowly.

He faced Carol and kissed her gently on the lips. She put an arm around the back of his head and returned the kiss, hard.

"Enough," Dexter said. "Out."

Daniel stepped out of the car and felt a chill even in the hot summer sun of San Diego. From the front, Dexter walked out and handed Daniel a Rabbit's Eye. He took it, inhaled deeply, and crept toward the front door. Opening it slowly, he called out, "Dad?"

No answer. That was good. That was something.

Daniel put on the Rabbit's Eye. JB appeared in his living room.

"Daniel," JB started, "you must be wondering why you had to come home."

He rolled his eyes and thought about punching JB, even if he only existed in virtual reality.

"There are two things you must do. They will be hard, but they are, in fact, designed to help you." JB smiled, but Daniel didn't trust him. Not one bit.

"The first is to make a call."

Daniel sighed. "I don't have—"

"You don't have to use your own phone," JB continued. "I'm making the call right now for you using the Rabbit's Eye. You'll hear the voice on the other end through the headset. Good luck, kid."

JB vanished, and Daniel heard the sound of a telephone ringing through the headset. He looked around the room. Nothing abnormal was enhanced through the 4D lenses, not yet, anyway. He sat on the couch in the living room.

Through the Rabbit's Eye, a voice said, "Hello?"

It was only one word, but Daniel recognized it immediately.

"Mom?" He could barely get the word out. A lump had formed in his throat.

"Oh, God. Danny? Is that you?" Did she sound happy? Surprised, for sure, but could that be happiness in her voice?

"Mom," he whispered. "Mom, how are you?"

Silence on the other end. Then, "How did you get my number, Danny?"

Daniel felt like he had been punched in the gut. "That's what you ask me? Not, 'Hi, I miss you, how are you?' but 'How did you get my number?' Jesus, Mom."

Silence again. Then breathing. Several breaths.

"I'm sorry," she said. "How . . . how are you?"

Daniel looked at Dexter, who was standing in the doorway.

"Not good," he said. Dexter took a step forward. "How are you?"

"What's wrong, baby?" Did she sound concerned? Really? Maybe.

Dexter shook his head at Daniel.

"Nothing," Daniel told her. "Just sad." He reached under the Rabbit's Eye to wipe his eyes. "Where are you?"

"Danny, I . . . I can't tell you that." She coughed.

"Why not, Mom?"

More silence. Then she asked, "How's your father?"

"Fuck him," Daniel shouted. He stood up and paced the living room.

"That good, huh?"

Daniel heard a noise by the front door. He turned and Dexter had stepped inside the living room.

"Who the fuck are you?" It was Daniel's father. Then he saw his son.

"Daniel?" He cocked his head like Michael Myers did when watching a victim die. "What the fuck is that on your head?" He laughed and shook his head. "What are you doing here? I got a call at work from . . . I don't know who . . . but he said that someone had broken into my house and that I needed to get home now."

Daniel stared at his father. JB had probably programmed that, too. Somehow, JB had located his mother's number and programmed this damn Rabbit's Eye not only to call her, but to call his father, too.

"Jesus, is that—"

"Yes, Mom. Dad is home." Daniel stared at his father, whose eyes opened wide with fury.

"Are you talking to *her* through that thing? What the fuck?" His father lunged forward and ripped the Rabbit's Eye off of Daniel's head. In the background, Daniel heard Dexter snicker.

On the ground, the Rabbit's Eye projected an image. It was Daniel's mother on the phone. Somehow the Rabbit's Eye must have accessed her phone camera. She gasped.

"I can see you," she said. The Rabbit's Eye must be broadcasting their image onto her phone, too.

"You bitch," his dad said. "Where are you?"

"Dad," Daniel said, "don't. Please."

He glared at Daniel. "Don't what?"

"She left because of you!" Daniel shouted. "You hit her and you hit me, and she couldn't take it! Don't you see that, you asshole?"

His father's eyes narrowed, and Daniel thought he heard a snarl.

"If either one of ya was worth anything, you wouldn't have gotten hit." His father's chest heaved, in and out.

"Mom," Daniel said, slowly turning away from his father. "It's your fault, too. You told me you couldn't see me cower to him. You remember that?" Daniel wiped his eyes. He couldn't let his father see the tears in his eyes. "But you're the biggest coward. You left, and never took me."

Daniel looked at his father. "Your hate, and her . . . her cowardice, I get it now. I get why I'm here." He wiped at his eyes again and swallowed hard. "That's who I was. Full of hate. Full of cowardice. But I don't have to be anymore. We can become . . . whatever we want to become. I'm here to . . ."

He licked his lips. His throat felt so dry. Dexter still stood in the corner of the room, and he was smiling. Daniel did hate him, but didn't Dexter deserve that? Daniel looked back at his dad and then to his mother.

"I'm here to tell you both good-bye," Daniel said. "It's not a good-bye because of hate or fear." He looked at his mother. "It's a good-bye because I deserve more."

His father slapped him across the face. Daniel tasted blood and wiped it from his lips.

"Only cowards have to hurt other people. That's how the scum of the earth manage to feel better." Daniel stepped up to his father, closer than he ever had before. He stared into his father's eyes. "Good-bye, Dad." Then without looking at his mother, he said, "Good-bye, Mom."

Through the Rabbit's Eye, JB appeared and Daniel's mom vanished. Daniel picked up the headset and walked out the door. He waited for Dexter to follow, and then Daniel slammed it shut.

He took the Rabbit's Eye into the back seat of the car and waited for JB's next clue.

Chapter Eighteen

"Fucking bullshit," Rose heard Dexter say to someone on the phone. She sat in the front seat of the rental car and looked at Daniel in the back.

Dexter slammed the car door and paced the gas station parking lot. The warm sun blazed through the car windows. Rose leaned back and enjoyed the warmth on her face.

For a moment, she considered running. Then she stroked the collar around her neck and sighed. "Daniel," she said, "play it again."

He held the Rabbit's Eye in his lap and pressed a button on the side of the headset. JB's image popped up through the lens.

"One down, many more to go. Yes, this is a competition. A race to the finish. But there's one twist." JB laughed, and Rose thought there would surely be more than one. "You must remember that we are a team, and no matter who wins, there must be that sense of team spirit. The next clue will not be given until at least half of the team has finished their individual challenges." JB folded his arms, smiled, and vanished.

"Why not everyone?" Carol asked and reached for Daniel's hand. They made Rose miss Wes all the more.

"Maybe, somehow, he knew not everyone would be able to finish," Rose told them and thought of Diane. She sat back against the window and wondered what terrible thing JB would make her face.

Would it be something about her brother? Her brother had died on a camping trip when she was young, and she still kept his picture in her purse. Rose's fear simulation during the first Halloween contest involved her brother. *But I've been through so much,* she thought. *Nearly burned alive. Permanently scarred. Kidnapped. Probably going to die.*

152

Am I going to die?

That question had rolled through her mind dozens of times since Dexter had taken her right from her very home. Then Diane was murdered—stabbed! By Brandis. Rose sighed and shook her head.

Is Wes going to die? Jaime? Bill? How many will die?

Dexter flung his door open and jumped in the front seat. One look in his eyes and Rose knew the question wasn't a matter of *if* someone else would die. It was a matter of *when*. And she had a terrible feeling that Dexter had planned on making sure she wouldn't survive. Maybe none of them would.

Dexter shook his head and breathed hard through his nose. Then he turned to Rose, and that terrible smile slithered upon his face.

"Let's start with you, firecracker."

She felt a chill, even with the warm sun still heating up the car. She closed her eyes and pictured Dexter's head exploding. That always made her feel better.

"So, first, that means back to New York. You'll have to get your riddle and get back in this game, too. Then to wherever JB wants to take you." Dexter started the car, and off they went.

*****

From California to New York, Dexter continued to lead them. JB's golden ticket allowed them access to private jets, too. They managed to bypass security this way. Dexter made Rose put on a little scarf. No one saw the collar, and they had their own private access to any transportation.

They arrived in New York late that evening, and the library had already closed. Once again, JB's ticket allowed them access to the library. Rose put on the Rabbit's Eye and fought the ghosts.

Then the bloody rabbit announced her special riddle:

Follow the Rabbit. Follow the Rabbit in Red.
You're not the only one to lose a brother,
The love here has too long gone unsaid.
To understand, you must start with their mother.

Then a new image appeared. It was one Rose recognized all too well, and she felt tiny hairs pop up along her arm.

It was a picture of a teenage JB. She knew that young face because of all the video tapes they had watched last year. He had long, dark hair. This must have been around the time of the Halloween dance at his school. Rose sighed at the memory of the video tape. Kids had tricked him and picked on him. The bullying had particularly bothered Wes. But at the end of the video, they all had heard JB hurting the bullies. The kids had tried something—but JB had hurt them, and by the sounds on the video, he had hurt them bad.

What was it they had called him?

She took a closer look at the picture. At the bottom, a phrase slowly appeared. It was the strange name they all had heard those terrible children call JB in the videos.

"Smell slime," Rose said out loud in the library. "JB Smell Slime." It didn't mean anything to her, and she still didn't understand it, but it must mean something. Why would that phrase be on the picture?

Rose looked over her shoulder at Dexter. He wore a Rabbit's Eye, too, but he must not have been able to see the picture. "What is it?" Dexter asked. "What are you looking at?"

"Nothing," Rose said. "Just thinking." She looked up at Dexter. "Did you hear my riddle?"

"Yeah. So who else lost a brother? One of the other students?" He crossed his arms.

Rose shrugged. "Must be."

So JB lost a brother, Rose thought. *And I lost a brother. And to do whatever he wants me to do—the love here has too long gone unsaid—I have to find their mother.*

JB's mother.

Rose knew JB's biography—what little of it was made available—as well as any of them. She had looked him up before even beginning the riddle contest.

That was the problem.

She knew that his mother was dead.

*****

Rose couldn't stop scratching at her neck and her arms. She wished she had a phone so she could Google, and she was dying to talk to someone about her riddle. Fortunately, they were now meeting up with the rest of the group. Dexter had talked with Boris, and they were going to take half of the group to go through their individual challenges.

Dexter breathed heavily through his nose. "None of you know someone else who lost a brother?" Daniel and Carol shook their heads. "This is stupid. How do we finish your challenge then?" Rose shrugged and avoided his eyes.

She had an idea. What she wanted to do was Google and see if she could find any information about JB's mom. On the ride to meet up with the rest of the group, Rose had an idea of where JB might want her to start.

A graveyard.

If his mother was dead but she had to "start with their mother," that seemed to be the most logical place. With the Rabbit's

Eye, JB could probably bring anyone to life. She shuddered at the thought—a little too *Psycho* for her taste, if that was his intention. But she needed to find out what cemetery JB's mother was buried at. And preferably get to it without Dexter knowing.

There was something about the picture that only she saw—the teenage JB. Something sad. Something not right. And whatever that was, Rose didn't want to share it with Dexter. He didn't deserve to know. There was something intimate and personal about his past that he wanted to share with the real rabbiteers, and Dexter shouldn't be a part of that.

How do I find the cemetery? How do I get there without Dexter?

Rose bit her lip and watched Dexter out of the corner of her eye. She needed a plan. She needed to talk with Wes, Jaime, and Bill.

A little while later, Dexter pulled up outside of a sketchy-looking motel. She followed his lead, and they walked into one of the rooms.

Wes ran and hugged her. She put her arms around him, and he kissed her. "Enough," Dexter said and pushed Wes off of her. Rose looked around and realized that they must have shoved everyone into this one motel room. It looked like the kind of place crack addicts would stay for the night.

"It's late," Dexter stated. "Shut up and sleep. We'll leave in the morning."

Wes grabbed Rose's hand and walked with her to a spot on the wall near the bathroom. He sat down, and she followed. Bill, Jaime, and Tara were sitting there, too.

"This is all we've done. Sit against the wall and try to sleep," Wes whispered. "But I couldn't sleep. Not one wink." He gave Rose a half-smile. "I was so worried."

She rested her head on his shoulders. "I'm okay. But I need to talk to you." She looked around the room. Dexter was talking to Boris and Brandis at the opposite wall near the door, and they glanced at her often.

Very quietly, she told Wes about the riddle, and Bill and Jaime leaned in to hear, too.

"So JB had a brother and lost him," Jaime said. "That doesn't necessarily mean he's dead. Knowing JB, it could mean anything."

Bill nodded. "It is weird to start with his mother. Didn't both of his parents die in a car crash?"

"Yeah," Wes whispered. "I remember reading that when I first heard of Rabbit in Red. Part of JB's estate came from the inheritance he received from his parents. I think, anyway."

Rose stretched her arms. "Yeah, that's right. I remember reading that, too." She looked around, making sure Dexter wasn't listening or watching. "Is it odd that JB showed me something that Dexter couldn't see?"

"The Rabbit's Eyes are programmed," Jaime said. "That's why they need us. JB deliberately set things up so just not anyone could see these things."

"We have to figure out where the cemetery is at," Bill said. "But how?"

"What do we do without Google?" Rose tried to joke. "Okay, think. Where do we go?"

"You were in a library, Rose." Jaime flashed a smile. "I know, I know. No way you could have looked stuff up with Dexter there."

"What about Smell Slime?" Bill asked. "That's obviously important." A look of worry flashed across Bill's face. Rose wondered what Bill was thinking, but then Wes interjected.

"Maybe," Wes said, "We just need *a* graveyard. That's why we have the Rabbit's Eyes, right?"

"You're a genius!" Rose kissed him on the cheek.. "Wherever we go tomorrow, I'll tell Dexter I have an idea and that it requires going to a cemetery. Hopefully, he won't be able to see what I see. And hopefully you're right and JB will leave another clue for us."

"Shut up over there!" It was Brandis. "Everyone sleep. Now."

Sure, Rose still had an explosive device around her neck. They were all in more trouble than they probably realized. One of those psychos could kill them at any moment, and they were out to take everything great about Rabbit in Red and keep it for themselves. It should be easy to just fall asleep on command. Rose rolled her eyes.

But next to Wes and her friends, Rose felt good. She looked over at Jaime and whispered, "And to think. You dated that douche bag."

Jaime smiled. "Don't remind me. What a hashtag D-bag."

Rose covered her mouth to stifle a laugh. It was the best she had felt all day.

Chapter Nineteen

Jaime woke up with a headache. She rolled her neck, trying to pop the stiffness.

"Up! Up and at 'em!" Brandis called out. Jaime rubbed her eyes. She must not have slept much, and certainly not all that well, but at least she had slept a bit.

She watched Bill wipe some drool off his chin, and she giggled softly.

"Whaa?" Bill mumbled.

She shook her head and hoped that someday she'd be able to make jokes about drool, messy hair, or stale breath. The more awake she became, the less she felt like laughing. She looked at Brandis and Dexter talking in the corner and wished she hadn't woken up to this nightmare.

"All right, let's get this over with," Brandis said and grabbed Jaime by the arm. He pulled her hard. She moaned and Bill jumped up.

"Get your hands off her," Bill shouted. In the corner, Jaime saw Dexter smile.

"We've done this before, or have you forgotten?" Brandis asked. Jaime got a whiff of his B.O. and she didn't care for it. He smelled like he hadn't showered in days. Had she really been attracted to him? She clenched her teeth.

Bill stood up tall. With his chest out and shoulders back, he looked taller than Jaime remembered. He was always the tallest, always the one to bend over when walking by ceiling fans and things like that, but she had gotten so used to it. Now he appeared to stand even taller, and Jaime wanted Bill to hit Brandis. Hit him hard. But then she remembered Diane. This wasn't just a bully you could punch and walk away from. Brandis and Dexter had guns, and they weren't afraid to use them.

"Whose turn is it today?" Jaime asked, trying to interrupt them. Bill didn't even blink, but Brandis turned and looked at her.

"Yours, darlin'. Time to revisit your suicidal uncle. Isn't that exciting?" Brandis opened his mouth when he smiled, and Jaime hated it. She could nearly feel the heat coming off Bill, too, and she knew she needed to calm him.

"Oh-right." She forced a smile at Bill. He left Brandis's eyes and locked contact with her. He nodded. They had bigger mysteries to solve right now, and they needed to stick together. No fighting, no—*well, nothing worse*, Jaime thought.

"You and Tara will come with me. Everyone else stays here." Brandis glared at Bill as he said the last sentence.

Jaime quickly interjected before Bill could complain. "I need Rose," she said, again locking contact with Bill. This was, in many ways, still a game they needed to play. They might not like the rules, but to win might require some extra creativity.

"Why?" Brandis asked.

Jaime spoke loud enough so Dexter could hear across the room. "Tara and I might be able to help Rose solve her riddle. We've got some ideas."

That did the trick. Dexter looked over and nodded.

"Fine," Brandis said. "Just the three of you. Bill and Wes stay put."

"Oh-right," Jaime said again and reached for Bill's hand. Brandis rolled his eyes.

"We go now," Brandis said.

Bill pulled her closer, even with Brandis watching. "Be careful," he told her.

"I will. You know I will." Jaime stared up into his blue eyes. She loved his messy, blonde hair. Maybe some morning, she'd wake up next to Bill in the privacy of a bedroom instead of this hotel room turned prison.

"Jaime." Bill squeezed her hands. He took a deep breath. She felt her stomach do a little twirl. "I love you."

He blinked hard. She could see the concern in his eyes, and they told her that he worried he might never see her again.

She felt warm and a hundred thoughts flew in her mind. This wasn't fair. None of it was fair. They deserved a chance. They deserved to be young and have fun and not worry about getting killed.

"I love you, too," Jaime told him. Bill looked beyond her shoulder for a moment, glaring at Brandis, she assumed. Then he met her eyes again and kissed her.

She returned the kiss. Her mouth was dry, but her passion made up for it.

"Enough!" Brandis snapped and pulled her away. She saw Bill had an evil twinkle in his eye, the kind that JB used to have whenever he announced a new game. Then he smiled, and Jaime smiled back.

She liked it when Bill was defiant.

Rose and Tara came to stand by her side then, and they followed Brandis out of the crappy motel and toward Uncle Tim's house.

*****

Brandis pulled up to her aunt and uncle's home. Her Aunt Megan and cousin Jennifer had stayed here, even after Uncle Tim's suicide. Jaime had always wondered how they did that. She knew that Bill and his mom had moved out after Bill's father was murdered inside their home. She didn't think she'd be able to say in a place where someone had died.

For a moment Jaime wished that her aunt and cousin would be home. Maybe, somehow, they could help. But no—that wasn't true. Brandis had a knife, a sharp, terrible knife that had killed Diane. He wouldn't be afraid to use it again, so Jaime hoped that her aunt and cousin would be gone. And of course, there was poor Rose, still wearing that awful collar. It would only take a click of a button. *Please be gone,* she thought.

They neared the garage, and Jaime remembered all the stories she had heard. Uncle Tim had done it in a work room he had built in the back of the garage. He had tossed some rope up into the rafters of the ceiling. Then he tied the rope around his neck, jumped off a chair, and let himself choke, slowly, until he died. Her family had told her that it wasn't instant—it wasn't high enough to be an instant snap of the neck. He choked to death, however long that took.

Jaime had been in this room only once after his death. She and her mom of course came over to do whatever it was people are supposed to do in tragedies. While her mom and Megan talked, Jaime wandered out to this room, stared up at the ceiling, and tried to figure it all out.

She never had figured it out. Not long after that, she had explored online forums for teens who had lost a family member. That was where she had met Bill. She smiled at the memory, as the car slowly came to a stop. After the forum on losing a loved one, she had found Bill again, this time on a horror page debating *The Shining.* It was as if their friendship were meant to be.

Brandis got out of the car and opened the back door. *How polite.* Tara, Rose, and Jaime got out and walked to the garage.

Of course, Jaime had seen this room one other time, unexpectedly. It was at that first weekend at Rabbit in Red. In the second round of games, JB had tested them on how well they could save the victims in popular horror movies. Jaime remembered saving Drew Barrymore's character in *Scream* and Marion in *Psycho,* but it ended with something much darker: she had to save her uncle. That was when she and everyone else at Rabbit in Red really started to question JB.

During that simulation, Jaime had to act like she was going to hang herself. Only then did Uncle Tim get down. She had to try to hurt herself in order to save him.

They approached the garage, and Brandis turned to her. "Do you know the code?"

She did, but she didn't want to tell him. Brandis grabbed Tara hard and shook her. "How about you?"

Tara moaned, and that was all it took for Jaime. "Stop! It's 1923."

Brandis pushed Tara back and entered the code. The garage door slowly opened, and Jaime exhaled a sigh of relief. No cars were here. Her family wasn't home.

"Here, put these on," Brandis said and gave Jaime and Tara a Rabbit's Eye. Jaime instantly felt sick. Tara was a part of this, too. Tara had told Jaime about her riddle after their little *Ghostbusters* adventure, but Jaime had told Tara to keep it quiet and not let Brandis or Dexter know.

"Why does Tara have to put this on?" Jaime asked.

She watched Tara hesitantly take the Rabbit's Eye. Tara usually looked older to Jaime than she really was, but right now, she saw a child's face and a child's fears.

"I don't want to," Tara whimpered. "I don't want to do this."

Brandis took out his knife. He pulled Jaime close, and she smelled his awful stink, like sewage and dead fish. She gagged.

"We don't have time for games," Brandis stated. "I want to know what your riddle was and I want to know now." He smiled then. "Oh, did you think we weren't going to check with your little sister?" Brandis whispered in her ear.

Tara's eyes grew wide and tears dropped down her cheeks. Jaime sighed. Everyone around her was in pain. She felt like she was about to snap, but she nodded at Tara.

"Go ahead. Tell him," Jaime said. She gritted her teeth and breathed hard through her nose.

"It said," Tara began, "Follow the Rabbit. Follow the Rabbit in Red." She coughed and wiped her face. "Be strong when others are weak. Be ready to face the ghosts of the dead. Only then will they find the answers they seek."

When Tara had first told Jaime about her riddle, Jaime assumed the ghost would be Uncle Tim. That Tara, too, would have to face his memory. But they didn't tell anyone because of the last part.

There were other questions they needed answered. Questions about JB. Things they wanted to keep from the bad guys.

If there was one thing Jaime understood, it was that JB encouraged them to work together as a team. The first competition had started with ranks and numbers, but that was just a front to ignite their competitive spirits, Jaime remembered JB telling them.

This isn't just about one winner, then. No, she thought. *There's always more to it, and JB was always a few steps ahead of them.* Well, until . . . she shook that out of her mind. Okay, so far, JB was only giving certain ones a little extra clue. Rose got the picture. Tara's riddle told her she'd play a part also. They'd have to come together—that was clear. Now if only they could keep that fact from Brandis and Dexter.

Brandis rubbed his forehead. "What answers?"

Jaime and Tara shrugged.

"Maybe things are more connected than we see," Rose said. "That's why JB wants so many people to be able to finish this part of his challenge before moving forward."

Brandis nodded. Rose wasn't lying, either. Some things were definitely connected.

"All right. Let's finish this here and see what happens." He shoved them into the garage.

Jaime and Tara put on their Rabbit's Eyes. They held hands and Jaime held her breath. As she had expected, Uncle Tim was waiting for them.

"Girls," he said and walked toward them. "It's good to see you." Jaime felt Tara squeeze her hand harder.

It wasn't just seeing him that made everything strange. It was his voice. It sounded just like him! How did JB do that?

"You can relax. JB didn't program any ghosts here. He says you've been through enough. Today is about answers."

Uncle Tim sat down and motioned for them to get closer.

"Of course, you have to find them for yourselves. I simply can't tell you." He smiled, and Jaime saw a little of JB in his eyes. He took a card out of his pocket and handed it to them.

Written on the card was *King's Chapel Burial Ground.*

Jaime gasped. It was a cemetery, maybe the one that would give them answers to JB's mother.

Uncle Tim stood up. He opened his mouth to speak again, but Jaime heard a scream from behind.

She turned around quickly.

She let go of Tara's hand. Her own hand started to shake, and she clenched her fists.

Was it a vision? Was it part of the Rabbit's Eye?

She blinked hard several times and shook her head. Then she took off the headset, but the vision remained.

It was Sid Malcom. Rose screamed again and ran toward Jaime and Tara.

Brandis's mouth opened wide. "What are you doing here?"

Sid snarled, and drool dripped from his mouth. Brandis held up his knife and pointed it at Sid, but his hand was shaking. Sid wore a black patch over his left eye, and for just a second that made Jaime feel good. She must have caused some real damage the last time they had met.

"Boy, boy, boy. They sure got you trying to be a big boy, don't they?" Sid laughed and walked closer. He had his hands behind his back, but Jaime saw a reflection from something shiny.

Slowly, Sid brought his hands out from behind, and he held a large machete. For a moment, he looked just like Jason Voorhees.

"What do you want?" Brandis asked. His entire arm shook, and Jaime thought for sure he was going to lose the knife. She didn't know what to think. For a second, she rooted for Sid—*yes, kill him. But, wait. Then what? No, never mind, please, Brandis, you better be able to take him. But then what?* It was a catch-22, and Jaime didn't like either possible outcome.

"For you to get out of the way," Sid said.

"You don't understand—"

"No, kid, you don't understand," Sid interrupted him. His good eye left Brandis and shot right over to Jaime. A sick smile formed on his lips, revealing stained, yellow teeth.

He didn't take his eye off Jaime, but he moved his right arm rather quickly.

Without even looking back at Brandis, Sid thrust a machete right into Brandis's stomach. Brandis made a strange noise—somewhere between vomiting and screaming, and then blood spurted out of his mouth. Sid stepped forward and held Brandis, only to push the machete in deeper. Brandis's blood soaked the front of Sid's shirt, and still Sid didn't take his eye off Jaime. There was something even creepier about it just being a single eye, and Jaime's skin erupted with goosebumps. Sid's tongue ran across his dirty teeth, and then he grabbed the machete with both hands. Laughing,

Sid lifted Brandis off the ground. His body squirmed and his feet shook.

More blood shot out of Brandis's mouth, and Sid lifted him higher. After what felt like an eternity of frozen time—*could this really be happening?*—Brandis fell limp.

Sid tossed him to the side like he was a bag of garbage. Then he stepped inside the garage and shut the door.

Never once did that smile leave his face. Until he spoke. When he spoke, the smile became a snarl.

He stepped toward all three of them.

He cracked his knuckles.

"Are you girls ready to join him?"

Chapter Twenty

Wes Pike hated not having Rose by his side. He sat close to Bill and squeezed his hands into fists. Some days he missed the little clown nose stress ball he used to take everywhere. He pulled at his t-shirt—Rose had helped him get rid of all the baggy sweatshirts he used to wear to cover up his extra baggage.

Perhaps even worse than not having Rose by his side was not being able to do anything about it. When she first went missing and Wes had raced to meet Bill, it at least felt like they were doing something about it. Now—nothing. They sat in this cramped hotel room that smelled like a locker room that hadn't been mopped during an entire football season.

"All right, fat ass, your turn." It was Dexter standing over him. Wes looked over at Bill. "Your boyfriend is coming too, so don't panic. I want the two of you with me. And also you, Danny."

Wes, Bill, and Daniel stood up. Looking at Daniel, Wes felt strangely comforted that he'd be with them, too.

"Repeat your riddle for us to hear," Dexter commanded.

Wes stuttered at first. He hadn't really thought about his own riddle, but he knew the time would come to once again face his fears. "Fuh . . . fuh . . . follow the Rabbit. Follow the Rabbit in Red. Clowns will laugh and children will run. Go to the oldest one where all visitors have fled. Time for you to have some fun."

Dexter frowned. "What does that mean to you?"

Wes knew exactly what it meant. He had told everyone that his fear of clowns started with Pennywise from Stephen King's *It*, but there was an earlier incident. His own real life *It*, something that maybe he hadn't fully understood until he encountered King's creation.

When he was a little boy, he had gotten lost in a little carnival funhouse. He had cried and screamed, and a clown had come to the rescue. The thing was—the clown didn't seem to be such a nice guy. He had approached Wes from behind, grabbed him by the shoulders, and yelled, "Boo!" Only after getting Wes to cry some more did the clown escort him out of the funhouse.

When Wes first saw *It*, he began to understand King's power. The author had taken something innocent, a childhood joy, and made it evil. In his later memories, Wes realized that he hated the clown in that funhouse for the same reason—it was supposed to be fun. A day at a carnival for a child should have been all cotton candy and laughter.

How did JB know about this?

"I need to go to a funhouse," Wes said. "A funhouse with the Rabbit's Eye." He gulped at the thought. Rabbit in Red used to have a funhouse. They had travelled though it during their first Halloween, but even then Wes had kept his eyes closed.

"The riddle also says I need to go to the oldest one. So use your phone and find the oldest funhouse in the country." Wes squeezed his hands again. He could really use his stress ball.

"Where all visitors have fled?" Bill asked. "That sounds like it's not just the oldest, but probably no longer in operation."

Wes had the same thought. "Yeah. An out-of-order funhouse with the Rabbit's Eye. Just what I'd like to do today."

Bill patted him on the back.

"Got it," Dexter said, looking up from his phone. *That took like a second,* Wes thought. It was as if Dexter already knew about the funhouse. "The oldest funhouse in the United States is also abandoned. Bar'l of Fun is in the Bushkill Amusement Park in Pennsylvania. That's not too long of a drive. Let's go."

Without a bathroom break or any preparation, Dexter pushed Wes, Bill, and Daniel out of the hotel room and into one of the rentals.

"How did you find that so fast?" Wes asked.

Dexter glared at him from the rear view mirror. "Huh?"

"The funhouse? How did you find it so fast?"

Dexter narrowed his eyes in the mirror. "It's called Google, you idiot." But Wes saw something in his eyes, something that told him Dexter knew more about all of this than he had told anyone.

Wes didn't press the issue, not now. He leaned back against the car seat, closed his eyes, and said a quick prayer that Rose was okay and that they'd all get out of this together.

*****

They arrived at Bushkill Amusement Park in about an hour and a half. Dexter appeared even more impatient than usual. He slammed the car doors, threw the Rabbit's Eye at Wes, and kicked him in the rear like he was an animal.

Wes grunted, but put on the Rabbit's Eye. He wanted to get this done quickly, too. The sooner this ended, the sooner he could get back to Rose.

Still, he felt the sweat begin to drip down his face the moment he put on the headset. The abandoned park had plenty of no trespassing signs, but they didn't pay any attention to those, of course. They each took a headset. The old amusement park, thanks to the Rabbit's Eye, was about to see life again.

Wes's first thought after looking out through the Rabbit's Eye: *Beautiful!* Except for that terrifying moment in the funhouse as a kid, he had always loved carnivals and theme parks. The Rabbit's Eye made the park bright—all the lights and sounds that one would expect had appeared. Wes even thought he could smell funnel cakes, and it didn't surprise him—this little device could do anything.

They walked through the park, past a Ferris wheel and rows of games. Carnies called out at them. "Hey kids, your first try is free!

It's on me! Everyone's a winner!" Wes smiled and waved, as if the carnies were real.

Up ahead, they saw the funhouse. A giant clown's face covered the entire left side of the building. It was white and looked more like a skull than a clown, but the blue eyes and red nose and lips signified that it was at least intended to be a clown. The funhouse was two stories, and on the top story, there was a balcony with red and green bowling pins as the fence. Stars and balloons were painted on the right side, and Wes heard that voice—always that voice—when he saw those. "Want a balloon?" He shivered.

Wes turned and faced the other guys. "This may just be for me, guys. Let me go first." No one argued.

Wes stepped into the entrance of the Bar'l of Fun. The inside had paintings that were even more terrifying. What about this was supposed to be fun? The paintings were of freaks—people with large noses or disproportioned faces. It reminded him of the old 80s movie *Funhouse*, the one about an actual freak.

Wes walked through a room with funny mirrors, the ones that made you really tall and thin or really small and fat. Wes couldn't really tell what was original to the funhouse and what the Rabbit's Eye was enhancing.

Until he saw the clowns in the mirrors. They all looked like the one painted on the outside. A clown skeleton with blue eyes. Its red lips dripped blood all the way down its shoulders.

"Welcome, Wes," the skeleton clown whispered.

Wes had overcome his fear of clowns before. In his first fear simulation at Rabbit in Red, JB had made Wes face his bullies. The bullies were kids who teased him in the locker room, and those stupid kids turned into evil clowns. Wes had overcome that. He could manage the Bar'l of Fun, too, right?

He kept moving forward, and behind bars he saw an oddly long donkey. The donkey turned its head, and the head morphed into a clown face. The clown barked at him like a dog, then its head busted right through the prison bars and snapped at him. Wes jumped back, dodged the attack, and ran forward.

Now he was in one of those spinning tunnels, and he couldn't find his balance. He fell, stood up, fell again, and resorted to crawling through the tunnel.

On the other side, a giant snake waited. It hissed at him, and Wes slapped at the snake. He grew up in the South. Snakes didn't scare him. *Come on, JB, whatcha got for me?*

The snake's head turned into a clown face, too, and Wes laughed at it. Clever, for sure, but comical, too. A long, thick snake, one you'd expect in a *Harry Potter* story, but with a clown face. It was a *Freakshow* all right, *American Horror* style.

Wes ran up some stairs, too long a flight of stairs for this size of a building. He ran and ran until he was out of breath, but he made it to the top. He was outside again, looking over the balcony with the railing made of bowling pins.

Then the bowling pins vanished. Wes lost his balance and threw himself back against the wall. The wall turned into a *Human Centipede* of clowns. Clown heads jammed into the back-side of other clowns, and Wes felt his stomach turn. Their arms reached for him and pulled him back. He flung his arms and dive-rolled to the opposite side of the balcony. Then he ran down the flight of stairs on this side into the other bottom half of the funhouse.

That was when he saw Rose.

She was tied up and back in the *Rosemary's Baby* crib.

Witches and clowns surrounded her. "What will you do to save me?" Rose asked.

"Anything," Wes said, and he ran through the clowns and witches, but when he got to her, she had disappeared.

In her place, the teenage version of JB appeared.

He was surrounded by his own bullies. The ones Wes had seen before—the ones on those video tapes who harassed him, called him names, and picked on him. The ones JB, in the end, had gotten the better of.

"Smell slime! Smell slime! Smell slime!" The bullies chanted and JB looked at Wes.

"What would you do to save me?" JB asked.

Wes stared at him. His chest tightened, and it was harder to catch his breath. "What do you want me to do?"

The young JB made direct eye contact with him. His bullies got closer and started beating him. JB stood there and took it. "You've overcome great fear, Wes, but you must be prepared to do more than just feel confident. Sometimes you have to fight. Do you understand?"

Wes nodded. He charged at JB's attackers, and they turned on him. Some morphed into clowns, and Wes punched them in the face. He kicked at their knees and groins and tossed them to the side.

One attacker after another charged at Wes, but he kept swinging his arms and kicking his legs. A roar came out of his mouth, and the last attacker approached.

It wasn't a clown. It wasn't a monster. It wasn't anything special.

It was a man.

"Sometimes," JB said from behind Wes, "the scariest monster is man. Are you prepared for that?"

Wes answered by charging at the man standing in front of him. He slammed the guy into a wall, and all the attackers had disappeared.

When Wes turned around, JB had changed back into the older man he had grown to know.

"Congratulations, Wes. My boy, I need you as much as I need anyone. Remember the power of names. They called me all sorts of terrible names, much worse than Smell Slime. But when you learn the meaning of that name, understand that sometimes we go to extreme measures to change the labels others have given us. Do you understand?"

Wes nodded.

"Now, return to your friends. They need you. The group is almost halfway through the fear simulations. Soon, you'll get the next clue." JB vanished.

Wes exited the funhouse and thought about what JB had to say. They were all here for a reason, right? It wasn't just their passion and knowledge of horror. It was that they all had experienced and understood their own horrors. Bill lost his father. Jaime lost her uncle. Rose had lost her brother. Wes had been bullied, just like JB. Wes understood the pain of losing self-esteem, the death of one's identity.

It sounded like JB had experienced that kind of loss, too. From Rose's riddle, he knew JB had also lost a brother. What else had he lost? What was it about Smell Slime?

He removed the Rabbit's Eye, and these thoughts flew away. Outside of the funhouse, Bill and Daniel stood behind Dexter, and Dexter had a gun pointed on someone.

That someone was Chester Malcolm.

Chapter Twenty-One

Bill rubbed his sore arm while waiting for Wes to explore the funhouse. How long had it been since he was attacked by Bonnie? His arm was sore, but he didn't think there was any permanent damage. Still, it'd be nice to be able to see a doctor and get it checked out. That was a fantasy though. Normalcy, a doctor's appointment, a soft bed: things that were once normal seemed like such a fantasy. He looked at Dexter, who didn't seem to care as much about the simulations or riddles anymore. He wore a constant frown, probably annoyed that they had to do so many of these individual challenges.

What was the end-game for Dexter? Bill tried to study Dexter's face. This wasn't just about money, was it? Bill's stomach soured, and then he heard footsteps coming from behind. He wanted a drink more than ever.

"What the fuck are you doing here?" Dexter snarled and pulled out the gun. He pointed it straight at Chester Malcolm.

Chester put up his hands. "Dexter, there's no need for that. Put down the gun. I just need to talk with you."

If anything, Bill saw Dexter's arms straighten, and the gun got an inch closer to Chester.

"I said what the fuck are you doing here?" Dexter's cold eyes didn't even blink.

"Bill, Daniel, are you guys okay?" Chester kept his hands up but looked at them.

"Don't talk to them. Talk to me," Dexter snapped, but Bill nodded softly at Chester.

"This isn't what JB wanted," Chester said. He slowly lowered his hands.

"You stay right there," Dexter barked. "And do you think I give a fuck what that old nut wanted?"

Chester tightened his lips and looked down. Then he shook his head. "I'm not talking about the challenges, Dexter. I'm talking about you."

Bill thought he saw Dexter flinch, just for a moment.

Chester continued. "Do you think JB kept everything to himself? I may not know everything, but he shared a lot with me. Including what he talked about with you."

What did JB talk about with Dexter? Bill looked from Chester to Dexter. He never would have admitted it to anyone, but Bill felt a pang of jealousy. A secret between those two? It didn't seem fair.

"What do you want?" Dexter repeated again.

"I want you to let the guys go," Chester said. "And then come with me. I've got plenty of other secrets to share." He smiled then, and Bill still had a hard time not seeing Captain Spaulding, the makeup and the costume Chester sported during the first Rabbit in Red weekend.

Dexter lowered his arm a few inches. Maybe his arm was just getting tired, or maybe Chester was getting through to him.

"What secrets?" Dexter asked.

"We could start with why he chose you." Chester took a step closer.

Dexter breathed hard through his nose. "Chose me for what?"

Chester looked over at Bill, like he was trying to tell him something telepathically. Then he looked back at Dexter. "JB had a dark past. There are things he did that you don't know about. I can tell you those things if you come with me. That's part why he chose you." Chester paused and took another step forward. "That's why he chose you to ultimately be his replacement."

Dexter definitely flinched at that. "Replacement?" Bill felt that odd jealousy again. Was Chester for real or was this all a trick?

Chester nodded. "It was his goal all along. Don't get me wrong, he loved you guys, too," he said looking at Bill and Daniel. "But he needed someone who understood . . . no, who possessed the ability to inflict actual horror on others."

Dexter raised the gun again. "I don't believe you."

Chester shrugged. "I have the papers to prove it. You don't need to go through all of this. I have the documents to end everything right now."

"Prove it." Dexter put his thumb on the back of the gun.

"I give you something. You give me something. That's how this works." Chester took another step closer.

Bill looked closely at JB's right hand man. How did Chester know they were here? If he knew they were in trouble, why didn't he bring his own gun or help or something?

Bill heard a noise from behind. Wes had just exited the funhouse, and his jaw hit the floor at the site of Dexter pointing the gun at Chester. Dexter glanced at Wes, but paid him no more attention than that.

"I should warn you," Dexter said. "If you try anything with me, I can kill Rose at any second. She's wearing . . . a special gift."

"You think I don't already know?" Chester laughed then, and Bill looked over at Wes. Worry spread across his face, too. *I don't get it. Why is Chester laughing?*

"You should know," Chester continued, "that I know you've contacted my brother."

Dexter's face turned red, and he looked down for a moment. Bill felt his throat dry up, and he looked at Wes again. *Sid is in on this, too?*

"My brother never was much for working with others." Chester frowned. "I'm giving you a chance here, Dexter. Leave the guys, and come with me. I'll show you a whole new world." Dexter looked at each of them and turned his eyes back to Chester. "Put the gun down, and come with me." Chester reached out his right hand.

Dexter lowered the gun. He looked over at Bill. *What was he thinking?* Dexter smiled, and Bill understood what was in his eyes. He had always thought it was blackness and evil. He wasn't wrong, that was for sure. He just didn't understand how evil or how dark. A tidal wave of darkness washed over his eyes, darkness creating more darkness, a depth no one could understand.

Dexter turned his attention back at Chester. "Listen, old man. I've got everything I want. Everything is working out. I will not be tricked. Not by you. Not by anyone." He opened his mouth and laughed. "Go to hell."

Dexter lifted the gun again, pointed it right at Chester's chest, and fired.

Chester's hands flew up over his heart and he collapsed.

*****

"Are you girls ready to join him?"

Jaime froze. Sid Malcolm, the man she saw in her nightmares—whether she was asleep or awake—stood in front of her.

He rubbed his left eye, which he had covered with a black patch. Even in the moment of horror, Jaime briefly saw an image of One-Eyed Willy from *Goonies*. Jaime smiled at Sid, remembering it was she who'd gouged out the other one. *Before it's all over, I'll take the other one, too.*

From the side, she saw Brandis's body shake, and blood continued to pour out of his chest. It soaked the concrete of the garage as quickly as a running hose. The ground turned red, and for a brief moment, Jaime thought of the lava game she used to play with Tara when they were kids. They'd pretend certain things in the house were lava, and they'd have to jump over them. Now the lava was approaching them, and so was Sid.

Sid swung the machete at the ground and let more blood fly off the metal blade, as if he were cleaning it. Then he grinned and walked toward them, slow and purposeful, a real-life Michael Myers.

No, a real life Jason. Jason liked the machete. Michael liked the butcher knife.

Is that what it feels like to go crazy? Thinking of childhood games and slasher trivia while a genuine madman stands in front of you?

Jaime swallowed hard and forced a smile. She looked over at Tara and Rose. Both stood frozen in shock. *This isn't just about me. I have to help them, too.*

"Hey, asshole." She spat on the ground near Sid's feet. "If you want me, put down that weapon that's obviously compensating for something, and come get me with your bare hands."

Sid snarled and held the weapon tighter. He looked over at Tara and Rose then back to Jaime. Then he showed his teeth and grinned.

"If that's what you want, bitch." He threw the weapon in the opposite direction and charged at her.

Jaime yelped and ran toward the door. The garage was attached to the house, but the damn door was locked. She glanced over her shoulder just in time to see Sid flying at her. Jaime quickly turned to the right, and Sid crashed into the door.

Rubbing his shoulder, he turned and faced her. Jaime walked backwards, and Sid marched forward one step at a time. "I'll kill you, you bitch! But first . . . first, you are going to get something else!"

He roared and lunged at her again. Jaime stumbled back into a table, and Sid threw her down on top of it. Then he jumped on top of her. She heard the table moan from their weight, and Sid punched her in the face. Not a slap, not a back hand. He made a hard fist and knocked her in the jaw.

Jaime cried out. The pain made her face numb, pins and needles in her jaw. She saw a flashing light. Above her, Uncle Tim appeared.

"Fight, Jaime, fight."

"Uncle Tim?" Jaime looked up at the ceiling, confused, as she wasn't wearing the Rabbit's Eye. *I must be losing it. That's where he hung himself. That's where he died. I'm going to die right where he did.*

Sid put his arms around her neck. "That's right. You'll join him soon enough. JB, too!" He slid his arms from her neck to her chest. He felt her up, his hands over her shirt, and she moaned. "Yeah, you like that? I knew you would." He ripped open her shirt and put his hands right on her breasts. This all was like a bad re-run. The last time Sid was on top of her, he had thought he had had her. Then he lost an eye. He wouldn't get her this time, either. She clenched her teeth.

He leaned closer and she could smell his breath. It was rotten, like spoiled milk and deviled eggs that had sat in the sun for days.

He put his lips on hers. Jaime let him. Just for a moment. Then she opened her mouth and bit his lips with all of her might. Blood gushed out and splattered her face, but she didn't care. She'd eat his fucking face if she had to. Anything to punish him and to get him off her.

"You bitch!" This time he slapped her with an open hand and held his mouth with his other. "I'll kill you. I'll kill you!"

She could focus on him more now, and she knew this was her chance. She dug her fingernails into his one good eye. Did she hear it pop? She spit out the blood that had splattered her face, and she clenched her teeth and clawed his entire face.

Then she elbowed him right in the jaw. He leaned back then, and she thought she had won. The thought only lasted a moment. He thrust all of his weight on top of her. Sid put his forearm right in her throat and dug in with every ounce of muscle and fat he had.

He pressed back and forth, and Jaime felt the air disappear. She couldn't breathe, and she felt her neck collapsing. Sid wasn't just trying to choke her. He was crushing her windpipe and trying to break her neck. She gasped for air but nothing came in. Nothing. The world turned black again, and Uncle Tim reappeared.

Sid cried an awful noise. He let her go, and the air rushed into Jaime's body. It was like being underwater longer than ever before and tasting air for the first time. She sucked it in. Uncle Tim vanished, and Sid came back into focus.

More blood gushed out, this time from his arm. Jaime didn't know where it was coming from at first. Then Sid cried again and fell off her.

Jaime saw Rose standing behind him holding the machete. She must have swung it at his arm and then at his back. She held the machete high over her head and swung it down on his body.

Blood shot up like she had struck oil.

Sid stopped moving.

Rose's chest heaved up and down, and Tara stood behind her, holding onto a pair of hedge trimmers.

Rose tossed the machete to the side and ran to Jaime. They hugged tight. Jaime closed her eyes and said, "Thank you." Jaime opened her eyes and looked out at her sister. Tara stood right over Sid's body.

"Tara. Come here," Jaime said.

Tara ran to her and hugged her hard as well. "Oh, Jaime! I didn't know what to do. I thought he was gonna . . . gonna . . . I didn't know!"

"Shh, it's okay. It's okay now. The bad guy is gone." Jaime held her sister close and rubbed her back.

"Bad *guys*," Rose corrected. "Two gone, but we've got more work to do." Rose looked more determined than Jaime had ever seen her. She wanted to get Dexter, too. That was good, Jaime thought.

Jaime let go of Tara and stood up. "That's right. There's no time to be sad or worry about what we've done. What would JB expect from us?" Jaime wiped the blood from her face. "Let me get inside and clean up. I'll grab one of Jennifer's shirts. Then we've got a cemetery to get to and more bad people to stop." She reached out for her sister. "Are you okay?"

Tara had tears in her eyes. "I know we won't be okay until this is over. So let's . . . let's stop them."

Jaime tried to smile, but her face felt frozen. "We will. We'll do whatever it takes."

Jaime felt Tara's warm face on her shoulders as they embraced, and she turned to look at Sid. Was he dead? Did they really kill him? She closed her eyes and wished away the nightmare. Jaime looked around the garage and found a couple tarps. She put one over Sid's body and another over Brandis's. She'd call the police and her aunt, once she got far enough away to not be stopped. Using a side door connected to the garage, Jaime went into the house, splashed water on her face, and grabbed some of her cousin's clothes. On the way back out, a voice spoke to her, and it was Uncle Tim. "Wishing and praying are fine, but nothing gets done without acting."

She opened her eyes, and another phrase floated to her mind, but this time it was her own voice.

Yes, whatever it takes. We'll finish this once and for all. Whatever it fucking takes.

Chapter Twenty-Two

This is crazy!

The thought went through Rose's mind as they left Jaime's aunt and uncle's place.

We should be calling the police!

I just saw someone murdered. Again!

Did I just kill someone?

It's like I'm living in a slasher movie.

Let's get Dexter next. Kill the asshole.

Her own thoughts surprised her.

"King's Chapel Burial Ground," Jaime said into Brandis's cell phone to load up the GPS. They had taken it off his body before leaving. "That's where we need to go."

Jaime sat in the driver's seat, and Rose wondered how the hell she could even think about driving. Jaime had nearly been murdered and raped, and right in front of her and Tara. Rose sat in the passenger seat and turned around to look at Tara in the back.

"You okay?" Rose asked.

Tara didn't move. Her face was pale, and her hair was a mess. Red, puffy clouds surrounded her eyes. She blinked slowly. *I'll take that as a no,* Rose thought. *But really, who is okay?*

She felt the collar around her neck and sighed. Eventually, someone would try to call Brandis, and he wouldn't answer. Would Dexter press his magic button? Rose swallowed hard. It would sure give him a good reason to, and Rose didn't think Dexter even really needed a reason. Would the remote work from that far away?

"How about you?" Rose asked Jaime. "You okay?"

Jaime huffed. "At least I have a clean shirt." She tried to smile. "No. No, I don't know what to do." Although they were dry, Jaime wiped her eyes. "You?"

"Shouldn't we call the police?" Rose asked. "This isn't some movie. We shouldn't be taking on bad guys and solving mysteries by ourselves. Right?"

Jamie exhaled hard. "You're right, but then what happens? The bomb squad tries to get that thing removed from your neck. What if they can't? And how do we even know there is such a thing nearby? Seems like something that only happens in the movies." She shook her head. "What if they lock us up, and we never finish this damn thing? What about Bill and Wes? What if we never get back to them?" Jaime's eyes weren't dry anymore, Rose noticed. "We finish this first."

Rose tugged at her seatbelt. There were too many questions and not enough answers. "We need a plan to get Dexter, then. Gotta find a way to get the remote away from him. Then we get to the police. With Wes and Bill, too. That way everyone is safe."

Tara grabbed the back of Rose's seat and pulled herself forward. "I want Mom. Jaime, call Mom!"

Jaime reached back to hold her sister's hand. "Me, too. But if we involve anyone else, we put them at risk. You understand that right? Mom can't help us. Mom can't help us!" Jaime pulled her hand back. "No one can! JB is dead, just like Uncle Tim. Brandis is dead. Diane is dead. Dad is a deadbeat! Mom—Mom would come, but then what? What if something happened to her?"

"Jaime, slow down," Rose said. The car lurched ahead at least twenty miles over the speed limit.

Jaime looked at the speedometer, gasped, and started to slow down.

"I just need time to think," Jaime said. She took a couple of deep breaths. "I'm sorry I yelled, Tara. I'm just scared, too."

They drove in silence for a few minutes. Rose's arms shook no matter what she did to try to stop them.

"Listen," Jaime said. "We'll figure out what's at King's Chapel. Then I'm dropping Tara off with Mom. Then you and I," she said gesturing at Rose, "will find Dexter and stop this. We stop it all."

Rose nodded and looked out the window. She had survived what could have been a fatal burning, and then she had saved Jaime by taking a machete to the man responsible.

They just needed to eliminate all the bad guys. Get rid of all the evil, right?

"Then we're done," Rose said, careful not to say everything she was thinking. "I don't care about the contest or JB or Rabbit in Red. I don't even care about this cemetery. Let's be done, Jaime. Done with it all." Rose looked at Jaime and reached for her hand.

Jaime didn't turn her eyes away from the highway, nor did she respond right away. She squeezed Rose's hand, and a few moments later, she said, "No. No, Rose. We're not going through all this for nothing. You can stop if you want. But I'm finishing it. All of it. Whatever it takes." Jaime ran a hand through her hair, but her eyes never left the road.

Rose crossed her arms and sat back. She'd make sure to take care of Dexter. She'd make sure her friends were safe. But then she was done. No more fucking riddles for her, thank you very much.

*****

Rose jerked her head up when the car hit something bumpy. *Did I really fall asleep?* She yawned and stretched out her arms. Looking around, she saw that they had entered a cemetery. Rose sat up and looked behind her. Tara sat in the back seat, her head pressed against the glass. Her eyes may have been open, but she wasn't looking at anything.

I know that look, Rose thought. *I looked at nurses and doctors that way for weeks. Maybe months.*

The car bounced on the uneven, cracked road that circled the cemetery. King's Chapel Cemetery. They were here all right.

Rose tried piecing together JB's riddles. JB had selected her, no doubt, because she had lost a brother. JB told her that she wasn't the only one, and to understand this situation, she had to start with his mother. Rose blinked her eyes several times, still adjusting to the daylight. She took a deep breath.

If it weren't for Jaime and Tara's simulation, they wouldn't know anything about King's Chapel. Rose wondered what Wes and Bill would find in their challenges. Wes had never lost someone the way she had.

And, of course, there's Bill, Rose thought. Bill acted as their leader more often than not. JB had treated Bill differently, too. He had been a father figure to Bill, maybe because Bill had lost his own. Regardless, she always thought Bill may have been JB's favorite. Bill or Jaime. If JB had favorites.

Jaime slowed down the car, and they exited by a sign that read, *King's Chapel Cemetery, 1630, Here were buried.*

Tara coughed in the back seat. "Jaime, I still wanna call Mom."

Jaime nodded but didn't respond. Rose wanted to call her mother, too, if truth be told. She couldn't wait to be out of this mess, done with Rabbit in Red forever.

"Soon, Tara, we will bury the rabbit," Rose told her. "We'll never have to look back again." She took a deep breath and exited the car.

Jaime and Tara got out on opposite sides, and Jaime grabbed the box with the Rabbit's Eye headsets. Rose took one without looking away from the sign.

"You okay?" Jaime asked.

Rose took a deep breath. She opened her mouth, hesitated, then shut it. Jaime may have asked the question, but the look in Jaime's eyes suggested something else. Jaime didn't exactly look at Rose. She looked beyond Rose.

Rose shrugged. "Let's see what happens with these things on. Ready?" Rose looked at Tara instead of Jaime.

"Do I have to do this?" Tara asked.

Rose started to shake her head, but Jaime jumped in. "The more eyes, the better. We need to be prepared for anything." Slowly, Tara reached for the headset.

They all put on and activated the headsets and moved forward. Nothing had changed, not yet, but the tombstones were creepy enough as they were. One tombstone sported a skull and crossbones. Another showed what Rose thought was a dancing skeleton, but a closer look revealed the skeleton putting out a candle.

"Death versus Father Time," Jaime said, like she had been reading Rose's mind. "Look. The skeleton is death. It's putting out the candle. Ending life. Father Time holds onto the hourglass, a symbol of the length of life." Jaime stepped closer and put her hand on the tombstone. "Father Time never wins. Life must end. No hourglass is forever."

Rose's stomach twisted and she felt sick. When was the last time they had eaten, anyway? She didn't want to think about death. She wanted to be numb, to not remember what happened earlier, to not worry about what was yet to come.

Then she heard Jaime gasp, and Rose looked up. In the distance, they saw JB. A younger JB, kneeling down by a grave. Rose, Jaime, and Tara approached slowly. When they neared him, Rose held her breath. Something about this simulation was different, and then Rose understood. This was more than enhanced reality. Somehow, they were seeing a memory.

Tears rolled from the young JB's face. That wasn't acting. Rose didn't know how he did it, but she sensed that they were seeing an actual memory.

JB looked to be in his late teens or early twenties, college age. He had shorter hair though, shorter than she remembered from the last video they saw.

Those damn VHS tapes. Sometimes she wished she had never seen them. What was their purpose anyway? To get them to question JB more? Like they needed that. And the last tape they saw, something happened, something off camera. Did JB kill someone? That's what was on everyone's mind. He had basically paid people to torture him or people who would let him torture them, much like their own simulations. He wanted to experience the role of victim and villain. He expected all his students to do the same.

"I wish you were here, Mom." JB sat crossed legged on the ground near his mother's tombstone. "I've made some changes, and I want to apologize. I want you to hear it from me first." JB put his hands on his knees and looked straight at the tombstone. "Maybe I went too far. But I have my reasons. I just hope you understand. I had to. I have to become . . . someone different."

He sighed and looked down. "I don't know if anyone will ever understand. That's why I wish you were here. You'd understand." He looked up and smiled. "If you didn't, you'd tell me it would all be okay. And even when things weren't okay at all, you'd still say that. 'Everything is going to be okay.' I need that now."

He lowered his head again and wiped his eyes. "I miss you so much." JB stood up, looked around the cemetery, and said one last thing. "I love you, Mom." He kissed the tombstone and walked away, rubbing his eyes some more.

Rose wanted now, more than ever, to grab the phone they took from Brandis and call her own mom. She'd been gone how long now? She didn't even remember, but certainly her parents and some of the others had notified the police that they were missing. That was good, right? The cops would be out here looking for them, too.

But more than that, she wanted to hear her mom's voice. She wanted to tell her mom that she loved her. Her dad, too. Rose stared at the tombstone of JB's mother. She thought of Bill. She looked at Jaime and Tara. Both had tears in their eyes. Parents wouldn't be around forever.

No one would be. No one was here forever. She rubbed at her collar.

"Rose, do you see that?" Jaime asked, pointing at the tombstone.

"Oh my God," Rose said. She covered her mouth. "Wait, what?"

"Jaime," Tara said. "Jaime, what does that mean? I don't get it. What does it mean?"

Rose moved closer to the tombstone and read the first line out loud. "*So the place was called Taberah because fire from the Lord had burned among them.*"

"I don't know what it means," Jaime said and shook her head.

"I've heard it before," Rose said. She paused for a moment and let the memory resurface. "Eleven. It had to do with how many new recruits would be invited to Rabbit in Red. Chester or someone said it last year. You weren't there. You were—" Rose stopped and looked at Tara. "Things were just getting started. I remember the quote because I wrote it down later. It seemed so out of place."

"So what does it mean?" Jaime asked.

"It's a quote from the Bible. A verse. From Numbers. I really don't know what it means," Rose said. "I looked up where it was from but that's it. I just figured it meant God liked setting people on fire or something. It sure fit with last year's theme."

Jaime nodded.

"You guys," Tara said. "Her name. His mom's name. Did you see that?"

In smaller letters underneath the Bible verse, Rose read the name of JB's mother. "Huh?"

"I . . . I don't get that, either," Jaime said and put her hands on her hips. "Her last name isn't the same as JB's."

"His mother's name," Rose said, "is Pamela Be—"

Rose couldn't finish. She froze and Jaime grabbed her hand. Beyond the tombstone, someone approached.

Someone approached very quickly.

It was Bonnie Villa, the one who had attacked them at Gein's old property in Wisconsin.

Bonnie locked eye contact with Rose, raised the knife in her hand, and sprinted right at the three of them.

Chapter Twenty-Three

Daniel stared at the back of Dexter's seat and imagined all the ways he could strangle the bastard. They were driving again, and Daniel sat immediately behind Dexter. Bill took shotgun—*how nice would it be to have a shotgun right now?*—and Wes sat on the other side in the back.

Things kept getting stranger and darker. Daniel had had to face his father and his mother, and now Chester had been killed. How many more would die? And for what?

Daniel wished that Carol was by his side. He had never fit in with Wes or Bill, and he never really liked them anyway. If Daniel was the stereotypical jock they made him out to be, then they were just nerds.

But none of that mattered now. What mattered was what was going to happen next and how this all was going to end.

They had left Chester bleeding to death, having just been shot in the heart, outside the funhouse. Then Dexter had pointed the gun at them, forced them back in the car, and sped off without saying so much as a curse word.

Examining Bill and Wes, Daniel wondered just how far they'd go for their friends. They were both in love, or at least they thought they were. They'd probably do just about anything, including risking their own lives. But what about that device around Rose's neck? That ruined everything. Dexter was strong, but Daniel thought he could take him, especially if he had some backup. They'd have to get the gun away from him and knock him out fast before he could do anything to Rose, but if they timed it right, they could do that.

Daniel had seen enough horror to understand one thing about the psychology of a man with a weapon. The gun was Dexter's golden ticket. He'd do anything to protect the weapon, and that gave them some kind of advantage. Or at least hope. If Dexter focused entirely on the weapon and keeping the gun, then maybe they could trick him.

Maybe.

"You're going the wrong way," Daniel said.

"Shut up," Dexter replied without even looking in the rear view mirror.

Daniel huffed. He could play this game. "What about Bill's simulation?"

"Don't you worry about a thing, princess." Dexter chuckled I got it all under control."

Daniel crossed his arms. "You sent Brandis to do Jaime. Probably in more than one way." Daniel snickered. "You've got Rose's, Wes's, mine, a few others. You know how close JB was to Bill, right? I just wouldn't want to miss that. That's all I'm saying." Daniel looked out the window trying to feign disinterest. "Could be important."

Daniel saw Bill glare at him. Bill probably didn't want to revisit old ghosts, but that wasn't exactly what Daniel had in mind. He just hoped Bill would understand. Dexter looked back at Daniel through the rear view mirror, then spoke to Bill. "What exactly did your riddle say again?"

Laughing, Daniel jumped in before Bill could reply. "That's the best part. You're gonna get to see him all fucked up." Daniel smiled. It still felt good to play the asshole.

"What's he talking about?" Dexter asked Bill.

"Tell him," Daniel said, giggling. Still staring out the window, Daniel muttered. "Do not pass go. Do not collect two-hundred." He glanced up at Bill then. *Did he understand?*

Bill shuffled in the front seat. "By the time Jaime and Rose get back, you'll have more than half of the fear simulations solved.

You'll be able to move on to the next challenge and finish this." Bill looked down at the floor of the car. "You don't need mine."

Perfect, Daniel thought. *Keep it up, Billy-boy.*

"Tell me what your riddle was," Dexter demanded.

Bill sighed hard. "You won't like it."

"I'll be the judge of that," Dexter snapped.

Daniel could almost see the wheels turning in Bill's head. Come on, Bill. *Do not pass go. Do not collect two-hundred dollars. Do you get me?*

"Follow the Rabbit. Follow the Rabbit in Red," Bill started. "He won't walk the green mile, but he'll die alone. You need answers, and remember what he said. Behind the glass, pick up the phone."

Excellent, Bill. Couldn't have said it better myself. It almost made Daniel think that was Bill's actual riddle. *Could it be?*

"It's about your father," Dexter said. He pulled over on the side of the highway and parked. "Or about the guy who killed your father. Right?"

Bill nodded and turned his head away from Dexter.

"Your father's killer is behind bars. No death penalty, no green mile." Dexter smiled, and Daniel grinned, too. The little bastard felt good just because he had figured out the fake riddle. Assuming it was fake. "We have to go to where your father's killer is. In jail." Dexter turned all the way around and looked at Wes and Daniel in the back seat.

"Danny, after all of this, you are still an asshole." Dexter laughed hard. "*Oh-right*, Bill, let's go meet your father's murderer. Where to? I assume you've known for some time where he's at."

Bill nodded slowly and told him. Daniel smiled in the back seat and leaned against the window.

They'd be at a prison, with cops and guards and all sorts of people who could help them. Daniel breathed the slightest sigh of relief, knowing Bill must have figured out his clue. Just like in Monopoly, they needed to stop what they were doing and go directly to jail. Maybe there was still a chance to find a way out of this mess.

Now if only he could get Dexter to go inside, too. Get him away from his gun. Do something that would prevent him from reaching his little remote, too. Then maybe, just maybe, they'd have a chance.

Dexter pulled the car back onto the highway, waited for the next median exit, turned the car around, and headed toward Illinois.

They were off to see Jason Lamb, the man who killed Bill's dad, and if they could get lucky, maybe they'd be able to leave Dexter in a cell right next to him.

*****

Bill understood what Daniel was trying to do, but he sure as hell didn't know what they were going to do once they arrived at the prison. Put on the Rabbit's Eye and see what the cops do? Dexter wouldn't let them walk inside a place full of police, would he? But if Bill could get close enough, then maybe they'd be able to get some help.

Somehow, Bill had forgotten about Jason Lamb. There was so much going on. To think—his confrontation with his father's murderer was like a scene from *Goosebumps*. Everything since then was like a wedding in *Game of Thrones*. Bill folded his arms and pressed his head against the driver's side window. He pretended to sleep, but he spent the long drive thinking about everything, and there was a lot to consider.

Lamb had known not only about JB and the "Smell Slime" nickname, but he had also known about the videotapes. He had told Bill to watch the tapes, and then Bill would understand.

Where's Jaime? The question interrupted everything. He hadn't had a phone on him for days, but he still felt little phantom vibrations. For a moment, he'd forget about the fact that he and Wes and Daniel were on a road trip with a psycho. He'd smile, wondering what Jaime was going to say, and then the smile would fade away when he realized he had no phone and that she certainly wasn't texting him.

Was she okay?

She had left with Brandis, and that worried Bill. He knew that she'd never fall for Brandis again, but why was it he still felt a pang of jealousy when he thought about that? No, Brandis could really hurt her, as well as Tara and Rose. Brandis had murdered someone in front of all of them, and he could do it again.

Oh, God, let her be okay.

This had to end soon. He longed for the simple things like holding her hand while watching a horror movie, not holding her hand out of fear because they were living in one.

Bill's thoughts bounced from Lamb to Jaime to Dexter to JB to the videotapes to basically everything. His head hurt like someone had taken a hammer and hit him from inside his skull. It was a constant pounding.

Hours passed by, and he drifted from one thought to another and in and out of small doses of sleep. Finally, Dexter took the exit Bill recognized from his own road trip not that long ago. The one that led to the prison that housed Jason Lamb.

Dexter pulled over about a block away from the prison after driving around a couple times. He looked closely for cameras, trying to make sure they couldn't get spotted. Then he turned to Bill and said, "Here's what's going to happen. Walk around the outside with the Rabbit's Eye. If anyone stops you, tell them you're Pokémon hunting. See if anything happens, and come right back here." Dexter took a deep breath and turned to Wes. "No matter where Rose is, I'll fucking kill her if any of you are playing with me. Talk to a cop and boom!" He took out the remote control device and shook it at Wes. Then he faced Bill again. "You got that? You try to get help and she dies. I want the answer to these riddles, and that's it. Okay?"

Bill nodded. Daniel handed him a Rabbit's Eye from the backseat. They locked contact for a second. Bill knew Daniel had set this up so that they could get help, but Bill didn't know how he would do it.

He stepped out of the car and walked toward the prison. Running a hand through his messy hair, he put on the Rabbit's Eye. He turned it on, but he nothing out of the ordinary happened.

Think, Bill, think! Then he got an idea. He'd just have to walk around the prison long enough to make Dexter believe it.

He paced and paced, looking back over his shoulder ever so briefly. After about five minutes on wandering around, he took a deep breath and went for it.

Bill sprinted to the back of the prison, completely out of sight from Dexter. Throwing himself against the outer brick wall, he thought for sure someone would come out and question him any moment. But, surprisingly, no one took notice. He waited here, breathing hard, and counted to sixty in his head. He had to be gone just long enough for Dexter to believe the little tale he had come up with.

After sixty seconds, Bill took another deep breath and charged back at the car. Dexter was already standing outside the car and approaching with Wes and Daniel following along. Dexter's face twisted at the sight of Bill sprinting right at him. Bill put on the breaks and took off the Rabbit's Eye.

Panting, Bill said, "You . . . you have to . . . see for yourself." He handed Dexter the Rabbit's Eye. Dexter simply stared at him. "It's . . . it's JB and Jason Lamb, working together." Bill wiped sweat off his brow. "And . . . and . . . they're asking for you."

Dexter cocked his head to the side, but he took the Rabbit's Eye. Bill had thought if he could get Dexter around the side of the building, out of sight of anyone walking in or out, and then confuse him with the Rabbit's Eye, then maybe they could jump him right then and there and finish him at least.

It sounded like a good plan, but then Bill's face contorted in surprise. Someone was walking toward them very quickly, and she looked pissed off.

Majorly pissed off.

Bill had seen that look before, more times than he could remember.

Dexter took the Rabbit's Eye from Bill with his right hand and adjusted the gun in the back of his pants with his left.

She must have seen what Dexter did because her hand went up over her mouth. Then her face knotted in anger, and she reached into her purse and took out what looked like a small club, a baton maybe. Her walk evolved into a sprint that may have been faster than Bill's, and she ran toward Dexter and swung the baton at the back of his head.

Dexter fell face first on the road, and Daniel jumped on his back. He grabbed Dexter's hands, and Wes dove for the remote control device in Daniel's pocket. Wes retrieved it and handed it to Bill, and then Sally Wise reached over and took the gun away from Dexter.

"William! What the hell is going on?" His mother stood there with a baton in one hand and a gun in the other right outside a prison. Out of nowhere, Bill laughed. He couldn't help it. So much rage and frustration had built up, and there stood his mother. They had been suffering for days, not really knowing what to do, and in less than a second, his own mom totally kicked Dexter's ass. Bill couldn't help but laugh, and it was contagious. Wes and Daniel started cracking up, too.

"Boys, I don't find any of this funny," Sally told them. She tried to cross her arms, but the gun and the baton were in the way. She looked at the weapons and frowned, then swung her arms by her side. They laughed all the more.

"Mom, you . . . you don't under—" Bill couldn't finish. The only thought that bounced through his tired mind was that his mom looked like Cherry Darling from *Planet Terror*, and that only made him laugh more.

He bent over from laughing so hard, and his mom kicked him in the leg. Kicked him!

"Sorry, Mom." He took a deep breath, but he couldn't have forced the smile away. For the first time in days, he felt safe. He lunged forward, wrapped both arms around her, and hugged her hard.

She hugged him back, and he felt the cold metal from the weapons press against his back. He had to force back another case of the giggles. Pulling away, she said, "Now, tell me what's been going on. I've looked everywhere for you. Everywhere!"

"What made you come here?" Bill asked.

Sally breathed through her nose and locked contact with him. "There's something you need to see. Something I saw on a videotape. That's what led me here."

"What? What tape do you have?" Bill felt his entire body cool, like the blood had poured right out of him.

"Some videotape of JB," she said. "Something you need to see."

"Where is it, Mom?"

"Back at our house."

Bill turned to Wes and Daniel. He was sure they wanted nothing more than for all of this to be over. To call the police now that Dexter wouldn't be able to hurt Rose, but now, more than anything, all he wanted was to see what was on the video tape.

"We have to see that," Bill said. "We have to see it now."

"Yes," Sally said, nodding. "I think you do."

"What about him?" Wes asked, pointing at Dexter.

Bill looked at Daniel. "Throw him in Mom's trunk. We'll deal with him later," Bill said. With the help of Wes and Daniel, Bill scooped up Dexter and did just that.

Bill resisted a nervous laugh, thinking of the crimes they were committing right outside a prison. The desire to laugh quickly vanished, though, when they got inside the car and drove away.

There was a videotape he needed to watch.

Chapter Twenty-Four

Jaime reached out for Tara, and they ran away from Bonnie. Already a step ahead of them, Rose flung a door open, and the three all piled in the front. Rose took the driver's seat, and Jaime reached across from the passenger seat and inserted the key. Jaime turned the key in the ignition, and Rose floored it.

Bonnie slammed her fists against the driver's side window, and Rose screeched. Bonnie yelled, "Get out of the car! Get out, or I'll drag you out!"

Rose turned the car around and sped out of the cemetery, leaving Bonnie behind. "That was too close," Rose said.

"You okay?" Jaime asked Tara, who had ducked down as low as possible. Slowly, she lifted her head. Her hair was a mess and her tears puffy from fatigue and frustration.

"I want Mom," Tara whimpered.

Jaime nodded and looked over at Rose. "That's where we have to go. Home."

"Yes," Rose said, never taking her eyes of the road. "We need to put all of this shit behind us. Why do we even care? We should care about our lives." Jaime watched a tear roll down Rose's cheek. "And the lives of our friends. Who knows what's happening with Wes and Bill?"

Rose sighed, and Jaime turned away. Of course, she cared about the lives of her friends and family. She wanted to get Tara back home, and she wanted to make sure everyone else was okay, but she felt an obsession, a dark craving, growing inside of her.

"Okay," Jaime said. She wanted to get Tara away from this mess, but she didn't tell Rose why else she wanted to go home. She needed a computer and a phone. She needed access to information. That name of JB's mother's tombstone? Maybe a Google search would help her figure out its meaning, or if it meant anything at all.

She'd do that, and Rose could stay with Tara and their mom if she wanted, but then Jaime was getting back in the car and getting the others. Whatever it took, she'd get them away from Boris and Dexter. And whoever wanted to finish would go with her.

A loud beeping emanated from the back seat, interrupting her thoughts.

"What's that?" Rose asked.

"It's coming from the Rabbit's Eyes," Jaime said. "Tara, hand me one."

Tara's eyes were freshly wet, and Jaime's chest hurt when she looked at her sister. Hadn't Tara been through enough? For a second, Jaime missed the days where they'd sit in her bedroom, and Jaime would write a story for her sister. Tara, never much a horror fan, still wanted to do whatever her big sister did. But not anymore, it seemed.

"Tara, the Rabbit's Eye, please?" Jaime asked. Tara shifted in her seat, grabbed the headset, and passed it to Jaime without ever looking up at her.

"I don't recognize that noise," Rose said. "What does it mean?"

Jaime put on the headset. "I think there's a message for us." She turned on the Rabbit's Eye and, sure enough, there was JB. Jaime had to look down. At first, JB appeared to be floating in the middle of the highway, and it made Jaime dizzy. She closed her eyes and just listened.

"You have only one more fear simulation to complete before the next and final round of challenges. Congratulations on working as a team." Jaime's chest hurt again. She realized how much she missed his voice. "If you didn't get to experience your own fear simulation, they will still be available to you. But the time has come to finish our game. As soon as one more fear simulation has been completed, all of you will receive an alert as to the next challenge. Get ready."

And then he disappeared. "Did you hear that?" Jaime asked.

Rose rolled her eyes and said, "Who cares? We're done." She looked over at Jaime. "Right?"

Jaime sighed and looked out the window. She never answered Rose, and she suspected Rose knew what was really going through her mind. It wasn't too long before they neared Jaime and Tara's home, and when Rose turned onto Jaime's street, Jaime sat straight up.

"Stop the car!" Jaime leaned forward. "Don't go down there. Pull over!"

Rose slowed the car and pulled over to the side.

"Do you see that?" Jaime asked. "Oh, shit. Do you see that?"

"I do," Rose said, "and I think we need to go down there."

Tara, who had hopped in the back seat, leaned forward and asked, "What is it?"

"Fuck," Jaime mumbled.

"We need to go to your house," Rose said. "It has to end."

Rose and Jaime looked again down the street. There were several police cars outside of Jaime's house. Obviously, Janet Stein had called the police. Maybe Jennifer and Megan had seen the mess at their house—a dead boy and a dead man, all right where Uncle Tim had died. God, they must be a mess.

Jaime turned to the side and faced her. "Yes, it does. But not like this. That—that's the end for us. Not for Rabbit in Red. Don't you want answers?"

Rose shook her head. "I want to be safe. I want Wes and Bill and everyone to be safe. Us, too."

Jaime dug her fingernails hard into her palms. What could she say to convince Rose? "Don't you get it?" Jaime continued. "If Dexter or anyone else gets the keys to Rabbit in Red, to all of JB's power and money and God knows what else, we will never be safe." Jaime slammed her fist into the side of the door. "I want to be safe, too! I want Tara to be safe and you and everyone. That means finishing JB's challenge. It means that we have to be the ones who win. It means following the rabbit until the very end."

Jaime locked eye contact with Rose and stared deep into her eyes. Rose had been through so much too, and the scars on her face would always be a terrible memory for her. But Jaime also had scars. Scars on the inside, and she didn't want them anymore.

Rose looked over to Tara. "What do you think?"

More tears ran down Tara's face, and she wiped them away. "I really wanna go home." She took a deep breath. "But I trust my sister. If she says we won't be safe till this is over, then I wanna help. I will help, and I will fight, too." She sniffed back the tears.

And it's all your fault. You really should stop this.

She shook her head. "Let's go, Rose. Turn around. Let's finish this on our own terms."

Rose groaned, but she turned the car around and drove back to the highway.

It was time to get the others.

*****

They drove through the evening toward the crappy motel where Dexter, Brandis, and Boris had kept them. Jaime hoped everyone was still there—she desperately wanted to talk to Bill about what they had found on JB's mother's grave, but she also just really wanted to see him. He'd make the crazy in her head go away, she hoped.

"So, how are we gonna get everyone out of there?" Rose asked. Jaime watched her hand feel around that terrible collar, and for a moment, Jaime doubted her decisions. Maybe they should have gone straight to the police. Maybe they would have been able to remove that device and give poor Rose some peace.

It was Tara who spoke up with the first idea, though. "Guys, we pull the fire alarm. That will get everyone out."

Jaime nodded. "Yes, and then we can take count of who is all there. Or send a signal or something."

"I like that," Rose said. "We need to get them a message. A sign that our friends will understand." Jaime felt the car speed up, and she smiled.

They approached the motel at night, and darkness and silence surrounded the place. Jaime darted across the road to a gas station and picked up some lighter fluid and matches. Then she raced back behind the creepy registration office, waving at Rose and Tara to let them know she got what she needed.

"This one's for you, Bill," she whispered as she shot the lighter fluid on the side of the motel. Then she took out a match and set it on fire. Yes, she thought, it's a good thing Rose and Tara stayed behind on this one. Once the lighter fluid caught fire, she knew she didn't have too much time. She sprinted across the motel, ducking under the registration office window, and pulled a fire alarm that was placed by the vending and ice machines. The alarm sounded throughout the motel, and she had a terrible flashback to the alarm at Rabbit in Red, just before it had burned down.

Running faster than she ever had before, she nearly slammed into their car. She jumped inside, and they all watched as their friends slowly exited the motel, led by Boris. Jaime counted each one and looked desperately for Bill and Wes. The flames from the lighter fluid were dissipating, and she hoped someone would see it before it was too late.

Carol and Julie appeared to be the first to see it. Jaime saw Carol point across the motel, and Julie's eyes followed. Looking back, Jaime hoped the numbers were still blazing, and they were.

She had written the numbers "217" across the side wall and set it on fire. Boris noticed and shoved everyone back in the motel. Then he walked out, grabbing Carol by her arm and taking her with him. Jaime looked all around, and no employee or anyone had even seemed to notice the fire alarm. Boris and Carol rushed across the motel. Evidently seeing the alarm, he pushed it back up and silenced it. Jaime wondered how much time they'd have before the fire department showed up, and she wished everyone would move quicker. Then Boris went up one flight of stairs, perhaps wanting to see what was behind door number 217.

Nothing, you idiot, Jaime thought. Carol would know, though. 217, of course, was the shout-out to *The Shining*.

"Did you see Dexter?" Jaime asked.

"No. Did you see Wes or Bill?" Rose replied.

"No. Shit," Jaime said. "Okay. Now's our chance. We get everyone out. Wherever Bill and Wes are, Dexter must be with them."

"I didn't see Daniel either," Rose said. "What about Carol? If Boris sees everyone running away, he may hurt her."

"You get everyone out of our room. I'll take care of them," Jaime said. Then she looked back. "Tara, you stay here."

Jaime exited the car and raced upstairs after Carol. Rose ran toward the motel room where everyone else stayed.

Once on the second floor, Jaime hid in the shadow of a tree that hung overhead. She watched Boris bang on room 217. No one answered, and Jaime saw him say something to Carol. Carol winced at the words, and then he shoved her forward. They were walking back, right in Jaime's direction.

She slid back, hiding right by the stairs, hugging the wall as tightly as possible and holding her breath. Carol walked right by her, and then there was the man who looked so much like JB.

Jaime jumped out. "Carol, MOVE!" Both Carol and the man jumped and turned around. "MOVE NOW!" Carol ran to the wall and hugged it just like Jaime had a second ago, and now Jaime charged at the man.

With all of her might, she shoved him right at the top of the stairs. He plunged backward, rolling down, hitting his head on the concrete steps and metal railing as he fell. Wasting no time, Jaime grabbed Carol. "Who else is here? Dexter?"

Carol shook her head. "Just him. He's been watching us since you all left. Dexter's out with Bill, Wes, and Daniel."

Jaime nodded. "Okay. Follow me, and fast."

They raced to the bottom of the stairs. Was the man dead? He was certainly unconscious at the very least, and Jaime searched his pockets. There was another gun, a knife, and the one thing she needed the most. The keys to the van. She grabbed everything, and they ran to the vans.

Rose had everyone outside, lined up against the van. Jaime waved at the group and unlocked the side door. She motioned for everyone to get inside.

"Wes and Bill aren't here," Rose said.

"Yeah, neither are Daniel or Dexter," Jaime replied.

"We have to get them," Rose stated.

Jaime agreed. "We'll drive all night. They must be at their fear simulations. We'll get them." She turned around to wave at Tara and check on Boris's condition. Tara looked okay, and the man still laid unconscious at the bottom of the stairs.

"You take the van," Jaime said. "I'll take the car and follow. Better to have two vehicles. Just in case."

Rose nodded and said, "Okay. Let's hurry. I've got a bad feeling." She rubbed at her collar, and Jaime felt a sting of terrible guilt. What would Dexter do to them for this?

As Rose got in the driver's seat, Jaime ran back to the car with Tara. She jumped in and they drove away from the motel as fast as they could.

They hit the highway and headed west.

From the backseat, the Rabbit's Eye beeped at them.

Jaime looked over at Tara. "Put it on. See what it says."

But she already knew it could only be one thing. Someone—and it had to be either Bill or Wes—had just finished a fear simulation, the last one needed for everyone to move forward.

The game was almost over.

Chapter Twenty-Five

They left the rental parked close to the prison, and Bill wondered if anyone would find that suspicious. He sat in the passenger side of his mom's car, and the guys were in the back. Except for Dexter. Dexter got the luxury of mom's trunk, and Bill laughed out loud at the thought.

"What is funny about any of this?" Sally Wise asked.

I have a kick-ass mom, he thought. But he shook his head and said, "Nothing."

The drive seemed to take forever. Bill sighed every time he looked at the speedometer because his mom stayed about five miles under the speed limit. "Can't you go any faster?" he asked

Sally rolled her eyes. "You want to get pulled over? Jesus, Bill. There's a body in the trunk of my car."

He couldn't stop his legs from bouncing or his mind from wandering. What did his mom see on the tape that made her drive to that prison? And where was Jaime? *Oh God, let her be okay.*

"What's on the tape?" He couldn't take it any longer.

His mom groaned. "Best you see for yourself."

"Oh my God. I cannot take it! Mom, please?"

"Why don't you start by telling me where the hell you've been? What's going on, Bill?" Now he felt the car pick up some speed. Not much, but a little.

"I was kidnapped, Mom. We all were. I had no way to call you. Now what's on the tape?"

"Kidnapped? Jesus fucking Christ! Are you okay? What happened?" The car nearly swerved off the road.

"Mrs. Wise," Daniel said from the backseat. "You do realize you just knocked someone out and threw him in the trunk, right?" Bill felt a giggle coming on. *I'm losing my mind,* he thought.

"Technically, you guys threw him in the trunk," she said, resuming a slower driving pace. "Okay, start from the beginning. Tell me everything."

"Then you'll tell me about the tapes?" Bill asked.

She nodded, but didn't say anything.

Bill started from the beginning. Halloween weekend nearly two years ago. He described the simulations—"you remember, Mom? From parents' weekend last year? But that wasn't all we did."

He swallowed hard. He had never told her this part. "We had a fear simulation, too. I had to . . . to relive that night. To face Dad's killer."

Watching her closely, he saw her lips tighten and her eyes narrow. "Go on," she said.

Then he talked about Hellfire and everything that went wrong when JB started the horror college. Bill only had told her the most basic of details, and never about the videotapes.

"At first, we thought Daniel somehow found the tapes," Bill said, keeping his eyes on the road and not looking in the backseat. "But it turned out to be Sid Malcolm, someone who worked behind the scenes. Chester's brother, one of the main assistants."

And now Chester was dead. *Jesus. How many lives will be lost before this is over?*

"What would Daniel want with the tapes?" Sally asked.

"Well—"

"Let me," Daniel said, interrupting Bill. "I wanted them to hate JB. I didn't get it at first." Bill turned around and looked at Daniel. "I guess he was trying to help, trying to get us to overcome fear. But I . . . I didn't get it. I wanted them to hate JB as much as I did."

"He was too scared to get it," Wes said, shuffling in the back seat. Daniel didn't admit it, but he didn't deny it either.

210

"But I only encouraged that distrust. I didn't do anything to anyone," Daniel said, turning away and looking out the window.

"So what was on all of the other tapes?" Sally asked. Bill thought he felt the car pick up a little speed again.

"The first was him as a child," Bill said. "He was re-enacting a scene from *The Exorcist* with a friend."

"They got worse," Wes said. "The second tape was a Halloween night." Wes lowered his face. "He told us some kids hurt him and took everything from him. They called him names."

"Smell Slime," Daniel said.

Bill's mom sighed heavily.

"Mom, what do you know?"

She shook her head. "Keep going."

Bill huffed but continued. "The third tape was when JB was in high school."

"A Halloween dance," Wes said.

"Yeah," Bill said. "It was almost like *Carrie*. They tricked him into asking out a girl or something. The girl said no, and the assholes all mocked him. But after the dance . . ." Bill looked at Daniel and Wes in the backseat. No one, it seemed, wanted to say it out loud.

"The kids tried to hurt him," Bill said. "But they didn't. JB hurt *them*. Badly. He even said that he would kill them if they ever tried to hurt him again."

Sally nodded, but didn't look at Bill. "Was there more?"

Bill looked out the window. "It got worse."

"Tell me," she said.

"The next couple were in college," Bill continued. "JB paid people to hurt him. And then he paid people he could hurt. He said he wanted to know real pain."

"Like Hellfire," Wes said. "He did for real what he programmed for us, virtually."

"And you never thought that was totally fucked up?" Sally asked.

"They were obsessed with JB," Daniel said. "And you thought I was the bad guy?" Bill turned enough to see Daniel glare at him.

"I was never team JB," Wes said. "I just wanted to be with Rose and protect her."

"Look how that turned out," Daniel said.

"Fuck you, man," Wes said. For a second, Bill thought Wes might hit Daniel.

"Boys! Stop. Continue the story, please," Sally said. Bill watched them glare at one another and then told his mom about the last thing they had seen on a videotape.

Bill closed his eyes and recalled the tape.

He stood up and looked in a mirror. "I don't recognize myself." He took scissors and started cutting his hair. He turned it into an uneven mess, but suddenly the JB they recognized began to appear before them.

He looked straight into the camera. "I can use the monster in me to create. Or I can let the monster die and do nothing at all. The latter is not an option. I'm sorry. I hope one day you'll forgive me." He picked up a long, sharp butcher knife. He faced a direction off-camera, something they couldn't see. Then he lifted his arm high up over his head, and just when he was about to bring the knife down, the video feed became disoriented. Lines squiggled throughout, and the sound cut off. Then the screen went to black.

He described this to his mother and then asked, "Now, can you tell me what you know? For the love of God!"

"First, I want to know about the kid in the trunk. What all has happened since you left?"

Bill sighed, but he told her everything. Dexter and Boris had some kind of plan to take JB's estate and Rabbit in Red for themselves. But it was so much worse than that. Bonnie, one of the other assistants, had attacked them, and Bill still didn't understand why that had happened. Brandis turned on them and killed Diane. Dexter kept an explosive device around Rose's neck. God knew what was happening to Jaime and Rose right now, too. And then Dexter just shot Chester Malcolm. Everything was a mess.

The last thing he told her was his own riddle, one more fear simulation to experience.

"Follow the Rabbit," Bill said. "Follow the Rabbit in Red. It's a childhood memory you'll never forget. Start in your old bed. Move forward but beware the silhouette."

By the time Bill told his mom everything, they were in his hometown. He barely had time to blink, and they were driving down the street of his childhood.

The trees touched in the middle of the street, like neighbors shaking hands. Sally Wise never questioned Bill on returning to their old house. After Arnie Wise, his father, had been murdered by Jason Lamb, Bill and his mom had stayed with his grandparents. Eventually, they got a new place of their own. They hadn't returned to this old house in years.

"Mom?" Bill coughed. "What if someone lives there?"

"Someone does," she said.

"How do you know? Who?" Bill asked, narrowing his eyes.

She didn't answer, but she pulled up in the driveway. "I believe you'll need one of those head things." She put the car in park and faced her son. "Bill, I don't know if I get all of this. Part of me wants to run to the police right now and then go home and open a great big bottle of wine." She forced a very small smile. "But I've heard enough to know that you have to finish JB's challenges. It's not for me to spoil or tell you what I know. You have to see it for yourself." His mom's eyes were wide, as if she couldn't believe what she was saying.

"Knock first," Sally said.

"Who will answer?" Bill asked.

Sally reached out and patted Bill's knee. "This is your story, Bill. Good luck."

*****

Bill put on the Rabbit's Eye and knocked on the door. It opened slowly, making a creaking noise that Bill remembered from his childhood. He guessed the new owners hadn't fixed that.

Holding his breath, Bill waited to see the face behind the door. He felt an immediate gag in his throat. He had expected this on some level, sure, but it didn't stop the emotional uppercut that punched him in the gut.

"Dad!" Bill wanted to run and hug him, but it was only virtual reality. The figure looked exactly the way Bill remembered: brown, messy hair, big glasses, and a smile that he never wanted to forget.

"Billy, I'm so glad you're home." Even the voice sounded real. Bill looked over his father's shoulder at the TV. His dad followed his gaze and motioned for Bill to come in. "I had it ready for you. I thought we could watch it together."

The title screen to *Gremlins* flashed on the television screen. Bill felt his arms weaken and tears poke at his eyes. They had watched this together every Christmas.

Bill shook his head and tried to escape from the thoughts. This was too real, too scary. *Too scary because . . . I could . . . yeah, I could completely forget about everything else and stay right here forever.* But would that be so bad?

Yes, it could be, he almost said out loud. *I have my mom— alive—right outside. My friends, too. And of course, Jaime. I need to figure out what I'm supposed to do here.*

"Dad, what's going on?"

Arnold wise shrugged and smiled. "I love you, kid. You know that?"

"I do. And I love you, too."

"Oh-right. Let's watch the movie."

Bill looked around the living room and as far as he could see through the house. Whether it was virtual or real, he wasn't sure, but everything looked the same. How long had it been since he had seen his childhood home? Ten years? It felt like a museum, and it felt like he had never left all at once.

He sat down on the couch with his father, and they watched the movie. Only a few minutes had passed. The father in the movie had just purchased Gizmo, and a boy told him the famous rules to take care of the creature. Then the room shook, and Bill turned toward his father. But his father was gone, and the room was dark.

A noise came from the kitchen, and Bill walked, reluctantly, toward it. Once in the kitchen, the cabinets opened and slammed. That couldn't be real, could it? Had to be another Rabbit's Eye enhancement.

From behind, back in the living from where he came, he heard voices. This was like a nightmare, Bill thought, when he looked back at the living room. It was no longer a living room at all. It was a college dorm room.

The college dorm room he had seen in JB's videos.

JB stood with a rope in hand, and another man lay face down on his dorm bed. JB sat on top of the man and carefully placed the rope around his neck. He pulled hard, JB's face turning a bright red from the strain. Bill could only imagine what the other guy must have felt.

Too much time passed, and Bill thought that surely the man would die, but no, with his left hand, he slapped at JB's leg like he was tapping out of a wrestling match.

JB let him go, and the man stood up. He looked down at the floor and rubbed his neck. JB handed him some money. As he took it from JB, the man looked up.

Bill gasped. It was the same man from the first video Bill had seen, but he didn't make the connection then. Of course, he was younger here, but Bill hadn't really seen much of the guy except pictures. He hadn't seen this man up close until recently.

The man that JB paid to hurt was Jason Lamb, his father's killer.

"Same time next week?" Lamb asked. JB nodded. Then the room whirled, and Bill had to close his eyes. When he opened them next, the living room had returned as Bill remembered.

But JB was standing there. It was the JB he remembered.

"Oh, Bill," JB said. He lowered his head, and Bill gulped. What had he just seen? "Bill, I'm so sorry. It's . . . it may be my fault that your father is dead."

Bill looked away. He suddenly felt cold, and he balled his hands into fists. "I don't understand."

"I never meant to create a monster. Lamb liked pain. I wanted to see what it was like in a controlled environment. Lamb and I partnered together for that entire year. Sometimes I hurt him. And sometimes he hurt me." JB stepped closer to Bill, but Bill still didn't look up.

"I've been watching you since you were a little boy," JB continued. Bill looked up at that. "Rabbit in Red wasn't built in a day. I had already produced several films and had the foundation to Rabbit in Red built the year your father was murdered."

Bill blinked several times. "You watched me since I was a kid?"

JB nodded. "I kept an eye on Lamb. What separates madmen from the rest of us is reality. There's a line. Believe it or not, I saw that line, but Lamb never did. He wanted to go . . . always to another level."

"Is that what's on the last tape?" Bill asked.

JB didn't answer.

The living room whirled again, and Bill quickly shut his eyes. The next time he opened them, everything was dark, except for a light coming from upstairs. He walked toward the light, toward the direction of his childhood bedroom.

And his parents' bedroom.

Walking up the stairs, he heard Jason Lamb say, "Where's your son?"

That was one of the questions that had haunted Bill. How did Lamb know that he was there? Lamb had said that he had scoped out the house, but Bill was convinced there was more to the story.

Bill kept walking upstairs, dreading this moment. Sparky, the family dog, would be up there. Would Bill have to relive this again? JB had already made him go through it once before during the original fear simulations that first Halloween.

Bill got his answer a second later—everything froze. And then everything rewound, like he was watching it backward. Lamb walked down the stairs and out the door, the living room whirled again, but this time Bill refused to even blink. What was he watching?

JB and Lamb were back in JB's dorm room.

"You can't quit this," Lamb said.

JB's hair was shorter than the previous videos. He didn't look older exactly, but the hair did something—it was closer to the JB Bill had known.

"I must move on," JB said.

"I'll tell the world what a freak you are," Lamb said and stepped closer.

"The time has come for us to go our separate ways." JB stepped forward, opened the door, and motioned for Lamb to leave.

Lamb huffed. "Fine. But what I do next, you only have yourself to blame." Lamb grinned and marched out the door.

The room whirled once more, and Bill still managed to stay focused. The old living room came back, and JB once again stood in front.

"Your final challenge Bill is simple. Now that you know the truth, I ask for your forgiveness. Will you forgive me?"

JB reached out a hand as if to hug him, but Bill didn't answer or move. He tried to process everything. "So, what are you saying? Why did Lamb pick my family?"

"Because you were home," JB said. "He had grown up in the same town as you, actually. After college, he moved back. He looked for happy families to hurt. He wanted to hurt them to hurt me. Do you understand?"

Bill shook his head. "Because we were home?"

"It was both planned and random," JB said. He sighed and looked away. "I never had evidence, not in the beginning, just my suspicions. But I kept my eye on you, and once you truly got into the horror genre, I knew that I had to bring you to Rabbit in Red."

"The riddles? The contest? Was any of that real?"

"Oh, sure. And you really did win. But I also asked questions that I knew you'd get right."

Bill gulped. He didn't know what to say or what to think.

"What I did to Lamb caused him to be a madman," JB said. "I stopped working with him. He chose to hurt other people, including you and your family. But we also wouldn't know one another today if that hadn't happened."

Bill felt hotness rise in his throat. "Jesus, is that supposed to be some kind of condolence? I wish I had never met you then! I wish Rabbit in Red had never existed! Fuck you, and fuck forgiveness.

You can keep your goddamn money and everything else and take it to the grave."

Tears ran down Bill's face, and JB started to say something else, but Bill tore off the Rabbit's Eye. He opened the front door to his old house, and he slammed the Rabbit's Eye on the concrete. He jumped on it again and again, and then he looked up.

His mother had tears running down her face, too.

Bill opened his mouth, but no words came out. He lost all sense of feeling.

Standing behind Sally Wise was Dexter Lange, and Dexter had a knife to her throat.

Dexter looked at Bill, smiled, and then pushed the knife against his mom's throat.

Chapter Twenty-Six

After filling up for gas and grabbing some much needed food, Jaime, Rose and the rest of the rabbiteers decided to split up.

"Are you sure this is a good idea?" Leroy asked.

"Yeah," Annie said doubtfully, "we know what happens to people in horror movies once they go in different directions."

"It's just for the sake of time," Jaime told them. "Rose and I will drive. That way we can drive by the funhouse that Wes would have gone to, and then to Bill's house." She looked at Rose for confirmation, and Rose nodded. "You guys fly to Chicago using the golden tickets and get to Bill's ASAP. We'll meet up there."

"What if no one is there?" Leroy asked.

"Then we meet at the final destination," Rose said. Her lips tightened and Jaime saw the worry on her face. There was a final destination, and Jaime worried what they'd have to experience.

"All right," Leroy said. "But you shouldn't go alone. Almost everyone that's been killed has been—"

"Girls," Rose said. "We know." Rose shook her head. Jaime and Rose had decided, for the time being, to not tell them about Brandis or even Sid. Jaime wanted to finish everything with as little distraction as possible, and she had managed to convince Rose to keep quiet, too. But Leroy was right.

"Jimmy, Carol—you come with us," Jaime said. They had worked well together last year, and as much as she hated to admit it, they should have one guy with them.

For a second, Jaime thought Leroy looked a little offended that she hadn't chosen him, so she said, "Leroy, you lead this group. You and Annie. We need to get everyone to the final destination safely. Okay?"

Leroy nodded, and the rabbiteers went their separate ways. Jaime drove, Rose sat in the passenger seat, and Carol, Kent, and Jimmy sat in the back. Jaime wasted no time hitting the highway.

"Don't you think we should tell them?" Rose whispered.

Jaime glanced in the backseat. Two of the new recruits from last year, two of the strongest, Jaime thought, if you didn't count poor Diane. Tara sat in between them. Then Jaime looked at Rose and nodded.

"Guys, we should tell you something that we didn't tell the others," Rose said. "We didn't want to scare them any more than we needed to."

She told them about Brandis and Sid. She told them about JB's mother's tombstone and what it said. And then they discussed the newest riddle and the final destination.

"Let's play the riddle again," Carol said. They took out one of the Rabbit's Eyes and replayed JB's message.

"Friends, you have worked hard as a team to overcome fears, and it's time to move to the last part of our challenge." It wasn't the rabbit's voice for this one, which made Jaime and the rest of them think this would be the final test. It was JB who said, "Follow the Rabbit. Follow the Rabbit in Red. Beneath the ashes, a phoenix will rise. Some skin dies and some skin sheds. Are you ready for the final surprise?"

"I have chills," Carol said.

"Me, too." Jimmy rubbed his arms.

"Do you think . . . do you think somehow he's alive? JB?" Carol asked.

Jaime shook her head. "He's certainly done a lot of twisted stuff, but we attended his funeral. That would be pretty shitty to put us through that if somehow he was alive."

"Wouldn't be the first shitty thing he's done," Rose said, rolling her eyes.

"True," Jimmy said. "If not that, then what's the final surprise?"

Rose sighed. "Somehow, Rabbit in Red is probably back. That's what it means right? From ashes to a phoenix." She cranked her neck around to look at the guys in the back seat directly. "You know what? I wish it would stay buried. It's been nothing but a nightmare."

Jaime swallowed hard. "It's not JB's fault, though, is it? He wasn't the crazy asshole who nearly killed you and nearly . . . killed me. He's not the fucker who orchestrated all of this and kidnapped us and made us go through hell." Jaime realized she was speeding and let off the accelerator a bit. "That wasn't JB," she said quietly.

She felt Rose staring at her. Then Rose said, "What if it was?"

Jaime shook her head, but the thought was planted. What if, just what if, somehow JB had darker plans? What if he *wanted* Sid or Dexter to do this? No, that was just not possible. *Is it?* The problem with JB was—always had been—that you just didn't know how far he would go.

They drove through the night in silence until they arrived at the funhouse. Rose had said that Wes had described his riddle to her, of course, and she had heard of this place before.

Slowly, Jaime drove through the parking lot. This place wasn't just closed for the night. It had been closed down for a long time by the looks of it. But there was one car sitting in the parking lot. Jaime drove by it, but didn't see anyone in it.

"Be right back," she said, parking the car and jumping out to look at the other car.

Jimmy shook his head. "Why does she say things like that? Doesn't she know what that means?"

"Shut it," Carol said, but Jaime heard the slightest laugh from the back. It was good that they could laugh, even if it was a little awkward.

Looking around, Jaime didn't see anything but darkness and some faded lines that used to mark parking spaces. She crept toward the car, and a warm summer breeze blew at her hair. She brushed the hair out of her eyes and stepped toward the vehicle.

It looked like a rental, and she had seen plenty of those recently. Too clean, no personal stuff inside, and she was about to turn away when she saw . . . what was that? She leaned closer, pressing her face against the driver's side window. Not quite able to make it out, she tried to open the door, and she emitted a slight gasp when it opened.

It was under the radio in the dashboard, and Jaime knew what it was without having to look any closer.

It was a golden ticket.

She grabbed it and ran back to the car. "Oh my God," Rose said when Jaime got back inside. "Whose could that be?"

"Let's look around," Jaime said, and before anyone could agree or disagree, she drove closer to the amusement park's entrance.

"What if the cops show up?" Carol asked.

Jaime shrugged. "We're just driving around looking for Pokémon. Gets you out of anything, right?" She exited the car, and the others followed. They walked around the side, looking for an easy way in. "There," Jaime said and pointed at a dilapidated chain link fence. "We can slide under, or climb over. Your choice."

Jaime's arms shook, maybe from a lack of sleep or a sudden surge of adrenaline, and she grabbed the top of the fence and jumped over. She didn't bother looking behind to see how the others entered. She just kept moving forward.

"I've got a bad feeling about this," Rose said from behind.

Jaime simply nodded. She had the same feeling, but it was more like a magnetic force driving her forward.

And then she saw it.

Jaime ran to the body. It was Chester Malcolm, and he was covered in blood, his own blood from the looks of it. Not knowing if she should touch the body, Jaime shouted, "Chester! Chester!"

He didn't move.

"God, is he dead?" Jimmy asked.

"Check to see if he's breathing," Carol said.

Jaime nodded and put her head close to Chester's mouth. She listened for breathing, but didn't hear anything.

Then, a cough! A great big puff of air blew at her face, and she felt wet. "Chester!" She looked directly at him, and he coughed again. She wiped her face and looked at her hand. Thankfully, it was only saliva. She worried it would be blood, and anyone coughing blood had to be bad, she thought.

"Are you okay?" It was a dumb question, Jaime knew, but she didn't know what else to say. Chester stared up at her but didn't answer.

"Call 911," Carol said. "We need an ambulance now!"

Jaime reached for her phone, and Chester's hand shot out and grabbed her arm.

"No." He coughed more, but it didn't sound as bad. "You have to . . ." More coughing. Very quietly, he said, "We have to get to the boys. They're in a lot of trouble."

*****

When Bill Wise saw Dexter with a knife against his mom's throat, everything froze. He heard the wind whistle and saw, ever so slowly, his mom's hair dance in the breeze. Then Dexter moved the knife against her throat.

He blinked hard, willing himself to act. *I can't lose my mom.* He heard his heart beat in his ears, and these few seconds felt like hours. He clenched his fists.

"You fucker," Bill said. "What is wrong with you?" Then he lunged forward, quicker than he had ever sprinted. He reached them and pulled his mom away from Dexter. Without pausing, he tackled Dexter to the ground. Dexter slashed the knife through the air, but Bill dodged and slugged Dexter in the face with his good arm. Then he punched him again with his bad. Wincing in pain, Bill slugged three times then four, but Dexter rolled him over after the fourth.

Still with his knife in hand, Dexter reached up high and swung it down. Bill flinched and tried to move but was pinned to the ground.

This is it. Jesus, that's it. This is how I go. Bill lifted his arms in a race to block the attack, but it was too late. The knife came down fast, and the blade plummeted toward him.

Then Dexter flew—no, soared—off of Bill, right before the blade nearly ended his life. Turning his head, Bill saw Daniel on top of Dexter. Daniel must have pushed Dexter off him and now was holding him with a choke from behind. Squeezing until his own face turned purple, Daniel squeezed and Bill could see Dexter's neck and Daniel's arms both bulging. Quickly getting up, Bill looked over at his mom. *Oh, God, don't let her be dead!* He ran toward her, but then he heard Daniel cry out. Dexter still had the fucking knife and had swung it into Daniel's leg.

Bill turned to help and saw Wes. Wes stood tall, arms extended, face stoic. He had both hands clenched around a single object: Dexter's gun. Dexter had had a gun and a knife that they had taken from him. Somehow he got the knife back, but Wes had the gun. Bill looked back over at his mom, praying that she was okay. He wanted to run to her, but he knew if they didn't stop Dexter right here and right now, this night would never end.

Bill looked at Wes, who stood with the gun pointed directly at Dexter. His arms shook but his body remained perfectly still. Bill knew this was the moment where they stop the bad guy for good. Or they risk a moment like this again.

Bill ran to Wes's side. "We have to stop him," Bill said, reaching out his hand. *If Wes isn't ready to shoot him, I will. I have to.*

They heard Daniel moan. Dexter pulled out of the choke, shoved Daniel aside, and sprinted toward Bill and Wes.

Wes pulled the trigger.

Bill didn't look away. Dexter put both hands over his chest. His face twisted in what Bill thought must be both pain and shock, and then Dexter fell to the ground.

Bill ran, ignoring Dexter's body, straight to his mother. She lay there, unmoving, and Bill's heart jumped into his throat.

"Mom, are you okay? Mom!"

She wasn't moving.

"Mom, please!" Bill felt a moment of hope. There was no blood, not really. A couple of dots across her neck, some redness, but that was all. But why was she unconscious? He grabbed her hand. He squeezed it, and he closed his eyes, thinking, cursing, praying.

Bill opened his eyes, released his hand, and felt for a pulse on his mom's neck.

His mom sighed. She slowly opened her eyes. "Billy?"

Bill cried and threw his arms around her. "You're okay? You're really okay?"

She sat up, slowly but on her own. She felt around her neck and chest. "I . . ." She coughed, and Bill reached for her hand. But then she smiled. "I'm okay. I think he must have barely pierced the skin, if at all. He . . . maybe he wanted to scare you. I don't know."

She continued touching her neck as if to be certain. "I just passed out. I felt the cold blade on my throat, and I was out."

She reached out for Bill, and he hugged her again and put his wet cheeks against her shoulder. When he pulled away, his mom looked around and breathed deeply. She must have been taking in everything that had happened.

Dexter's body remained on the ground. Bill couldn't help but think of Michael Myers. Would Dexter get up again last minute? Was he really dead?

"You did what you had to do, boys," she said after a minute. She stood up, brushing dirt off her jeans. She looked over at Wes and Daniel, standing tall but frozen. Then back to Bill. "This may sound crazy. No, I know it sounds crazy." Sally took a deep breath, "But you have to finish. You all have to finish."

"What?" Bill hadn't thought about what would happen next. His mom had nearly been murdered, they all had almost been killed, and they had taken a life. Sure, it was a psycho dude who deserved it, but this wasn't normal. *This isn't okay. Am I in shock?*

"That headset of yours went off while you were in there. You have to listen to it." She brushed her hair out of her eyes. "There's . . . ugh, I wish this were over. I do. I don't know what the hell I'm even saying, but you have to know the rest of the story. You have to finish. I get it now." She shook her head, and Bill wondered if she had hit her head on the ground. "I do. I get it. I'll stay here and call the police. I'll tell them everything. But if they come now, you'll never finish. They won't let you. And you have to finish."

She reached out to Bill. Then she looked over at the body on the ground again, then to the two boys standing by it. Daniel put one arm around Wes and the other was rubbing his leg where Dexter must have stabbed him. *Shit, we have to take care of that, too.* Wes had dropped the gun and leaned into Daniel. *Stranger things have happened,* Bill thought.

227

"Mom, I can't leave you," Bill said turning back to face her. "I don't care about this anymore."

She smiled at him. "I'm okay. Honest. He got out and grabbed me," she said, referring to Dexter. "He put the knife up to my throat and told your friends that if they moved, he'd kill me. That's when you came out. You saved me, Bill. You really saved me."

Bill hadn't thought of that. He had saved his family in a simulation before, but this was real. And then a terrible thought popped in his head: Was this part of JB's plan all along, too?

"I know more than you realize, kid." She straightened her shirt, took a look at the bloody front, and then gave up. "Go. You have to go. You have to finish this. Do you understand?"

Bill shook his head. "Are you sure?"

Sally sighed. "Don't question me, or I'll lock you in your room and never let you out."

Bill looked over at Wes and Daniel. "Are you guys okay? Can we do this?"

Wes looked up. His eyes were dark, and Bill thought he was holding back tears. "I want to get Rose and finish this. And then go home."

Daniel nodded but didn't say anything.

"Oh-right," Bill said. "Where are we going?"

Wes frowned. "Back to Rabbit in Red," he said.

Chapter Twenty-Seven

They drove back to Bill's home, but Sally stayed behind with Dexter's body. She would tell the police everything and they'd face the consequences later. Bill still thought she must have hit her head when she fell.

He rubbed his forehead at the hypnotic passing of the streets. They all needed to freshen up a little if they were going to be seen at all in public. Then they'd drive to the airport to use JB's Golden Ticket and hop on a flight to LAX.

He looked over at Wes, the first friend he'd made at Rabbit in Red, when he was just the chubby kid in the baggy sweatshirts who packed a few too many Snickers bars and squeezed a red clown nose when he got stressed. Bill knew that Wes hadn't cared for JB pretty much since that first Halloween weekend, and now because of JB—whether directly or not—Wes had killed someone.

Their lives had become a horror movie. "You okay?" Bill asked.

Wes didn't answer. He stared out the window, seeing something Bill couldn't see. Bill turned to Daniel in the back seat. Daniel shrugged, and Bill resumed his attention on the road. Everything would be okay in the end, right? It had to be.

They stopped at a CVS to get something for Daniel's leg wound. Fortunately, it was a smaller cut on the outside of his leg. Bill thought it needed medical attention, but Daniel convinced them that he could wait until the next day.

"We don't have time," he said. "I'll be okay. I promise."

When they got to Bill's house, they showered, and Bill found some clothes for each of them. They fit Daniel okay, just a little long, but on Wes they were too long and too tight. But no one laughed or said a word. Nothing was funny anymore.

They got back in the car and drove to Chicago Midway Airport. Bill wondered what his mom was doing and what she was going to say to the police. If they told the truth, they'd all be in trouble. They were adults now, and Wes would be leaving the crime scene. Even if it was self-defense, it wasn't smart to leave, was it?

The airport clerks swiped their golden tickets and smiled at them. Bill wondered what all these employees must have thought. They boarded a direct flight to LAX, and once they were in the air, Bill thrust forward in his seat. "Shit!"

"What?" Daniel asked. Even Wes turned to see what why Bill was cursing.

"The video tape! Mom had the damn video tape at the house!"

Daniel sighed and lowered his head.

Would they ever see what was on it?

A few hours later, the plane landed in LAX. They used their tickets to get another rental, and they drove to Hollywood and into the backlots where Rabbit in Red had once consumed an entire block.

It had been a half a year now since the buildings had burned, but when they pulled on the street, Bill could almost still see the ashes and the fires.

"Weird, isn't it?" Daniel asked.

Bill nodded but didn't answer. Weird was an understatement. They pulled up to where the front of the building used to be, where a *Killer Klown from Outer Space* had once welcomed them. There was no clown today, no giant hall decorated like *It* or *Hellraiser*. There was, simply, nothing.

"Wait, we're forgetting something," Daniel said. He reached into the carry-on bag that he had brought and pulled out the Rabbit's Eyes.

Yes, Bill thought. His eyes grew wide. *Why didn't I think of that?*

Daniel handed one to Bill and then Wes. Wes took the headset very hesitantly. Bill, on the other hand, put it on quickly. Clicking the power button on, Bill gasped.

The lights to Rabbit in Red came back on. Over the dirt, the studio had been brought back to life. There was the clown, and, walking closer, it greeted Bill.

"Welcome, Mr. Wise."

Bill ran forward, and there was the main hall. It was back to the *It* theme of the first year, but it had changed a bit, too—it looked more like the remake than the original. To his right was *The Shining* hall, to his left *Halloween II.* It was like seeing Rabbit in Red for the first time.

"What do you guys see?" Bill asked.

"Look—the commons!" Daniel said. "Not *Candyman,* but *Carrie.* From the first year."

Was that a smile on Wes's face? He still hadn't spoken, but his expression shifted. Not happiness, Bill thought. But curiosity at least. That was something.

They continued walking forward, through the commons to where the game chambers once stood, to beyond where all the additional studio rooms used to be.

They walked through the entire studio, and they kept walking, as if drawn, back to where *The Wicker Man* cages had been built. To the room where Sid Malcolm had confronted them and JB had died.

Bill saw something that caught his attention in the distance. "Look!"

They ran to what had been the edge of this room. Bill looked around and took off his Rabbit's Eye. "Do you guys think . . . do you think this is the spot where JB died?"

He watched Wes gulp, and both Wes and Daniel took off their headsets, too. Wes looked up at Bill with heavy eyes.

"I think we should wait for the others," Wes said finally.

Daniel put on the Rabbit's Eye again and then took it off. "Yeah, whatever is here can only be seen through this. And, uh, I think we know what it means."

Bill put on his headset to take a closer look. It was a tree, an oddly shaped tree. It reminded Bill of the wicker used to trap JB. But below the tree was a line of blood. More than blood, it was ooze. It looked like they could go through the tree, through it into a new dimension, a new reality of Rabbit in Red.

"The Upside Down," Wes said.

Bill gulped. "Yes. From *Stranger Things*. It makes perfect sense."

"If there's more to see at Rabbit in Red, then it's through there that we go," Daniel said.

"I agree with Wes," Bill said. "We should wait. This is something we do together."

"Unless . . ." Daniel put on the Rabbit's Eye again. "Unless we want to win."

Bill's stomach turned. "Hey, what?"

"There's a winner to this, right?" Daniel asked. "Someone who gets JB's cash and whatever?"

"Don't man," Bill said. "Don't be that guy."

Daniel looked at the allusion to the Upside Down from *Stranger Things* and then back at Bill and Wes. Would he betray them again?

Then he took off the headset. "Right. Right. We wait."

They stood up and walked around the perimeter of Rabbit in Red without the Rabbit's Eyes. About an hour later, a car pulled up and parked right behind theirs. And then another, and another.

The rabbiteers had arrived.

Bill, Wes, and Daniel ran and greeted everyone. Daniel limped a little as he walked but other than that didn't seem too bad. He started to catch them all up with what had happened, and Bill and Wes kept looking and waiting for Jaime and Rose, but they weren't there. Neither was Carol, and Daniel walked back to Wes and Bill.

"Where are they?" Daniel asked.

The rest of the rabbiteers put on their headsets and explored the ground, but Bill, Daniel, and Wes sat down outside and waited.

And waited.

Another hour passed. Finally, a new car showed up.

The three jumped to their feet and ran toward it.

The car parked, and out of the driver's seat, Bonnie Villa exited. She wasn't the only one. Thomas Lance, the assistant who had dressed as Pumpkinhead, exited the passenger seat. Michael Quinn, who had dressed as Sam from *Trick R Treat* got out of the back. He was followed by Marcus Everett, the man who had once shot at them during *The People Under The Stairs* simulation.

It was four of JB's former employees. And one of them had attacked Bill for real. He rubbed his shoulder.

Bonnie snarled at Bill. She walked around the car and opened the trunk. She gave Michael a butcher knife. She gave Marcus a gun. Then she picked up a chainsaw.

She faced them, pulled the cord on the chainsaw, and laughed. Then she yelled, "Stop them! Even if you have to kill them. Stop them!"

*****

Jaime pulled up in front of Bill's house. *Crazy that this is how I get to see it,* she thought. And of all people, it was Tara who actually knew the address.

"I looked at the house on Google maps one night," Tara said. "We text sometimes, you know."

Jaime knew that Tara had become close to Bill. They were even closer after Jaime was attacked last winter. For a long time, Jaime hadn't been in the mood for any kind of normal conversation with friends or family, but her sister talked with Bill a lot.

They parked in front of Bill's house, and another car pulled up behind them. Jimmy waved, and Jaime waved back. He had driven Chester's car, with Chester in the passenger seat. Chester refused hospital treatment and insisted on going with them. It wasn't the first time this week that Jaime made an emergency stop at Walgreens to patch someone up who probably should be in a hospital. Chester had claimed the bullet had gone through his upper chest near his shoulder and that all he had to do for now was stop the bleeding.

"There are bigger things to worry about, and we have to act fast," he had said.

Chester walked out of the car, and Jimmy put an arm around him. "I'm okay, kid. But thanks." Jaime frowned at him, and Chester said, "Seriously. This isn't actually my first time getting shot."

Jaime shook her head, and Rose and Tara walked up to the front of Bill's house. Rose knocked on the door, and they heard a yelp.

Someone screamed from inside. Jaime ran to the front door and listened. It was quiet. Too quiet. Like someone being forced to shut up.

Jaime pounded on the door. "Bill! Are you in there? Mrs. Wise?"

She put her head against the door but didn't hear any noise. "Bill!" Tara yelled this time. "Bill, if you're in there, say something now or we will break the door down!" Jaime almost smiled at her sister.

Then they heard movement, steady and soft movement toward the front door. It opened, and behind it stood Bill's mom.

"Jaime?" She looked at everyone. "What are all of you doing here?"

"Is Bill okay?" Tara asked.

Sally looked down and nodded. "Yeah. They went back to Rabbit in Red." Sally folded her arms and looked beyond them, out into the street.

"What happened?" Rose asked. "Are you okay?"

"It's a long story," Sally said. No one moved, and Sally kept looking around. Then she looked at Jaime and Tara. "Oh, you girls." She sighed and shook her head. "All right, come inside. Quickly!"

Sally led them into the living room, and Jaime looked around. Was this where Bill watched so many of the horror movies they used to talk about?

"Have a seat," Sally said. Without looking away from her, Jaime slowly sat down. When she did, Jaime saw movement further back in the house.

"Who's back there?" Jaime asked, standing right back up.

"Eric, it's okay. You can come out," Sally said. A tall man with light brown hair walked out. He looked younger than Bill's mom. Maybe in his thirties. Actually, Jaime thought, he looked an awful lot like Bill.

"This is my brother," Sally said. "He had to help me with something today." She sighed.

"What happened?" Rose asked. "Please. We just want to get this all over with, too."

Sally swallowed hard and wiped her lips. "You're Wes's girlfriend, right?"

Rose nodded.

"That's what I thought. Listen, I don't know if I should even be the one to say."

Rose stood up. "What is it? Is Wes okay?"

Sally nodded but looked away as she did. "Physically, yes. They were with—"

"Dexter," Rose said. "We know. What happened?"

Sally pursed her lips and looked Rose in the eye. "Dexter's dead." She walked closer to Rose and looked at the device she still wore around her neck. "You don't have to worry about that anymore."

Rose touched the collar gently. "Where's the remote Dexter had?"

"You don't have to worry about that now, either," Sally said.

"What happened?" Tara asked. "Did Bill kill him?"

Sally shook her head.

The way Bill's mom stared at Rose told Jaime the answer. Rose must have known, too.

"Wes," Rose said. It wasn't a question, but Sally nodded. "I hope he blew Dexter's head off."

Sally flinched. "The boys were very brave and very strong," she told Rose. "And believe me, I wanted to keep them here, but I know they have to finish. I know you all have to finish. I get it," Sally said. "But I made one mistake. I should have gone with Bill. I never should have let him leave. I was . . ." She looked at Eric then back at the rest of them. "I had to take care of Dexter. That's why I called my brother. We're taking care of it."

Jaime took a step forward. "Then let's go. We'll go together. Let's finish this."

Sally nodded. "Yes. But first, I think you should see something." Sally left the room for a minute. When she returned, she was holding a VHS tape.

"Let them finish this first, ma'am," Chester said.

Jaime had nearly forgotten he was in the room with them. She looked back, and Chester leaned against the front door.

"You know what's on this?" Sally asked him.

"Yes, ma'am. I have a sneaking suspicion that I do." Chester looked over at Jaime and Tara and smiled ever so slightly.

"What's on the tape?" Jaime asked. She turned quickly toward Bill's mom. There was something about that smile on Chester's face that she didn't like.

"Trust me," Chester said. "When you finish JB's challenge, you'll know everything. Right now, that's just another distraction." He walked closer to them and put a hand on Tara's back. She jumped at the touch. "If Bill and the others are already back at Rabbit in Red, then we need to get moving. Now. They may still be in trouble."

"What kind of trouble?" Sally asked.

Chester frowned and looked away.

"Tell me," Sally said.

Chester looked up. He may have been older than Bill's mom, Jaime wasn't sure, but in this moment, he looked like a kid getting in trouble.

"Not everyone wants you guys to finish," he said.

"Bonnie!" Jaime said. "Bonnie attacked us way back at the first simulation at Gein's property."

Chester nodded. "She's not the only one, either. Rabbit in Red isn't safe."

"Tell me something new," Sally said and rolled her eyes. She stormed off, but returned a minute later with a bag. "Let's go. Now." She opened the door, and everyone walked out except her brother, Eric. "Call me if you need me," she said to him. "Just, uh, let's wait till this is over to involve the police. Okay?" Then she shut the door.

Everything else happened very quickly. They drove to Chicago Midway airport. They used the golden tickets to get on a plane, and Chester conveniently had an extra for Bill's mom. They flew to LAX and arrived before nightfall.

On the way, Jaime kept mostly silent, thinking about what could have been on the videotape Bill's mom had. And why did she have it?

She thought about what Rose, Tara, and she had seen on JB's mother's grave back in Boston. She thought of all the riddles, all the videotapes, that name—that stupid name—of Smell Slime, and then she closed her eyes.

She dreamed of Sid Malcom. Sid pressing his body against her. She dreamed of Brandis. Brandis kissing her last winter, then Brandis killing Diane. Then Sid killing Brandis.

"I'm not done with you yet," Brandis said in her dream. He smiled, and his face morphed into Sid's face, and Sid stuck out his tongue and licked Jaime.

She woke up in a cold sweat. The plane had landed at LAX. They exited quickly, got a couple of rentals, and drove to Rabbit in Red.

Her heart beat hard, like she was driving to an execution. She closed her eyes as they drove past the spot where Sid had taken her. He had dragged her to his van, but she had escaped. He hadn't been able to hurt her then, and he sure as hell wasn't going to be able to hurt her anymore.

She opened her eyes, and she saw flames. Huge flames! A fire had engulfed Rabbit in Red again. She blinked hard, several times.

No, there was no fire. *I'm seeing things again,* she thought.

In the distance, she heard screams. And a chainsaw. And then a gunshot.

Unlike the flames she thought she saw, Jaime knew those were real.

They got out of the car anyway.

And ran toward the screams.

Chapter Twenty-Eight

Bill and the rest of the rabbiteers ran toward the illusion they had seen of Stranger Things' *Upside Down*. Behind them, they heard the roar of the chainsaw and even gunshots.

"Is that real?" Kent asked.

"Yes!" Bill kept running. "Faster!" The chainsaw Bonnie had attacked him with was no prop, and he had a feeling that the guns weren't props, either. The days of game chambers and movie props were long gone, but he still needed the Rabbit's Eye to find the exact entrance. Bill put it on, and then behind him he saw a car pull up in the distance. And then another. Two girls exited the front of the first vehicle—Jaime and Rose.

"Wes!"

"I see them!" Wes had stopped running.

"We have to keep going," Bill said. "They'll find us."

Wes shook his head. "But look what's in between us!" Across the ground that had once stood this magnificent studio, Bonnie Villa led three angry looking men right toward them. Bill sighed. And then he saw someone else step out of the vehicle.

"Mom?" Bill squinted, but he knew it was her. His mom had come with Jaime and Rose.

Daniel ran right in between Bill and Wes and said, "Let me handle this." Neither had time to respond before Daniel darted right at the four former employees of JB. Even with a little limp, Daniel was fast. Bonnie's chainsaw rumbled and one of the men fired his gun at Daniel. Daniel sprinted close to them and then darted back, but in a different direction then the rest of the crew.

"They're taking the bait," Wes said. His mouth fell open as he watched.

"Wait for it, man," Bill said. "They don't seem to have noticed the others who pulled up."

Wes nodded and watched Bonnie, Marcus, Thomas, and Michael all chase Daniel. Daniel cursed at them and taunted them, and, like Wes, Bill couldn't believe they were chasing just him. *There's like twenty of us right here, but they choose just one.*

And then it hit Bill. Daniel was the only real muscle in the group. Whatever they were thinking, they must know that. *If they catch the muscle, then the rest of us, physically, won't be as difficult of a challenge.*

"Now!" Wes yelled and ran toward Rose and Jaime. Bill didn't know if he had waited long enough, but it was too late. He joined Wes and raced ahead.

Bill looked over his shoulder. There was screaming, but Daniel kept running and he was faster than anyone. *He's going to be okay.* He nearly stumbled over some rubbish, but he kept running, and in moments, there was Jaime right in front of him.

He ran into her so hard he nearly knocked her over, but once he regained his balance, he hugged her and pressed her tightly against him. "Jaime, oh God, are you okay?"

She hugged him back, and her body felt incredibly warm. "There's so much to tell you, but now isn't the time. Where do we go?"

His chest hurt. He didn't want to pull away, but he knew they couldn't stay here long. Bill looked over his shoulder and saw Wes hugging Rose, and then he saw Tara standing alone with a look of terror on her face. He pulled away and hugged Tara, too.

"It's gonna be okay. You trust me, right?" Bill asked.

Bill felt wetness from Tara's eyes on his chest, but she moved her head up and down ever so slightly. He let her go and hugged his mother, too. "What are you doing here?"

"I shouldn't have let you go," Sally told him. "Everything happened so fast. Dexter's body isn't going anywhere. I can help more here than waiting on the damn police and answering questions.

I'm sure we'll be answering questions for the rest of our lives. Forget that now. I'm here and I'm gonna help."

Bill nodded and then he saw Jimmy and Chester. Chester's face looked terribly pale.

"Bill," Chester said, "we don't have much time."

"Let's go," Bill said, and they ran back to the group.

Daniel kept an eye on them in the distance, and he tried to run in a direction so that Bonnie and her crew wouldn't see the new arrivals, but one of them must have noticed. They stopped chasing Daniel, and they stood in the distance. Then Marcus shot at Bill's group.

"Faster!" Bill yelled.

When they caught up with the others, Bill put on the Rabbit's Eye. "I don't know where we're going or what will happen, but I know where we start." He took several deep breaths. "If you have a Rabbit's Eye, put it on. If not, just follow me." He reached for Jaime's hand, and she gave it to him. He squeezed it and hoped that all of this would be okay.

Then, off to the side, a scream distracted them. It was Daniel. He fell to the ground, and the four attackers raced toward him.

"What happened?" Bill asked.

"I saw it! I saw it," Carol cried. She put her hands up to her face. "Oh, God, I think they shot him." She started to run toward the attackers, and Rose grabbed her.

"No," Rose said. "I know it's hard. But they'll hurt you, too."

Bill felt his entire body shake as Bonnie and the others approached Daniel. He squiggled on the floor and tried to move, but she had caught up with him. Then she took her chainsaw and came down viciously hard right on his back. Daniel screamed, Carol shrieked, and all of them gasped.

"No!" Carol cried.

Carol's body twitched, and Bill reached out to her. His arm shook, too, and he felt a huge weight in his stomach. *This can't be happening.*

Daniel screamed again. Bonnie lifted the chainsaw up to her shoulders and came down again on Daniel. His body convulsed, and Carol cried out again.

A lump the size of a bowling ball formed in Bill's throat, but he said, "C'mon. I'm so sorry. But we have to move." He pulled at her, and Wes helped. Bill's mom put an arm around Carol, too. They approached the entrance of the Upside Down just as Bonnie and the others sprinted back toward them.

In the lead, Bill reached through the oozing tree that could only be seen through the Rabbit's Eye. He felt some kind of lever, and he grasped it. "Something's here. Brace yourselves," he said. "I don't know what's gonna happen." He counted to three very quickly, and then he turned the lever.

The ground below them shifted, and Bill reached out to Jaime, Tara, and his mom. They held on tight. It was some kind of elevator, and it lowered into the ground. Bill looked up, but didn't see Bonnie or the attackers. The floor dropped. Bill remembered thinking last year about just how big Rabbit in Red really was. There always seemed to be unexplored areas, and JB apparently had at least one more surprise left for them.

"How deep are we going?" Sally asked.

"I'm guessing this is like twenty-five feet now," Wes said. "And we're still moving."

From up ahead, Bonnie and the other attackers had reached the edge. Marcus pointed his gun down at them, and they shrieked. "Cover your heads!" Chester yelled.

The gun fired, and they screamed again.

The floor kept moving. Another blast from above and the buzzing of a bullet made them all scream more.

After a few more seconds, Bill looked up. He could barely see them. "Is everyone okay?"

"Check the person standing next to you," Sally said. "Make sure no one got hurt."

"Do you know where this is?" Rose asked Chester.

"JB kept plenty of secrets, Chester said. "I knew most of them, but this is new to me."

When they reached the bottom, Bill guessed they had to be nearly a hundred feet in the ground. Lights flickered in the distance, and directly in front of them, the virtual rabbit appeared.

"Welcome," the rabbit said, "to the final challenge. The victor of this final test will inherit the keys to the future of Rabbit in Red." It shrieked and spun and then hopped away. Then in front of them, JB appeared.

Bill took off the Rabbit's Eye and held it so those without could look inside and see JB.

He walked toward them.

"My friends," JB started, "my students, my family." He smiled, but his eyes were dark. "If you're seeing this message, you're at the end of the story. Endings always make me sad." JB took a deep breath. "It means, of course, that my time with you is at an end. I suppose to some extent I did all of this for a chance at immortality." He blinked several times, and Bill thought that JB almost looked like he was about to tear up.

"There are extra Rabbit's Eyes stored behind you, in case any of yours were damaged in previous simulations," JB continued. "Put them on, and let's get ready for one final adventure. I will pass on my estate, my inheritance, and my truth to the winner. You're under Rabbit in Red. It's a tunnel from one end to the other. All you have to do is get to the opposite side. There, you will be greeted by our rabbit, and the first to catch it wins. Good luck. See you at the finish line." JB vanished.

Bill put his Rabbit's Eye back on, and those who didn't have one got one of the extras that JB had mentioned. Chester and Bill's mom stayed put.

"This isn't for us," Chester said. "You all were invited here for a reason. Finish the game."

Rose stepped forward. "I don't know if I want it. If I won, I'd just . . . I don't know."

Wes reached for her hand. "I'm with Rose. Always. I don't care who wins."

Bill looked at Jaime and Tara. "Let's get to the rabbit together. We'll finish this challenge, but let's wait for everyone to get to the end. Oh-right?"

Jaime pulled away from Bill. "Can we split this?" she asked Chester. "Will it work that way?"

Chester shrugged. "I don't know. I knew JB always had a back-up plan in case something happened to him. But I don't know. I suspect, though, that even if you try to win it together, you'll need a leader to make some of those tougher decisions."

Jaime retuned to Bill and grabbed his hand. "I nominate Bill."

"Yes," agreed Wes, "at the end, we'll try to grab it together, but Bill leads us."

Bill shook his head. "No, you guys." He sighed. "We're all too close. I nominate Tara."

Her jaw dropped to the floor. "What would I do?"

"We don't know yet," Bill asked. "But I'd trust you even more than myself to make the right decision." He looked up at Jaime, but she shook her head.

"I trust my sister to do anything, but it's got to be you, Bill," Jaime said. "You found the contest in the first place, remember? You reached out to Wes. You've led all of us. It has to be you."

No one argued.

"I'd rather it'd be all of us," Bill said. "Let's just see what JB has in store for the final challenge."

They each put the Rabbit's Eye on and moved forward.

*****

Jaime made sure the Rabbit's Eye was on tight, and she let go of Bill's hand. Part of her wanted this—wanted to win, wanted everything she could get—but she held back those thoughts. Bill would do the right thing in the end, she thought. But would that be what she'd want to do?

Would there even be a Rabbit in Red in the future? JB's concept of a horror college might never come to fruition. Would Bill bury the rabbit? She sighed and shook away the thoughts. *Whatever happens*, she thought, *I'm at least going to finish this.*

But what do you really want?

She didn't have time for the voices in her head, not one second, but still she found herself considering. *What* do *I want?*

I want it all. I want Rabbit in Red to be the horror college it could have been. I want it to be real again.

She looked over her left shoulder, and Bill and Wes stood tall, ready to begin. She looked over her right, and there stood Rose and Tara. What did they want? Would it all just end, and they'd go back to a regular college or find some boring job?

"Let's go," Jaime said weakly, and they walked down a long, dark tunnel, many feet below where Rabbit in Red had once stood.

The rabbit hopped in front of them and mutated into a human with ghostly white flesh. Its skin oozed and rolled off the bones. "They're coming to get you, Barbara."

Jaime tried to step forward, but the zombie rabbit blocked her.

"I can't move," Wes said. "What's happening?"

"They're coming to get you, Barbara," the voice echoed.

Jaime felt a smile sneak up on her face. Yes, it was another riddle that needed an answer. If only she could forget what had happened above them on the land that once housed these great studios and focus on what was in front of her. It was more than a riddle, too. It was another game, and she knew what she had to say to win.

She didn't attempt to move. Standing perfectly still, she faced the rabbit. Then she said what she knew it wanted. "Stop it! You're ignorant!"

It vanished, and Jaime's smile grew. "It wanted the line," she said. "The next line in the show."

Bill let out an awkward sounding laugh. "Let's hope they're all that easy."

The rabbit hopped ahead, leading the way. They only took a few steps when it changed into a bat and flew over their heads. Then it spoke. "Does this word not sound like the midnight call of the Bird of Death? Do not utter it, or the images of life will fade—into pale shadows and ghostly dreams will rise from your heart and feed your blood."

"What's the word?" Wes asked.

"I know," Rose said. "Nosferatu." The bat screeched and flew away, and the rabbit reappeared in front of them, hopping forward once again.

Jaime took a deep breath and followed. This is too easy, she thought. What surprises does JB have around the corner? She looked as far ahead as she could, but it was pure darkness except for the virtual rabbit in front of them.

As they followed the rabbit, a voice called from overhead. "You're now outside. Let my voice be your guide. Keep a steady stride. Into the further you go."

"That sounds like JB," Tara said.

246

"I think it is JB," Bill told her.

"But that line is from—" Wes couldn't finish. The rabbit spun and turned into a demon, a black and red creature with long claws. The demon howled, and Jaime fell backward. Jimmy caught her and pushed her back up.

Jaime opened her mouth to speak, but the demon beat her to it. It howled again, and this time she felt pain, crippling pain all throughout her body.

That's more like it, Jaime thought.

"Jesus, man, what is that?" It was Leroy yelling from behind.

"It's like getting burned all over again," Carol told him. Jaime caught a glimpse of Carol's lips. Her face was covered by the headset, but her mouth told a familiar story. Carol was familiar with the pain, thanks to Hellfire. Carol looked like she just wanted to get out of here.

The thought left as quickly as it had come, and Jaime felt another pain—it was paralyzing and she could barely move.

Bill grunted next to her. They needed to say the name. That was what the *Night of the Living Dead* and *Nosferatu* tests were all about, but that was just a warm-up.

How do we stop the pain? Jaime couldn't say the question out loud, and the more she struggled to speak or move forward, the more it hurt. She realized what she had to do. She remained perfectly still. Maybe it was about tolerating pain, not fighting it. There was always something more to JB's tests.

She closed her eyes and tried to relax every muscle in her body. The demon still howled, and she saw the others falling. They shook with pain, many on the floor. Bill tried to move forward, but Jaime knew that wouldn't work. Once her body was completely relaxed, she was able to yell what she needed.

"Insidious!"

The demon's face twisted as if it had been stabbed. It gave Jaime a dirty look and flew away.

"How did you do that?" Bill asked.

Jaime ignored the question for the moment and turned to her sister. "Are you okay?"

Tara nodded. "It really hurt. But . . . but it's gone now."

Putting an arm around her shoulder, Jaime said, "Be ready for more of that. The Rabbit's Eye is programmed to make you feel as well as see." Jaime turned back to Bill. "You had to relax and not fight it."

The rabbit came back and hopped forward. Strobe lights flashed ahead, and the tunnel became a funhouse of horror.

JB walked through the flashing lights, and he smiled at them, but as he did, his face vanished. He was nothing but bone and muscle, and the word "Obey" flashed. Jaime nearly tripped over something, and, looking down, she saw a pile of bones. Then the tunnel shrunk as they walked. They would have to crawl through the next section.

Moments later, on their knees, they were paralyzed once again. A man stood in front of them, and he pounded a stick on the ground. Jaime studied it, but it was hard to see. Each time he hit the ground with the stick, a shock of pain shot up through her knees. She tried to focus, to look closer, but then he'd hit the floor again.

"My knees!" It was Tara's voice, and Jaime studied harder, trying to understand the challenge in front of them. She tried to mute the pain. Looking closer, she saw the stick had a silver head and was decorated with a wolf. *What's that from?*

The answer was on the tip of her tongue, but then a new shock of pain would scatter her thoughts. *Focus, dammit!*

The man recited a line. "Even a man who is pure in heart, and says his prayers by night may become a—" He stopped in mid-sentence and slammed the stick on the ground again. More pain shot up through Jaime's body.

"It's *The Wolfman*," Wes shouted out.

"Yeah!" That was what was on the tip of her tongue, but there was more to it.

"It's the poem they recite," Jimmy said. "I know this one!"

The man with the walking stick repeated the line. "Even a man who is pure in heart, and says his prayers by night may become a—"

Jimmy shouted out the next part quickly before the man could cause any more pain. "—wolf when the wolfbane blooms and the autumn moon is bright!"

The man vanished.

Then dozens of images flashed before them. A two-horned devil wearing a long Christmas-like robe waved at them. An older man with an eye patch stood next to someone with a skull mask and crazy hair shooting in all directions. The tunnel narrowed, and they had to form a single line.

"Are you okay?" Jaime asked Tara. Tara crawled behind Jaime, Bill behind Tara, and Jaime couldn't tell the order after that.

Images continued to flash around them. An older woman stuck her head in an oven, and then took off her pants and threw a dirty diaper at them. They heard the sound of a heart beating, louder and louder. Jaime took deeper breaths. It was getting harder and harder to breathe.

Then she couldn't move any further.

Someone shouted from the back. "What's going on?"

"I'm stuck," Jaime yelled.

Another image appeared, this time directly in front of her. It was a man with a theatrical mask, pure white, covering just half of his face.

"Phantom!" Jaime said. But nothing happened.

It stared at her, and then its face changed into a hundred faces. Michael Myers, then Jason, then Freddy. Pinhead, Chucky, Dracula, Frankenstein's monster, a werewolf, Leatherface, and more. Jaime couldn't move. She was stuck, forced to watch the many faces of horror.

Finally, it paused on just one.

It was JB.

It was the face she saw of him as a child on the video where he reenacted *The Exorcist*. Then his face aged, and she saw him as a teenager and a young adult. It ended on the face they all knew so well. The man they never fully understood.

"Who am I?" JB asked.

"JB," Jaime said.

His head shook from left to right.

"Who am I?" he asked again.

"Jay Bell," Jaime said. Once again, he shook his head no.

"Who am I?"

Jaime didn't know what to say, so she tried that strange nickname.

"Smell Slime." This time JB's face smiled, but it still said no.

"Jaime," Tara said from behind. "The name we saw on the tombstone. His mother's name." Tara coughed. "Use that."

Yes, Tara's right. There was a reason they saw that name, but Jaime felt a chill thinking about it. Something clicked—it had been clicking all along since the day JB had shown up at her graduation—but she wasn't sure she wanted it to click.

"Jay Bellstein." Jaime swallowed hard after she said it.

JB's head nodded. "You may enter." Jaime moved forward through the tunnel into a new room, and she was finally able to stand. One at a time, each of the others had to say JB's name. His real name.

They passed it along like a game of telephone. Bill walked up to Jaime. "Bellstein?"

Rose said, "That's the name on his mother's tombstone."

Wes brushed dirt off of his shorts and said, "And the way they say it—they don't pronounce it the way you think they would. It rhymes with Smell Slime."

"So those kids in the videos," Bill said, waiting for everyone to exit the tunnel and enter this new room, "they changed Bellstein to Smell Slime?"

"You saw *The Exorcist* video he made," Rose said. "He liked working with weird, slimy things. Kids are weird. It's a strange nickname but it makes sense."

"Except that it doesn't," Wes said. "Bellstein? I don't get it."

"I do," Bill said. "That's what on the last tape, isn't it?"

Jaime nodded—she had a feeling Bill was right—but pushed the thought out of her mind. There was an explanation, right? There had to be, of course, but she didn't know if she wanted to hear it. Bill looked like he was already connecting the dots, and she had, too. She just wasn't ready to say it out loud, not yet.

Before they could say anything else on the subject, a loud boom distracted them. Jaime threw her hands up over her ears and looked over at the tunnel. Was that a gunshot?

Out from the tunnel came Sally Wise and Chester Malcolm. They stood in the room with them now, but behind them came out the ones Jaime had hoped she wouldn't have to ever see again.

It was Bonnie Villa and the three others who had attacked them.

Bonnie had dragged her chainsaw all the way down here, but it was silent. The men had guns, and one had shot his gun into the ceiling.

"This is as far as you go," Bonnie said. "Any further and we will kill each and every one of you."

Bill reached for Jaime's hand, and she took it.

A voice shouted, "That's enough, Bonnie." It came from in front of them, from a part of the underground they had yet to see. Bill recognized the voice immediately, and he pulled Jaime close.

It was Sid Malcolm. Out of the shadows, he walked closer. He had his own gun, too, and he pointed it right at Bonnie.

He stood with a patch over one eye, and his other looked like a bloody beet. Could he see out of it?

"Sid?" Bonnie asked. "How did you—"

He shuffled forward, and Bonnie quieted. As he got closer, his eyes shifted from Bonnie to Jaime, and he grinned sadistically. Bill saw Sid holding his side with his free arm. Sid said, "Think you got me, huh? Close, maybe. But I ain't dead yet."

Sid coughed, and blood came out not only from his mouth, but some trickled out from his eyeball. Close, for sure, Jaime thought. *Have we learned nothing from all this horror? We should have checked that he was really dead and not just have driven away so quickly!*

Chester moved forward, and Bonnie and the others who had taken him didn't try to stop him.

"Sid, listen to me. We can help you, if you let us."

"Shut up! You shut up. You never wanted to help me. All you wanted was to be the next JB." He squinted hard with his one not-so-good eye, and Jaime could tell Sid definitely couldn't see too well. But somehow he'd made it all the way here. *How?*

He coughed again and wiped more blood off his chin. "They don't have any idea what it took to create all of this, do they? All the sweat. All the tears." He paused and looked at Jaime. "All the blood."

"Let me help you," Chester said and reached out a hand. "Give me the gun. We will get you the help we should have gotten you long ago."

Ignoring his brother, Sid faced Bill and Jaime. "Do you know what it took to build this? Broken relationships. Broken families. My mother—"

"Our mother," Chester interrupted, "would still take care of you. She always has, hasn't she? Last summer, didn't you stay in your old bedroom every day and still she took care of you?"

"Shut up!" Sid faced his brother. "Mom isn't the same because of that monster, and you know it. She still thinks—"

"Let me help you, brother."

Sid lifted his gun higher and pointed it right at Chester.

"Fuck you," he said. Then he fired the gun. The bullet hit Chester's face, and his cheek blew apart. Blood splattered the wall. Bill's mom ducked but got sprayed with blood, too.

Jaime's heart beat hard in her chest, but she stood still. Everyone stood frozen. The others have guns, Jaime thought. Why don't they use them?

"Sid," Bonnie said, her voice calm and steady. "We want the same thing. We want to make sure Rabbit in Red gets buried once and for all." She swung the chainsaw to her other arm. "Help us."

Sid licked his lips. "All you want is JB's money."

Jaime saw Bonnie flinch. "We want what's ours!" Bonnie said. "We want what we deserve."

"You were his slaves. You deserve nothing." Then he pointed his gun at her. Marcus, Thomas, and Michael pointed their guns back at Sid. Jaime could only hope they'd kill one another.

Then from behind Sid, another man walked forward.

Could it be? No, no way. But it couldn't be a simulation, could it? She had taken off the Rabbit's Eye. Could it be the doppelganger?

Or was the man walking out from behind Sid really JB?

Chapter Twenty-Nine

"My friends," JB said. Jaime felt vomit rise up in her throat, and she squeezed Bill's hand harder. Could this be for real?

Then Sid turned and shot the gun at him without hesitation.

The bullets went straight through him, and JB stood as tall and strong as before.

It was a simulation, but it was more than that, too, somehow.

"Sid, you won, didn't you? You managed to kill me, and now you have my kids trapped down here with you." JB shook his head.

Jaime looked at Bill, and he wore a similarly confused expression.

"What the fuck?" Sid asked and fired the gun again at JB.

"I'm not real, you asshole," JB said and laughed. "Perhaps my greatest sin was pride. Too much pride in my creations. This is my consciousness—or a part of it at least—immortalized in the technology of Rabbit in Red. It allows me to respond to you. Like Siri, but with my personal history also programmed to generate accurate responses." He smiled. "You could never beat me, Sid."

There it is again, Jaime thought. *That fucking pride. Maybe if he hadn't spent so much time trying to figure out all of this technology he'd actually be alive.*

"Funny," Sid said. "Let's see you stop a bullet." Sid swung his gun at Jaime, and Bill threw himself in front of her. Sid laughed, and JB yelled.

"Get away from them! Let them finish, Sid. Let them finish the game!"

"That's all you ever cared about," Sid said and shook his head. His eyes narrowed, and he locked contact with Jaime. But it wasn't her he wanted, not this time anyway.

Behind Jaime, Tara hid and held onto her sister's t-shirt. Without any additional warning, Sid fired the gun.

"No!" Jaime yelled and lunged, trying to cover Tara completely. All of a sudden, she felt warm and numb. What had just happened? She looked at Tara, and her sister screamed.

"Jaime!"

Tara's shirt was bloody, and Sid laughed. Jaime reached for her sister. "Oh, Tara!" She saw blood on Tara's shirt, but, looking closer, she realized the blood wasn't coming from Tara.

It was coming from her own body. She had been shot. Her eyes darted to her chest, and she patted her body frantically looking for the wound.

There it was. A bloody hole on the right side of her chest just below her shoulder. She touched it and looked at her hand. The blood was so bright and warm, but Jaime didn't feel pain. She looked from Tara, to Sid, and then to Bill.

Then—*boom!* Another gunshot. Jaime grabbed her sister.

"Are you okay?"

Tara nodded. "Are you?"

Jaime shook her head. "I don't know. We have to get out of here."

More gunshots. Jaime turned around and saw Bill fly back on the ground, like he did a back-hand spring but landed on his face.

Sally yelled, "No!" and charged at Sid. More gunshots. Too many! The air became dusty, and it was hard to breathe.

Jaime looked behind her. "Together. We run. Knock him over, run him down, and let's go!" She saw a few nods from the others behind her, but the air became thicker, and the shots were deafening.

Jaime ran, holding on to Tara. Sid stood in front of them, and he turned the gun again at Jaime. Jaime closed her eyes and charged as fast as she could. She knocked him down, and Sid released an "Umph!" Then they ran right on top of him. She hoped he'd be trampled to death.

"This way!" JB called from up ahead, and they followed his image. They entered a new room, and the walls shook. From behind, the gunshots had stopped but Jaime heard Bonnie's chainsaw roar to life.

The new room shook harder. Was this part of JB's final challenge? "Bill! Where are you?" Jaime called. There was no response. Tara held on to her still, but her grip weakened.

"I can't reprogram what's happening, girls," JB said. "You have to survive this. On the other side, all the answers await."

"I don't care about the fucking answers anymore," Jaime said. "I have to get Tara out of here."

JB didn't respond, and his image disappeared.

Then the walls screeched. The ceiling lowered, and the ground shook. Jaime couldn't breathe, and she couldn't see anyone else. "Rose? Wes? Bill! Where is everyone?"

No one answered, and the room shrank. She and Tara were forced to lay flat on the ground.

Jaime closed her eyes. They were being buried alive.

"Stay with me, sis. It's another test. Just another test."

Then the room shifted again. Like a Tilt-a-Whirl, Jaime and Tara spun apart from one another. Then wooden panels thrust through the ground and covered Jaime, just like being in a coffin.

Jaime tried to steady her breathing. JB's tests were about overcoming fear, and she knew if she panicked that she'd lose. Now, though, she began to feel a throbbing pain near her collar bone. The pain made her want to win, and suddenly she cared about the ending again. She had to win, not for the game, but so that she could get her sister to safety.

Dirt rained down on her, and her chest felt heavy. She could taste it in her mouth, hundreds of feet below the surface of where the studios once stood, real dirt poured down on them. Jaime thought she heard a cry near her. "No, stay still, Tara. You have to stay still."

Jaime heard a louder cry and then punching sounds. "Stop it, Tara!"

The room shifted more, once again like a spinning carnival ride. Jaime remained perfectly still, even as more dirt fell upon her. Minutes passed, and as the room continued to spin, she heard several screams. *What happens if you move?*

She listened closely, and she thought she heard the ground opening and closing. *The people who move—somehow they're being tossed out?* Maybe that wasn't such a bad thing, considering what was behind them. Or who. But Jaime stayed still, perfectly still even though she could barely breathe and couldn't see anything.

She had never experienced such pure darkness. *This is what dying is like, isn't it?* She held her breath as long as she could and took quick, soft inhales through her nose only when needed. Even then, she inhaled some dirt. *It's another experience. We have to know what it feels like to die.*

The room shifted and spun once more. Then after one more minute, the wooden panels that surrounded her opened, and the dirt was released. She jumped out and entered a new room.

In front of her, the image of the rabbit spun. She knew it was the final destination. The rabbit had turned green, like it was ill and dying. It looked weak, more like a zombie than a living creature. This was the moment when the rabbit could be saved and reborn. It didn't have to be buried. All she had to do was touch it, and she would win. All of JB's estate would be hers. She'd own Rabbit in Red.

Where's Tara? Jaime shook her head violently. *I need to get Tara to safety. We all need to get out of here!*

She couldn't take her eyes off the rabbit, though. She walked closer, reaching out her hand and then pulling it back. Bill was supposed to be the one! That was what they'd agreed upon. Jaime looked around. No one else was here. Not yet.

She circled the sickening green rabbit. The rabbit was half in the earth, half out. Waiting to be saved or to be buried once and for all.

Maybe I should just do it, she thought. *What if one of the others runs for it? Sid could be here, or Bonnie.* Jaime stepped closer to the rabbit.

"Jaime?" It was Bill's voice. She spun around and caught herself wincing at the pain near her shoulder.

"Bill, are you okay?"

He nodded. "The gunshot grazed my bad arm. It hurts like hell, but I'll be okay. What about you?" He walked quickly toward her and looked at her chest. He spun her around and looked at her back.

"Oh, God." Bill covered his mouth. "How do you feel?"

Jaime shook her head. "It hurts. More and more by the second." She swallowed hard. "Have you seen Tara?"

"No." Bill examined Jaime closer. "We gotta get you help." He looked around the room. "We have to get out of here!"

"Guys?" Another voice. It was Wes, and next to Wes stood Rose.

Bill ran to them. "You guys okay?" They nodded.

"What do we do?" Wes asked, staring at the rabbit.

"Jaime's been shot," Bill said. "We have to get her help. And my mom, Tara—where are they?"

Wes and Rose shrugged, and their eyes shifted from Jaime's injury to the rabbit, spinning and glowing in a hue of green.

"Guys, the only way out is to finish this," Jaime said.

Bill put an arm around her shoulder.

The four walked toward the rabbit. "Let's do it together," Bill said, and they nodded. They walked slowly, and Jaime held her breath again. This was the moment. This would give them not only the keys to Rabbit in Red, but it would give them all of JB's estate. And the answers they had wanted for so long, too, right?

They reached out their hands. "On three," Bill said. "One, two—"

"Stop!" Jaime snapped her head around. It was Sid Malcolm. Jesus, was he Jason Fucking Voorhees or something? The son-of-a-bitch wouldn't die! Sid had hold of Bill's mom.

"If you touch it, she dies," Sid said. It looked like he tried to blink, and a drop of blood leaked from his eye. He put his gun right on Sally's temple.

"You look surprised that we got through." He laughed, which morphed into choking and more spitting up of blood. "Being still isn't hard when you've been threatened. Oh, and I did you one favor." He grinned. "You won't have to worry about Bonnie or the other assistants ever bothering you again. They're rotting in hell with my brother and your stupid . . . stupid JB."

He really was like Jason, or maybe more like Freddy, Jaime thought. A real nightmare. Sally's eyes widened, and that got Jaime's attention. She watched Sally's eyes shoot straight to Bill. Sally blinked hard, twice, like she was trying to send a message. Then she swung her arm down hard and fast like a wrecking ball and grabbed at Sid's groin. She squeezed, and Sid yelped, too. Bill charged at them. He tackled Sid, and the gun flew out of his grip. Bill hit Sid over and over in the face, and Jaime picked up the gun.

"Bill! Move," Jaime said. He looked up, and he ran to her.

"Jaime—let me." He reached out his hand. "You've done enough. Let me help." The gun shook in her hands.

"He has to die, Bill," she said. "We won't be safe till he's dead."

"I know," Bill replied, "but let me do it for you."

Jaime shook her head. "It has to be me, Bill. I have to end my own nightmare."

Sally cried out. "You kids. Jesus! Give me the gun and I'll take care of this. Then we get out of here, okay?"

But before she could reach for the gun, Sid shot up and screamed. He reached for Bill with both arms. Bill rolled out of the way, and then Jaime pointed the gun at Sid's head.

She pulled the trigger, and another deafening boom echoed off the walls. A corner of Sid's head blew off and splashed against the wall like a broken egg.

Sid staggered backward, and Jaime pulled the trigger again.

The bullet went right into the one not-so-good eye. Then Sid fell backward.

They all stood motionless. Dust and debris had flown everywhere, and it took a couple minutes to settle. Jaime dropped the gun and reached for Bill's hand.

Jaime looked at Bill closely, and she realized he didn't know what to say. She felt stronger than she had ever felt. She wasn't the princess who needed a guy to save her. She'd finally taken care of Sid Malcom. She had finally destroyed her nightmares. She didn't think she was in shock. In fact, she had completely forgotten about the pain in her chest and hadn't felt this good since their dark night first began. She closed her eyes for just a second, remembering what Rabbit in Red had looked like on fire, remembering how she felt after escaping from Sid's vehicle outside of the studios all those months ago. Then she opened her eyes and smiled. The nightmare was over.

"Let's finish this, and let's get out of here."

Then more noise came from behind, and they realized several of the others had finally made it out. They looked at the original four leaders to Bill's mom to Sid on the ground.

"Hey," Jaime said.

"Should all of us touch the rabbit?" Wes asked. Jaime knew that look on his face. He wanted to get the hell out of here.

Carol stepped out from the shadows. Her eyes were wet, and Jaime felt an incredible pain for her, knowing that Carol would never see Daniel again.

None of them would.

"You were the original four," Carol said. "It makes sense for you to be the ones. We trust that you'll do whatever is right."

Jaime nodded and squeezed Bill's hand. The four of them walked toward the rabbit.

"On three again," Bill said. "One, two, three!" They grabbed the rabbit, and the green light morphed into a bloody, bright red that shot out from all directions. Then a wall shifted just beyond the rabbit.

They walked through the rabbit and into the new room.

The virtual JB awaited them, and he motioned them inside. It was a small movie theater.

"Let's watch that last tape," JB said. "And then I've got one more thing to finally show you."

Chapter Thirty

Jaime and Bill sat down in the front, hand in hand. She looked over at Bill, worried, not knowing what to expect and knowing exactly what was going to happen all at once.

Before the screen turned on, she heard a banging from the side, like someone was knocking on the door. She looked over at Bill, who shrugged, and then she felt around the side of a wall. Jaime discovered a lever, and behind the lever was more pounding. She pulled hard and a part of the wall opened.

Standing on the other side was Tara.

Jaime hugged her. "Ow," she said holding her chest. "Tara, you're okay?"

"I'm okay," she said. Behind Tara, the rest of the rabbiteers appeared, apparently everyone who didn't make it through the final challenge. "The Rabbit's Eye came on and directed us down here," Tara said, answering the question Jaime was about to ask.

She put an arm around her little sister, and they took a seat. Everyone gathered around the screen.

The screen in front of them wasn't big, and there were only about a dozen chairs. When the screen lit up, though, it brightened the dark basement room like the sun had risen.

The first part they recognized. They had seen this much before and they knew it all too well. JB talked about leaving a woman who he had loved. Then he cut his hair, and finally he swung a knife down at something. They had yet to see what had really happened at that point.

The virtual JB paused the tape again at that spot. "We must take a step further back in the past to understand the present."

The tape showed JB sitting in a small apartment. He had long hair and wore a Wolfman t-shirt.

"You recording?" *It was another man's voice.*

"Yes," JB said.

"Good. I want this on record in case . . . well, if I go down, you go down. Understood?"

JB didn't answer, but the other voice continued. Bill's grip on Jaime's hand tightened at the sound of the voice.

"All of this . . . this play between us. It's not real. You want a horror masterpiece? We have to make it real." The camera didn't show the face of the man speaking, just the back of his head.

"What do you suggest?" JB asked.

"It's like—the end justifies the means. There are bad people out there. We can make the world a better place by getting rid of them. And you'll get what you want. No more paying people to hurt." The man lit up a cigarette. "Do it for the art."

JB shook his head. "I don't know."

"Then let me do it for you. For us," the man said.

JB shrugged but after a moment said, "Okay."

"And I'll be your right-hand man?" the man asked.

Jaime squinted. Was that Chester? Maybe Sid? Who was this man speaking to JB?

"Yes," JB told him. "I'll agree to that."

"Put it in writing."

"Okay, Jason. I will."

Bill squirmed in his seat and squeezed Jaime's hand.

The video jumped ahead. JB and Jason were in a dingy apartment room, and Jason spoke while pacing back and forth.

"It was such a rush, man. You have to do it next time with me. The adrenaline! Afterward, shit, Jay! Think about the possibilities!" Jason's entire body shook.

"No," JB said. "I have thought about the possibilities. We can't do this. It's not that I don't . . . appreciate it on some level. But . . . but, no, this isn't the horror I want to create."

"You can't just end it," Jason said. "You signed a contract with me."

JB sighed. "I never wanted any of this to be real. Don't you get it? Art isn't real. The movies aren't real. But they take us to new places, and they give us the greatest escape. If you make it real, then how does that make it an escape from reality?"

Jason laughed. "Those lines will blur someday. You'll see."

JB frowned. "I don't know. But I do know that this— whatever this was—is over. We are not hurting people."

Jason walked closer to him, and they stood face to face. "Oh, Jay. You don't get it. I have no interest in fantasy. I only have interest in pain. Pain in reality."

"I'm leaving," JB said. "This was all a giant mistake."

"You'll regret this," Jason said. "I promise that you'll regret this."

JB picked up his video camera. "Good-bye, Jason." He walked toward the door and turned it off.

Bill's hand felt cold and sweaty. The virtual JB approached Jaime and Bill, and he spoke.

"Bill, I'm sorry. Jason Lamb went on to become a real monster. He hurt a lot of people. I didn't know you or your family, but I kept an eye on him." He paused. "Then after that terrible night when he hurt your family, I kept an eye on you." JB tried to smile. "You see, my boy, you developed a great love of the same stuff I loved, and I knew before I even opened the doors to Rabbit in Red that I would want you here."

He opened his arms a bit, as if he wanted to hug Bill. "Can you forgive me? It was my obsession with understanding real pain that led to Jason Lamb's behavior. In a way, I am responsible. For that, I'm sorry." JB looked over at Sally. "I owe you an apology, too, Mrs. Wise. I wish I could take that part back. I do. But you and Bill—you'll never have to worry about anything ever again. You're getting a part of this estate—more money than most people can even imagine. It's the least I can do."

Bill stood up and wiped tears from his eyes.

"Please, Bill," JB continued. "Now is the time for forgiveness. No more hate."

Bill opened his mouth, but nothing came out. He turned to Jaime. "It's okay," she said. "Somehow it will all be okay." He took her hand and sat back down.

"I spoke with him, you know," Bill said. "To Jason. I went to see him." He put his head down, and Jaime heard a gasp in the room. "He knew about Smell Slime. He knew what we were doing, or some part of it anyway. How could that be?" He looked up, perhaps expecting the virtual JB to have a stronger reaction.

"He followed what I was doing as much as I followed what he was doing," JB said. "I did some things to try and hide from him, but it must not have worked. You'll understand in a minute." He paused for a moment. "Bill, if there's one thing I can promise you— he won't ever be getting out of prison. I have files and evidence of multiple crimes that will keep him there. Forever."

JB paused again. It was as if the computer simulation was trying to process what to say next. "You have to forget about him. Sometimes, to move on, you have to forget the people who hurt you."

Then JB turned and faced Tara and Jaime. "There's more that you need to understand. I love you both, so much." JB sighed. "Let the past speak for itself."

The screen lit up again, and JB took them back to his college graduation. He looked a bit younger here than he did in the previous video.

Jaime thought of Rose and what they saw at JB's mother's grave. That name. Now it was she who squeezed Bill's hand as she braced herself to hear it.

The graduation speaker called off a series of names. "Doris Beacher. Cynthia Beale. Patrick Beck." Each graduate walked up on stage and shook hands with several people.

And then: "Jay Bellstein."

Jaime knew she would hear it. It was the same last name she had seen at JB's mother's grave.

The video on the screen jumped around. It went back to one they had already seen, the one with the kids picking on him and calling him names.

"Smell slime, smell slime!"

The video played in the background but was silenced.

"But—Bellstein?" Jaime asked. "Why did you change it?"

"Keep watching." Virtual JB vanished, and the video moved forward.

JB sat at a kitchen table holding a newspaper. He spoke directly into the camera.

"I don't know who will ever watch these. Or who I'll ever show them to." He sighed. "But I want to document my shame." He held up the newspaper. "It's clear to me that Jason Lamb is becoming what I only hoped to create on film. He's a real monster." JB shook his head. "Today, I'm changing my identity. Jay Bellstein is no more. I'm done with horror. Done!" JB slammed his fist on the table. "Look at what I've created! I never wanted that." He lowered his head. "So today, I officially quit. No more horror studies. No more horror movies. I will get a normal job and a normal life. And so that Jason never finds me, I must change my identity, too." He smiled.

"I've always been haunted by The Exorcist bells. It's time I get rid of Bell once and for all. So, today, I become Jason Stein." He laughed. "Brilliant, yes? Taking the first name of the guy I hate so he doesn't find me? Yeah. It's not a bad idea. I don't have to kill anything except part of my last name. Say hello to Jason Stein."

Jaime let go of Bill and put her arms around Tara, who sat on her left. Tara asked, "You mean—"

"Yeah," Jaime said. "Yeah."

"But how?" Tara asked. "Why?"

Jaime couldn't answer. They watched the tape show a montage of other images.

There was Janet, Tara and Jaime's mother. There was Janet with JB. Or Jason, as she must have known him. There was Janet and JB's wedding picture. His hair was long, long enough that the average person never would have recognized him as the person he was later in life. He was much skinnier, too. He sure looked different, but Jaime recognized him instantly now that she had connected all the dots.

Tara turned to the virtual JB.

"You're our . . . our dad?"

JB nodded.

"But we've spoken to Dad on Skype," Tara said.

JB shook his head. "An actor. Someone I hired to speak for me."

Jaime stood up. "Why hide it? Why leave us?"

JB pointed back at the screen. The final tape resumed.

He looked straight into the camera. "I can use the monster in me to create. Or I can let the monster die and do nothing at all. The latter is not an option. I'm sorry. I hope one day you'll forgive me." He picked up a long, sharp butcher knife. The video played the scenes they never had seen before. He looked into a mirror and hacked away at his hair with a knife. Then he screamed and punched the mirror. He held up his bloody knuckles to the camera.

"I tried. I can't work a nine to five. I can't be a husband or a father. I'm not that person. I died the moment I became Jason Stein. It's not your fault, Janet. It's not anyone's fault." JB wiped tears from his eyes. "I have to leave. I have . . . a different purpose.

One day, you'll see. One day, our daughters will have more than they ever dreamed possible. I will work to make that happen, but I can't do it here. I can't." He grabbed more of his hair and slashed at it with the butcher knife.

"*I must go back to Jay, and I must retire my last name.*" He shook his head. "*But I can't go back to Bellstein. I won't. I accept that my life will always be haunted. Haunted as the bells in* The Exorcist. *It's Jay Bell from here on out.*"

The video ended, and it felt like the air had been sucked out of the room. Jaime had so many questions, but she didn't know if she even wanted to ask them. She looked at the virtual image of her father. This now was all she had.

The end of the last tape—it was about killing his identity for the second time. First, Jay Bellstein, then Jason Stein, then finally Jay Bell.

JB. Their father.

She blinked, and no one spoke. It gave her a minute to think. *So this is why you were at my high school graduation? This is why you were at Uncle Tim's funeral! He was your brother.* All those riddles made more sense. Everything had been connected.

This is why you were never around when Mom was here last year. It was always Chester or some other assistant who did your usual work when Mom was here. Every single time she was in the studios, JB had been conveniently absent.

It sure explains why he took such an interest in Tara and me, she thought.

So many thoughts, but she didn't know what to say.

The virtual image just stood there, waiting for one of them to break the silence.

She asked the question that she always wanted to know.

"Do you know why Uncle Tim killed himself?"

JB blinked slowly and then gestured back at the screen. *Oh, shit,* Jaime thought—*another video?*

"Tim," JB said to her uncle. There he was—*the man that Jaime always thought of as her real father. "I know it's a lot to ask."*

"I understand. I'd do anything for you." Tim smiled, and *Jaime ached at the sight of him. "So I'll become Tim Stein instead of Tim Bellstein. It's easier to say. No problem."*

"I'll arrange the legal paperwork," JB said.

"You've always been resourceful," Tim said.

JB grinned and asked, "How are you?"

"Okay," Tim said.

"No, how are you really? You know what I'm asking?"

Tim sighed. "It comes and goes, but I'm doing okay, really."

"You can always call me if you need help. You know that right?"

Tim nodded. "It's scary, if I'm being honest. Depression takes hold like . . . like a monster in one of your movies. When it does get me, I feel like I'm drowning."

"It's hard to get out of that without someone else," JB said. *"I'll always pull you up, but you have to try and let me know. Okay?"*

The video jumped ahead, and both were older.

"How can you do this, Jay?" Tim asked. His face twisted and his eyes glared at JB.

JB shook his head. "I'm sorry. I just need one more favor."

"I changed my name for you. Our family's name!"

"I know," JB said and lowered his eyes. *"All I'm asking is for you not to share my identity. I know Janet will be sad, and those girls, too. Be a father to them, will you?"* He walked closer to his brother and put an arm around him. He looked at Tim closely in the eyes. *"I wish you understood."*

269

Tim huffed. "I do," he said. "Don't you see? Your obsessions—that's your monster. Your drowning. Your depression."

JB sighed. "It's all I have."

"You have a wife, a beautiful girl, and a new baby. You have a wonderful life!"

"But it's not the life I wanted," JB said. "I'm sorry. You can always call me. But I have to go. I have a . . . a vision. Something that's going to take years and years to build. But once I do, I'll be . . . I'll be immortal."

Tim shook his head. "I don't understand you."

"I'm not asking you to," JB said. "And please, call me still when your monsters come. Okay?"

The screen turned to black.

"But he didn't," the virtual JB said. "I didn't check in like I should have. And he never called me after that. Oh, girls, there's a lot to tell you. I made so many mistakes. Leaving you two. Leaving your mom. Forgetting about my own brother."

JB shook his head and looked down. A moment later he continued. "But you have to understand, I created Rabbit in Red not just because it was my dream, but because I wanted something to pass on to others. I had hoped you would win the competition, and you did! You won it as a team. It's what I always had hoped for."

Tara looked at Jaime. "I don't want it."

Jaime held her sister closer. "You let it burn. There's nothing to give us. You got yourself killed. If you did to Sid anything like you and Jason Lamb did to others, it's no wonder he became a psycho." Jaime stood up. "You have nothing to give us." She reached for Bill's hand, and then turned to JB one last time.

"Rabbit in Red is dead. Its secrets will be buried here. I don't want a virtual father, especially one that left us." She felt a fire rise up in her throat.

"Look what has happened!" Jaime continued. "We almost died! This is all a fucking waste." She looked down at her chest. "I should get to a hospital."

She held onto to her sister and Bill, and then spoke to everyone in the room. "Come on. Let's go. Let the rabbit stay buried."

"There's one more thing I have to show you. Please," JB said. "I want you to see it before the world does."

"Oh my God, if this is another video—" Jaime started.

"My dear, it is, but it's not one of those. You've seen enough of the past. There's one last thing to show you." He paused and the old, sadistic grin grew across his face.

"This time, I'm showing you the future," JB said.

He didn't wait for a response. The screen came back on.

Opening credits rolled.

Rabbit in Red Studios present . . .

A Jay Bell production . . .

Starring . . .

Bill Wise. Jaime Stein. Rose Dawn. Wes Pike.

The names kept rolling and rolling.

Then a title screen: *Follow the Rabbit.*

And then the movie began.

Bill and Jaime spoke on their phones and were solving riddles. Then they met for the first time at Rabbit in Red. They watched everyone battle horror's greatest villains and explore the studios. Jaime gasped as they watched Tara's hair go up in flames How the hell did JB have that on video? They watched last year's new recruits run through Hellfire, and they held their breath when the studios burned. They watched JB die, and Rose get trapped inside.

They relived the past weeks, from Dexter taking Rose to the simulations across the country, to today. They watched real murders—Donnie, the professor they never met, JB, Diane, Brandis, Chester, Dexter, Daniel, Bonnie, Marcus, Thomas, Michael, and Sid.

Real murders. No acting, no extra special effects. Jaime heard Carol moan when they watched Bonnie attack Daniel.

When it ended and the credits rolled, JB spoke again. "I collected video everywhere, from cell phones to cameras in the studios to anything I could access outside of here. You can get video from anything that has a camera. Don't you see, everyone? You are my masterpiece. My final, glorious masterpiece." JB smiled. "We captured the heroes and the villains. It's genuine horror, just as horror should be."

Jaime didn't return JB's smile. She looked around the room. No one was smiling.

Wes stood up. "Didn't you tell Jason that you couldn't do that to people?" His body was shaking.

"Wes, my boy, I told Jason we couldn't be the ones doing the evil. I never caused what happened to you. I just caught it on tape."

"You watched your daughter nearly get burned alive," Jaime stated. "How could you do that?"

"My dear, much of this footage if not all was collected after the fact. A team put this together. A special team of editors." He moved forwarded and lifted his arms.

"This is the horror movie that will change everything," JB continued. "You are Rabbit in Red!" He laughed. "You always were, and you always will be."

Jaime looked from Bill to Tara then back to JB. Tears flew down her cheeks, and her body shook.

Wes put an arm around Rose and pulled her close. "You're the villain. You always were. Can't you see that?"

Jaime wished the real JB were alive and standing in front of her. Then she could have punched him, and it would have been real.

Instead, she settled for two little words.

"Fuck you," Jaime said and turned around. It was time to leave Rabbit in Red.

Epilogue

"There is no such thing as a happy ending. I never met a single one to equal 'Once upon a time.' Endings are heartless. Ending is just another word for goodbye."

— Stephen King, *The Dark Tower*

"The man in black fled across the desert, and the gunslinger followed."

— Stephen King, *The Gunslinger*

Epilogue

A decade had passed since Bill Wise and Jaime Stein watched *Follow the Rabbit* in a basement hundreds of feet below Rabbit in Red. Since then, it had become the number one downloaded movie in the world. It never hit theaters—too much potential for lawsuits. But it thrived on the back alley of the internet. If someone's family was able to get the film removed from one site, it just popped up on another, hopping from one place to the next.

Bill never watched it a second time. He had lived it, after all, and he wondered why people took such an interest in the real horror that others had experienced.

The first year after they were all burdened with interviews—from the media to more serious ones with police. Evidently, they had committed more crimes than Bill thought possible. Fortunately, they had the money to hire the best lawyers, and no one faced any serious consequences much worse than fines thanks to the wonderful United States legal system. They also, fortunately, didn't have to worry about the legal rights they had signed over to Dexter and JB's doppelganger. Neither of them were around to file any claims.

Now, ten years after that terrible day, Bill sat across from Jaime in a quiet coffee shop on Sunset Boulevard. He was in the middle of an article on the popular Fitz of Horror page that was previewing tonight's event.

To understand what's happening now, though, you have to go back in time. Ten years back in time.

A group of students who just wanted to study horror got a lot more than they ever bargained for. They lost friends and some even had to kill—in self-defense, or so they say.

The mastermind behind Rabbit in Red—Jay Bellstein, or Jay Bell, or JB or whatever you want to call him—really screwed up some kids.

Wes Pike shot and killed Dexter Lange.

Jaime Stein shot and killed Sid Malcolm, after her friend Rose almost killed him with a machete.

These "kids" and even some of their parents, like Sally Wise, were charged with a number of crimes. Let me list just a few of the charges.

Bill stopped reading and closed the page. He had given Fitz of Horror an exclusive interview about what was happening tonight. It was the first time he had willingly given an interview in ten years. He looked across the table at Jaime, reached for her hand, and she smiled at him.

When he took her hand, he played with the ring he had given her. Last year, he had taken her for a weekend getaway at the Stanley Hotel in Colorado, which of course was used as the Overlook in *The Shining*.

He had made special arrangements to stay in room 217, and he still liked pointing out to Jaime that the real room number was not 237.

They had stayed up all night on a ghost hunting tour of the hotel, and exactly at 2:17 a.m. Bill dropped to one knee and asked Jaime to be his wife.

She said yes.

They toasted with one glass of champagne. Bill had learned to be very careful with alcohol, too.

They hoped to be married next year. Wes would be Bill's best man, and Tara would be Jaime's maid-of-honor. Right now, they had other projects to work on.

After that final night, each of the rabbiteers had received a very generous amount of money from JB's estate, and the money kept pouring in thanks to *Follow the Rabbit*. Illegal downloads or not, it made money, and lots of it.

Rabbit in Red had never been more well-known. It could all be traced back to the first app they downloaded and all those riddles they answered. They had accepted the terms of agreement without reading them—who read those?—and that had given JB all the legal access he needed to their cameras and their lives. Ethical and moral debates popped up in college classrooms and Facebook feeds, and no matter what people thought of Rabbit in Red and JB, they sure talked an awful lot about them.

For better or for worse, Bill knew that would have pleased JB. He had achieved immortality.

Bill and Jaime finished their coffees, and Bill called Wes. "Are you sure you won't come?" Bill asked, getting into Jaime's car now.

"Rose and I are very happy, man," Wes said. "She doesn't want anything to do with it. We love you guys. But you're crazy."

"How's Jonathan?" Bill asked.

"We haven't slept in a month, but he's good. Can black kids have red hair? That would be pretty sweet, don't you think?"

Bill laughed. "We'll come visit the baby again in a couple months. Can't wait to see him again. You sure you won't come with us?"

"Jason's balls and Freddy's claws!" Rose yelled. "Tell Bill no already and come help me."

"You heard the lady," Wes said. "Good luck, Bill."

"Thanks, man." Bill hung up. He looked over at Jaime as she drove down Sunset Boulevard. "Are you ready for tonight?"

"Are you?" Jaime asked.

Bill thought of JB. "Your dad was one crazy dude, you know?"

Jaime nodded. "I still try to piece everything together. I don't think I'll ever understand him."

"Nope." Bill shook his head. "Me neither. Do you think Tara will visit?"

"She made it pretty clear that we have to go to her." Jaime laughed. "She's my favorite person, you know. Besides you of course."

"Of course." Bill smiled.

"I just love who she's become. A therapist. Can you believe it?"

"I can. Yeah. She was the strongest of all of us, I think. The really strong use their pain to help others."

"Did you ever forgive him?" Jaime asked.

Bill raised an eyebrow. "Huh?"

"From your final challenge. You told me once that all you had to do is forgive him. Did you ever?"

Bill breathed deeply through his nose. "I guess not. Not formally anyway. Have you forgiven him?"

Jaime frowned. "The jury's still out on that one, too."

"I don't think he really understood the larger consequence of what he was doing. He wanted to be immortalized in his creation." Bill paused and looked at her.

"In that, he succeeded," Jaime said.

"So, are you sure you want to do this?" Bill asked.

"You know, I think . . . I think this is how we begin to forgive him. If forgiveness is the ultimate challenge, then, yeah, I think we have to move forward." She smiled at him. "Of course, we don't have to go through with it, you know. We can always go live on a small island or something."

"No, I want to. I think." Bill laughed. "It's a chance to get it right. Without all the murder and stuff, right? To do it the way it was meant to be done."

"Exactly," Jaime said. "This isn't about honoring him. It's about honoring all of us who believed in him."

They pulled up outside the front of Rabbit in Red studios. It had never looked bigger or better. The building rivaled the biggest casinos in Las Vegas. Bill and Jaime had spent the last decade rebuilding it, and tonight was the beginning of a new journey. Jaime drove around back. They used a fingerprint key lock and eye scanner (all of her security required a thorough scan of the eyes, just in case a demon from her past showed up), and entered the studios.

They walked toward the commons.

At exactly 7:00 p.m.—or nineteen hundred hours, as Bill liked—they walked out to the main stage of the new Rabbit in Red commons.

In front of them, nineteen young faces smiled back. Bill and Jaime held hands and walked toward them.

"Are you ready to follow the rabbit?" Bill asked.

Everyone cheered, and Bill smiled.

"Your first challenge," Jaime said and gestured behind her. A rabbit spun, turning colors from green to red to white. It danced in its box, hopping over an axe, a typewriter with a missing letter, chocolate mousse, and more. It was engulfed in a box and blood poured out.

Then it spoke.

Follow the Rabbit. Follow the Rabbit in Red.
From the steps of L.A. to the Great Northern,
Fools, eye-patches, a strong woman: don't end up dead.
Be ready to pay tribute to them when it's your turn.

Jaime and Bill continued to hunt the rabbit in red, and they knew someone would always follow them into the darkest of rabbit holes.

THE END

Acknowledgements

I wrote the first draft of the first book of this series in June of 2014. I'm writing the acknowledgements to the final book of the series on July 11, 2017. That's three wonderful years of my imagination living in this world. What a wonderful world it's been.

But I didn't get there by myself. If there's anything I've learned in the last three years, it's that collaboration is the key to success.

First, let me thank YOU, the reader. No matter what, this final book wouldn't be here if not for your enthusiasm for this series. Thank you for giving meaning to my dreams.

It would seriously take another book to thank all the people who have helped me get here. Instead, allow me to highlight a few exceptional people.

Brian McWilliams and Brandy Kennington were my first readers for every part of this series. They read it at its worst and helped it become its best. Thanks for putting up with me.

Kathy Teel professionally edited each book in this series. *Rabbit in Red* wouldn't be what it was without her.

Thank you to Camron Johnson, my cover artist. His imagination saw the rabbit in the best way possible, and I can't imagine better cover art.

Thank you to Bryan Fitzgerald of Fitz of Horror. Not only is he the voice of *Rabbit in Red* for the audio book, but his Facebook page was the first big page to consistently give shout-outs for the book.

Thank you to Deb Galloway, the first Barnes & Noble store manager to put my book on the staff-recommended and local favorites section. That's always been such a cool honor for me, and it fueled my motivation when I needed it most.

I've had great proofreaders, too. Jennifer Gadd and Elyse Zwicky helped with this series the most. Thanks for catching as many typos as you did. I sure make a lot.

Thank you Horror Block for sending my book—two of them—to tens of thousands of readers. That put me on the map. Thank you to SpearCraft Book Box, the Box of Dread, and BookLoot for including my stories in your boxes, too.

To all my readers and friends: How did I get so lucky to know you? Thanks for your words of encouragement. Thanks for following me online and interacting. It's been fun. And we're only just now getting started. See you again soon. The rabbit hole goes deep, and a new tale of darkness awaits.

Bonus:
Rabbit in Red Short Story
Contest Winner

Dear Readers,

For those who follow me on social media (www.facebook.com/chianakas or @joechianakas on Instagram or Twitter), you saw a special contest. I offered readers a chance to write a short story using a *Rabbit in Red* character playing in a number of different scenarios. The winning story, selected by a panel of independent judges, would be published as a bonus in *Bury the Rabbit.*

Why?

First, it's to celebrate what brought us to this trilogy: A love of horror. The trilogy may be over, but our love for everything horror never ends. This story, submitted by Matthew Daudish, perfectly illustrates a passion for horror.

Second, it's because I also wanted to put a spotlight on a fellow writer. It's not something I've seen in other books. This business isn't easy, and if I can introduce a few thousand people to Matthew Daudish or help another writer in some way, then that seems pretty awesome.

If you like this idea and want to use *Rabbit in Red* characters to re-create scenes like in the virtual reality of book one, or add a nasty element to Hellfire from book two, or even take them through real-world settings like in this final book, write your short story and e-mail it to me at joechianakas@gmail.com. I'll put them up on my blog and social media sites, and give you a shout-out, too.

Matt was born in Indiana and currently lives in Connecticut with his wife Ashley, their springer spaniel puppy Luna, black cat Seuss, and guinea pig Arya. Matt attended the University of Connecticut and graduated with a Bachelor's degree in Mechanical Engineering in 2012. He currently works as a manufacturing engineer, programming inspection machines that measure jet engine parts.

In his free time, Matt enjoys visiting local breweries, watching movies, reading, and writing short stories with horror themes. He also enjoys brewing his own mead and painting horror themed labels for the bottles. His favorite Horror movie is Hellraiser and his least favorite horror movie is Hellraiser Revelations. His favorite non-horror movie is The Last Action Hero.

You can find him on Twitter at @MJDAUDISH.

Here's his story. I truly enjoyed it, from the fun re-enacting of a classic horror movie to the lesson learned at the end. This is fun. Thanks, Matt, and congrats.

Enjoy, friends. Horror never dies!

Virtual Hell
By Matthew Daudish

Bill Wise wanted more practice on the virtual reality simulator.

He had done really well during the first round, in the simulators for *Freddy vs Jason*, *Evil Dead 2*, and *Fright Night*, but Daniel had still beaten him. Not by much, but still…. It would have been fine if it had been Wes or Rose or Jaime that he had lost to, but no, it had to be Daniel. Horror was his life, and it was frustrating to think that someone as despicable as Daniel could beat him in something he loved so much.

Aside from that, he was worried about what still lie ahead for them in the upcoming tests. Just because he had done well this round did not mean that he would do well in future rounds. Bill was worried that he had just gotten lucky. What if they picked a movie he didn't know as well next time? What if they picked a movie that he hadn't even seen? Bill devoured horror movies whenever he got the chance, but he would never be able to see them all. Who knows what movies JB might drag out to really test them?

And even IF he knew all the movies, Bill wanted more practice with the hardware itself. The system was impressive and had been fairly easy to figure out, but he didn't want to take any chances. It would just kill him if he lost next round by stumbling or screwing up a punch in a scene that he knew. The computer didn't know any better and would interpret a dumb physical mistake like that as a lack of knowledge about the movie. He also didn't want to risk tripping over himself in front of Jaime.

And if he needed any extra reason beyond all that, Bill just wanted to play for fun. This was cutting edge virtual reality equipment that JB was testing them on. How much did a system like this even cost? He could watch these movies a million times at home, but actually being inside them was a very awesome experience. Regardless of how this summer went and whether or not he won or lost, Bill intended to make sure that he had as much fun as possible and learned as much as possible while he was here.

Captain Spaulding was attending the virtual reality station when Bill walked up. No one else was around, luckily. He had left dinner with the intention of catching a round before anyone else showed up. Captain Spaulding gave him a devious grin and suited him up in the gear.

Bill stepped into the small room, once again feeling like a mouse in a ball. He strolled around to get used to the curved floor that moved with his steps. He felt confident, or so he hoped.

The screen over his eyes dimmed, and then presented a menu in front of him. The first round of the virtual reality test had used movies that JB has specifically selected for them, but there was a whole library of other movies to choose from that JB had also built into the system. Bill felt a thrill of excitement just looking through them. The menu only gave the name of the movies, and no details on the scene that would be played out from each, which made it much harder to predict. Bill recognized almost all the movies, aside from a select few. This was going to be a real tough decision. Should he pick something hard to challenge himself? Should he just pick something that he really loved, just for the enjoyment of experiencing it in this virtual reality environment? Bill scrolled through the options.

The Howling. Too hard. Bill had seen most of the franchise and he loved the practical special effects, but the plots were always so convoluted and hard to follow.

Saw. Awesome movie, but Bill had just eaten and didn't want to have to saw off his leg and lose his dinner.

American Werewolf in London. Bill had seen this movie a million times. Any scene would be way too easy.

The Grudge. Too scary. This was one of the first real horror movies he had ever seen, and the attic scene at the start had traumatized him for a long time – in a good way. Better to save that one for later.

Tremors. He almost chose this one immediately. Blasting Graboids with Burt was a video game that he had wanted to see released ever since he had first watched the movie.

Cabin in the Woods. This could be a whole virtual reality game just on its own, if it expanded past just what was shown on the screen.

Pieces. What was this movie? He hadn't heard of it. Bill made a note to himself to look it up later.

Hellraiser. A classic. He had seen the first movie on VHS a while ago, and recently binge-watched the rest of the franchise on Netflix after they all showed up there.

Final Destination. He loved this franchise for all of its creative kill scenes, but this would be a difficult one to replicate.

The Faculty. This was one of Bill's favorite alien movies of all time, aside from *Alien* itself.

Children of the Corn. Bill had seen this one once, and he still needed to watch the rest of the sequels.

Phantom of the Opera. Which one? There were so many movie adaptions of this story. He would have to tell JB that some of the entries like this one weren't specific enough. Or was that the point?

Bill kept scrolling through a few more, but then paused. He had made his decision.

Bill scrolled back, using the motion of his arms to control the menu, and stopped over *Hellraiser*. This was the perfect choice. He loved this franchise and had seen all of the movies in it, but he actually hadn't seen the first movie in several years at least. This movie would be awesome to see in VR, but still a challenge.

The first movie was a classic from Clive Barker, and the second movie was just as good. Some people even thought it was better than the first. The third and fourth movies were fun, but got a little cheesy. They were good but failed to capture the same mystique that Clive had developed in the first two. They also turned Pinhead into more of a generic slasher, which was disappointing to see. Pinhead from the first two movies was an entity that played by very specific rules and was almost a neutral character. Frank and Julia were the real bad guys in that movie. Pinhead was definitely not supposed to be a generic bloodthirsty slasher villain, Bill thought.

The next few movies after that were decent, but from what Bill understood, they had all started as random scripts floating around the studio that were loosely converted to add Hellraiser elements. They were okay, but had very random plots and didn't really utilize the awesome source material much.

The last movie, *Hellraiser Revelations*, had been abysmal. Doug Bradley seemed like a good sport and had played Pinhead for every other movie in the franchise, but this one was apparently where he drew the line. Bill had heard that this movie was filmed in just a couple weeks, and the only reason that they made it was to retain studio rights to the franchise.

Bill smiled, and then clenched his fist out in front of him to confirm the option. The view around him fizzled to a noisy VHS static screen for a few seconds before booting up into the virtual reality scene from the movie. The voice inside the helmet instructed him to "RE-ENACT THIS SCENE."

Bill's mind raced to place himself the second that the scene visualized in front of him. He was in a small neutral colored room. Based on the IV next to him and the strange gown-like outfit he was wearing, he quickly identified it as a hospital room. But where in the movie was there a hospital?

288

Bill was also lying face down on the bed, holding something in his hands. It didn't take much effort to identify what it was. It was the puzzle box that the characters used in the franchise to summon Pinhead and the Cenobites. Sometimes it was on purpose, sometimes it wasn't. It was moving in his hands, though. Half of the box slid up in triangular segments, rotated around the center of the box, and then slid back down in a new orientation.

Bill needed to think fast. The puzzle box was opening, which meant that he had very little time before the Cenobites or something else showed up. If he didn't play it right, the Cenobites would tie him down with hooks that would appear out of the air, and would rip him apart before he could get away.

He was definitely re-enacting the scene as Kirsty, the main girl from the movie. Luckily there weren't a whole lot of other characters, so it was easy to pin that down. If he had the box and he was playing as Kirsty, then that put him at least halfway through the movie. That meant that Julie had already discovered Frank, she had already brought home several victims for Frank, and that Kirsty had walked in on Frank and seen him half decomposed.

But what happened next? Bill's memory of this exact scene was a bit fuzzy. How had she ended up in the hospital? He didn't have time to dwell on it, because Pinhead was bound to show up any second.

He hadn't, yet anyway. Instead, the wall in front of Bill (Kirsty) split and slid apart, and fog rolled out of the space behind it. This wasn't Pinhead at all. This was something else. Nothing appeared, but there was some low rumbling noises echoing out of the gap. Was he supposed to go in there?

Bill racked his brain and started to recall the situation better. This happened after Kirsty had escaped the house and saw Frank. She had grabbed the puzzle box, ran down the street, passed out, and woken up in the hospital. She had solved the box and then opened this door, which led to a monster on the other side.

Bill climbed out of bed, slowly. He knew that she was supposed to go through the wall to explore, but she was cautious and wouldn't be running for it. Bill replicated this and slowly approached the wall, and then entered. He walked down a gray tunnel lightly rolling with fog. There were more noises ahead. Bill couldn't remember exactly what the monster ahead looked like, but he did know that he wasn't supposed to fight it. Once Kirsty saw it in the movie, she turned and ran back to the room. That was easy enough, Bill supposed. He kept going forward.

Even though he was expecting it, the monster still surprised him. It jumped out of the darkness and scrambled toward him, emitting a horrible noise as it came. It was taller than him, with a scorpion-like stinger and gooey 80s special effects-style plastic skin. There was a fanged face that looked like a mix of human and snake. Bill turned and ran, as he was supposed to do.

Bill fell through the gap back into the hospital room, onto his hands on the floor. He quickly turned around, but the door had sealed behind him, thankfully. Bill guessed that this was one of the primary failure points in the simulation. If he had stayed too long in the tunnel to fight the creature or analyze it, the door would have closed and trapped him inside to be eaten by the creature. The creature was making noises behind the wall, but Bill knew that it wouldn't break through.

This wasn't over yet, though. Bill turned to the other side of the room, knowing what was coming, as the light in the room turned surreal. Bill saw the IV drip reverse and blood flow upward into the IV bag. The TV started flashing strange images that looked like flowers, and the light fixture beside the bed shattered.

One by one, the cenobites zapped into the room with a flash of electricity. First Chatterer, then Butterball, then the girl Cenobite that Bill couldn't remember the name of, and then finally Pinhead himself. Seeing Pinhead while watching the movie was impressive, but seeing him in this virtual reality setup was amazing. Bill almost forgot that he needed to stay focused.

The Chatterer Cenobite rushed over and pinned him against the wall. Bill didn't struggle. In the movie, Kirsty had made it out of this situation by convincing the Cenobites that they wanted Frank instead. He could try struggling out of Chatterer's grip, but that wasn't part of the movie. It was all talk from here on out, if he wanted to pass this.

"The box. You opened it. We came," Pinhead said. None of them were moving. Bill wasn't struggling.

"I didn't mean to," Bill responded. He couldn't remember the exact dialogue, but he figured that JB wasn't expecting them to. If he could guide the conversation in the right direction, that should be enough to satisfy the test. Bill doubted that JB wanted them to simply memorize dialogue. If he were here, JB would probably be telling him that the characters behind the dialogue were what mattered, not the actual words they said.

Pinhead responded, "You solved the box. We came. Now you must come with us. Taste our pleasures." The girl Cenobite hissed at him.

This was real tough, Bill thought. One wrong statement and Pinhead would end the conversation and take him away. If he didn't respond quickly enough, he would also fail. Bill had to be quick to keep the conversation going in the direction that it was supposed to.

"Who are you?" Bill asked, trying to stall. He knew, but technically Kirsty didn't. What was he supposed to say next?

"Explorers in the further regions of experience. Demons to some. Angels to others."

"Someone escaped you. A man named Frank," Bill said, trying to cut to the end. Frank was what they really wanted, not Kirsty. That was his only bargaining chip here. He had to convince them to spare himself.

"Nobody escapes us," Pinhead said sternly. That wasn't true though, Bill knew.

"He did escape you. I just saw him. I took the box from him," Bill said.

Pinhead glared at him and frowned.

"Supposing he had escaped us . . . what has that to do with you?"

Bill wondered for a moment. He knew that his next comment would be that he could lead them to Frank. Bill said the line, and he saw Pinhead's face change as he contemplated it. Why did they actually need him, though? Frank was just hanging around the same house where he was taken by the Cenobites. That seems like it would be the very first place that the Cenobites would want to look if they were trying to track him down.

That was outside the scope of this test, however. Maybe Bill was remembering wrong, or maybe it didn't make sense. Either way, he was just here to say the line.

Pinhead responded, "I want to hear him confess himself, then maybe. Maybe."

The girl cenobite continued, "But if you cheat us . . .

"We'll tear your soul apart," Pinhead finished.

Bill had won! The Cenobites faded away and the room returned to normal. The visor faded, and the voice in the helmet congratulated Bill. Bill took off the helmet to give back to Captain Spaulding, but he was gone and JB was standing in his place outside the door to the virtual reality setup.

He grinned at Bill. "Congratulations. That was not an easy one."

"There's a good lesson to be learned from that scene, too, Bill. I didn't make my way to where I am now just by fighting. Kirsty made it out of that situation using her intellect rather than her strength. If she had struggled, she would have been killed."

"Lots of situations in life are just like that. Even if you don't win this competition, I want you and everyone else to walk away from this in a better spot than you started in. There are lots of lessons to be learned from horror movies. Sometimes you need strength to survive, sometimes you need smarts, and sometimes things just go wrong no matter what you do. Once you really understand that, life will start to make more sense."

Bill nodded. JB might be a crazy dude, but he certainly was a smart crazy dude. There was no way he could make it as far as he did without knowing stuff and making good decisions.

JB smiled at him. "Good luck next round," he said, and then turned and left. Bill watched him leave, and then walked back to his room, feeling a little more confident about the challenges ahead.

Thanks for following the rabbit.

Now, please follow the author:

Look for Joe Chianakas on Facebook at www.facebook.com/chianakas and on Twitter and Instragram @JoeChianakas. Visit his webpage at www.FrightFest4D.com for updates or to grab signed copies of his books.

What's next? Joe fell through the rabbit hole and is now deep in the Pit of Darkness. Updates on his new novel will be released on his social media.

***PIT OF DARKNESS, a* new novel by Joe, is coming soon.**

Magic is real, even if fifteen-year-old Lawson Russo can't remember. He and his best friend, Elle, discovered a Fountain of Youth when they were kids. But something dark and dangerous made them forget.

A monster lives below the Fountain in the Pit of Darkness. It kills whoever remembers its secrets, and a variety of forces have awakened forgotten memories and sleeping demons.

Lawson and other teens fight to discover the true meaning of the Fountain of Youth, and the Pit has sent a monster to kill them all. In trying to live forever, some will die young.